The Traitor

The Traitor

Sydney Horler

With an Introduction
by Martin Edwards

Poisoned Pen Press

Originally published in London in 1936 by Collins

Published by Poisoned Pen Press in association with the British Library

First Edition 2015
First US Trade Paperback Edition

10 9 8 7 6 5 4 3 2 1

Library of Congress Catalog Card Number: 2015938529

ISBN: 9781464204975 Trade Paperback

Poisoned Pen Press
6962 E. First Ave., Ste. 103
Scottsdale, AZ 85251
www.poisonedpenpress.com
info@poisonedpenpress.com

Printed in the United States of America

Contents

Introduction

The Traitor is a spy novel originally published in 1936. At first glance today, it seems a period piece, a reminder of vanished attitudes from a vanished world. But the book was a success in its day, earning praise from reviewers in the U.S. and Australia, and its author was one of Britain's most famous thriller writers, at the height of his fame. His sales were said to run into the millions.

"Horler for Excitement!" was the marketing slogan adorning the dust jackets of books by Sydney Horler. He knew his readers wanted a pacy narrative, vivid and varied settings (some of them overseas), and plenty of action, and *The Traitor* delivered. For anyone reading the book in the twenty-first century, there is a bonus. The story allows us a glimpse of the tensions and stresses within British society in the mid-1930s.

The First World War had been bloody and terrifying. Everyone knew someone who had been killed or wounded, and memories of the horrors of the trenches were slow to fade. As Hitler and Mussolini began to throw their weight about on the international stage, renewed international conflict became an increasing risk. Opinion was, however, divided as to how to deal with the aggressors. Some, like George Orwell and Winston Churchill, opposed appeasement, but others found it impossible to contemplate the calamity of another conflict; many were committed pacifists, and the Peace Pledge Union enjoyed massive support. Above all, the 1930s was a decade in which uncertainty and anxiety gradually gave way to fear of a formidable foe.

Against this backdrop, Horler crafted a story with two strands. The first, set in 1918, just before the end of the war, sees young Captain Alan Clinton in Paris, bewitched by the seductive agent Minna Braun, alias "Marie Roget." He spends the night with her in the hotel Lion d'Or, and his act of folly leads to the loss of over five thousand British lives.

The second part of the story is set seventeen years later, in the turbulent present. Minna Braun has switched allegiance from Germany to Ronstadt, a "new state" of sixty million people ruled over by the supreme dictator Kuhnreich, a Jew-hating fanatic. Ronstadt is, of course, a thinly disguised Germany, and Kuhnreich is Hitler. As his chief of Secret Police tells Minna, "War is coming—and that means that our secret agents must get busy." Europe has again become a battleground, and Minna is pressed into service once more.

Alan Clinton is now a colonel working for MI5. Other than his old friend Peter Mallory, however, it seems that nobody knows Clinton's shameful secret. Before long, it is not Alan Clinton but his equally gullible son Bobby who makes a trip to continental Europe and falls prey to Minna's seductive wiles. Will he betray Britain, and if so, what will be the consequences? The story rattles along to a climax at a military trial which takes place while Bobby's girlfriend races against time in a desperate attempt to prove that he is no traitor.

The long-term consequences of acts of cowardice or criminal stupidity during the First World War were a recurrent plot element in thriller and mystery fiction over the next twenty years, and featured in notable detective novels such as Philip MacDonald's *The Rasp*, Henry Wade's *The High Sheriff*, and the Agatha Christie classic *And Then There Were None*. But although in *The Traitor*, Horler offers a twist ending and a "least likely suspect" solution of the kind which became very familiar in whodunits written during the Golden Age of Murder, this was a time when sharp distinctions were drawn between thriller writers and detective novelists.

Edgar Wallace (whom Horler much admired), "Sapper," and Horler himself were prolific and popular thriller writers, but even in the 1930s, their books were as patronised by the literati as they were loved by vast numbers of readers. Dorothy L. Sayers—a highly influential critic, as well as a prominent author of detective stories—questioned their quality, saying in one review: "People sometimes complain that I am harsh and high-hat about thrillers...I give you my word that when I meet the least touch of real originality, or creepy-crawlery, or glamour, or humour, or sheer rollicking cut-and-thrust-and-have-at-'em combativeness in a thriller I hail it with cries of joy. But 99 times out of 100 I find only bad English, cliché, balderdash, and boredom." She and Horler had no time for each other, and it is fair to say that, while her reputation has endured, and Horler's has plummeted since his death.

The reappearance of The Traitor does, however, give a new generation of spy fiction fans a chance to judge Horler afresh, making up their own minds rather than relying on preconceptions. This is, surely, the great service which the British Library has rendered in retrieving long-forgotten works of popular fiction from its vaults. As many readers will do, I came to this book without ever having read Horler before. I had, however, read plenty of criticism of his work by commentators with even less enthusiasm for his work than

Sayers. And whilst the British Library makes no claims for Horler as a literary stylist, the dash and verve of this book give clues as to why he sold so well in his heyday.

Sydney Horler (1888–1954) was a journalist who published his first novel in 1920, and his first thriller, *The Mystery of No. 1*, five years later. The success of this book prompted him to become a full-time thriller writer, and more than one hundred novels followed. "Tiger" Standish, his most popular character, was a freelance secret agent. Horler was an industrious rather than innovative writer, but he developed the knack of keeping his readers gripped, and *The Traitor* exemplifies the type of British spy thriller that stayed in fashion until the likes of Eric Ambler and Graham Greene took the genre in a new direction.

Martin Edwards
www.martinedwardsbooks.co

Book I

Chapter I

The Messenger

The crossing had been particularly vile, the journey to Paris, if anything, worse, and Alan Clinton, as he stepped from the crowded carriage at the Gare du Nord and stretched his cramped limbs in an ecstasy of abandon, swore with corresponding gusto.

"To hell with this bloody war!" he cried, glaring about him.

"I quite agree with you, Clinton," said a voice behind his left shoulder.

Who the devil—? He turned quickly. Then he reassured himself with a forced smile. He had never particularly cared for Brian Fordinghame, especially since Fordinghame had apparently run to cover and got himself a safe and cushy job in the Home Branch of Military Intelligence. "M.I."—it was to laugh: if these gentry who were so cursedly careful of their own skins had served with him in the trenches for the past three years and a half, they'd know a lot more about Military Intelligence than they did at present!

A man of about thirty, lean and fit-looking, with keen, quizzical grey eyes, stood regarding him with a slight smile.

Thinking of what he himself was about to do, Clinton felt that those same grey eyes were boring into him; they seemed to have the faculty of looking right through his body into his very soul. It was disconcerting.

The man wearing the green tabs of an Intelligence staff captain now nodded.

"How are you, Clinton?" he asked.

It was perhaps because the sight of green tabs had, during the past twelve months at least, invariably irritated him that the other's reply was brusque.

"Oh, not so bad. And in any case"—ill temper coming swiftly to the surface, "it's a lot *you* know about the war, Fordinghame."

The other, disregarding the insult, refused to be ruffled. Instead, he smiled once again. It was an attractive smile—attractive in spite of its icy quality.

"Had a good crossing?" he asked.

"Lousy."

"Where are you going now?"

"My hotel. I want some sleep."

Fordinghame seemed determined to be friendly—and hospitable.

"I heard you were on this train, and I thought I would come along to the station and ask you to have a bite of food with me."

"Why?"

"Oh, no reason in particular," was the non-committal answer; "I just thought I'd like to have your company for an hour."

The words did something to soften the other's mood. Clinton's voice, as he spoke, contained an element of regret.

"Sorry, Fordinghame. I'd like to—but, honestly, I'm dog-tired. I *must* get some sleep."

"Where are you staying?"

"Oh—" he paused. "A little place I know. Cheap—that's a consideration, these days."

"Yes, indeed," agreed the staff captain. "Well, another time, perhaps. I shall be in Paris for a few days. When do you go up the line?"

"To-morrow, curse it!"

"Well, good-bye—and good luck!"

The man who had crossed to Paris with important dispatches raised his right hand in a corresponding salute and then walked quickly away to find some sort of a conveyance. In August, 1918, one was lucky to find a decent taxi-cab.

He wasn't lucky—and this increased his ill temper. The aged driver, who glared at him out of hideous, red-lidded eyes, was almost as much a derelict as the vehicle which—after a considerable argument, conducted with asperity on both sides—commenced to wheeze its way out of the crowded station.

Clinton flung himself back against the malodorous upholstery. The interior of the taxi smelt abominably, and, fresh from home, his nostrils had not yet become accustomed again to the vile stench of war. The fact was, he was thoroughly fed-up—if it hadn't been for Marie he didn't know but what.... But that, of course, was madness; and, especially now that he had his present job to do, the idea must not be seriously entertained. This did not prevent him, however, from wishing that a million miles separated him from everything connected with this cursed war. It was a hopeless ambition, for the end seemed as far off as ever. Even in London the never-ending horror had thrust itself upon him at every conceivable turn. In the theatres and music-halls one could not escape it; at the Service clubs the talk was of nothing else; even if one went out to a private dinner party one was pestered with questions about the trenches. The newspapers, the posters on the walls, the hoardings, even the shop-windows—God! How everything reeked of the beastliness!

And now, here he was back in the very centre of things—and within twenty-four hours he would be reporting himself.... That reminded him. With a swift clutch at the heart, his hand closed on the dispatch-case by his side. A wave of relief passed through him. He must be careful. Yes, he must be a damned sight more careful than he would be if he were actually in the trenches, for—if what that Major-General fellow at the W.O. had hinted at was correct—thousands of lives, instead of merely his own, depended on the contents of that case being handed over safely.

The reflection sobered him. And it brought the somewhat consoling knowledge that, if he were fed up himself, millions of other human beings were in the same boat. He must carry on; the job was not yet finished. And, in any case, there was Marie....

Twenty minutes later, the disreputable taxi drew up before a small but comfortable-looking hotel in a side street off the Boulevard des Capucines. Clinton had stayed at the Lion d'Or before; he had discovered this cosy hostelry some months previously, and he had a particular reason for choosing it now. So far as he had been able to ascertain, it was not frequented very much by Allied officers—a recommendation in itself.

The thought came, as he paid off the gargoyle of a driver, that Fordinghame might possibly have followed him to the place. Of course, the idea on the surface was ridiculous—but he took a keen look around all the same. These espionage fellows took themselves damned seriously, and one couldn't be too careful. Not that he had anything to bother about—if every Allied officer who slept with a French girl now and then was to be cross-examined...! Yet, all the same, he couldn't very well get those searching eyes of the Intelligence officer out of his mind. Funny, that Fordinghame should have been at the station at the very moment that he got out of the train. Had he been waiting for him—and, if so, why?

He told himself the next moment not to be such a damned fool. Any one would think he had something to hide—that he contemplated doing something shady.

Shrugging his shoulders, he walked into the hotel.

The dinner had been worth eating—which was something to say, in these days—and now Clinton was taking his ease. He was stretched out on a sofa in the private sitting-room he had engaged, when a distant siren brought him to his feet. Wrapped in the contemplation of his thoughts and the comfort induced by the meal, all sense of the war had temporarily slipped from him. But now the strident warning that enemy aircraft were paying another visit to the French capital brought him back to reality with a jerk. He cursed volubly.

The siren shrieked again—this time so loudly that the picture of the Emperor Napoleon with the tricolour draped over it, which was the most prominent furnishing on the opposite wall, seemed to his excited fancy to quiver.

Throwing aside the copy of *La Vie Parisienne*, Clinton crossed the floor. As he did so, a knock sounded on the door.

"Come in," he ordered irritably.

A waiter, wearing a much-stained suit, entered nervously.

"You rang, monsieur?"

Clinton remembered that he had touched the bell a few seconds before the first siren had sounded.

"Yes," he returned, "and you've taken a pretty long time answering it."

The man became obsequious.

"A thousand pardons, monsieur, but the hotel is so busy."

"I dare say. Still," pointing to the half-empty bottle of wine which had given him annoyance, "this wine's rotten—that's why I rang. I want it changed."

The waiter made a gesture of hopelessness.

"That will be difficult, monsieur. The war makes it very difficult to get good wine." Another gesture of hopelessness. "All Paris knows that."

"That may be, but this would take the first prize for muck—take it away."

The waiter, shrugging his shoulders once more, approached the small table, picked up the bottle and glass and prepared to leave the room.

"I will do my best, monsieur. I am sorry—"

Clinton, looking at the forlorn wretch—the waiter's sense of hopelessness had struck him during dinner—changed his tone.

"Oh, that's all right. Cut along now, and be back as soon as you can."

"Yes, monsieur." He walked to the door and then turned. A finger that shook pointed to a warning hanging on the wall. "It is necessary to remind you, monsieur, to read that notice. You must be very careful about keeping the curtains drawn. The law against showing any lights is very severe, with terrible penalties, and the siren has just sounded."

"I heard it myself—I don't happen to be deaf."

The waiter seemed inclined to linger. "No doubt by this time you are used to the air bombs, monsieur?"

The British officer laughed. "Well, we've had just a few in London, you know, not to mention the trenches. So they're expecting those Zeppelins here to-night, are they?"

A look of hatred flashed into the sallow face.

"Yes, monsieur; on every night that there is no moon we expect them now. Ah! *ces sales Boches!*" A grimy fist was clenched and lifted up.

Clinton watched him with barely concealed amusement. These Gallic melodramatics!

"Well, cut along now," he ordered again.

"Yes, monsieur." But the man still stayed. "If I had a Boche here. . . ." This time both hands were raised, whilst their owner went through the motions of choking a man to death. "We have the raids so often now that every one in Paris gets to hear the noise of the engines in his sleep." Some indistinct French which the British officer could not understand followed, and then the man spoke in English again. "The boom of those bombs on our poor city!"

By this time Clinton was getting sick of the fellow. Self-pity was all right in its way—but Paris was suffering from a surfeit of it. He looked at the fellow keenly.

"How have you managed to escape military service?"

The man put a hand to his breast.

"It is my heart, monsieur. Ah, but it is great sorrow for me. How gladly would I serve *la patrie*! How freely would I give it my life!" He threatened to become maudlin. The listener had the traditional English dislike of sentimentality. Besides, by now he was tired of the fellow's face.

"Well," he said, "if you take my tip you'll hang on here—and think yourself damned lucky to have got such a good billet."

The waiter's face changed. Hatred convulsed its ugliness. Absurd as it was, Clinton thought for a moment that the man was actually going to attack him.

"You joke, monsieur," cried the other angrily. "Every Frenchman loves his country—and would gladly die for it."

"A good many Englishmen have done that—poor devils! And let me tell you—by the way, what's your name?"

"Pierre, monsieur."

"Let me tell you, Pierre, that the trenches aren't exactly drawing-rooms."

"That I can well understand, monsieur; I have heard so many stories.... Yes, this war is terrible. And how will it end?"

"Oh, Jerry'll get whacked all right; don't you worry about that. He'll want some wearing down—but we shall do it."

"What a happy day that will be for France, monsieur!" (The speaker struck an attitude which, if Clinton had yielded to the impulse, would have made him double up with laughter.) "The tragedy of Sedan! The humiliation of Alsace-Lorraine! Ah, but they will all be wiped out upon the day that France enters Berlin in victory."

"Yeh. But I'm afraid there's a long way to go yet."

The waiter thrust his sallow face forward.

"Are you from the Somme front, monsieur?"

"No." A sudden suspicion came. "Why do you ask that?"

The fellow was ready with his reply.

"My brother is there—on the Somme front. He is with the artillery."

"I see. Well, I don't envy him; the Somme isn't any too pleasant a place nowadays."

"Don't I know?"

"How do you know?"

"I hear from my brother whenever he can write," was the quick retort. "The Boche, does he not make the—what you say?—offensive there, *n'est-ce-pas*?"

"I don't know. He's usually doing something of the sort." Clinton's patience was exhausted. "Look here, what about that wine?"

The waiter crouched humbly.

"Pardon, monsieur. I think too much of the war, but it is because of my brother." He turned and put a hand on the door. "But I go now."

Yet he could not leave the room without turning round once more.

"Monsieur, a thousand pardons, I forget. There is another British officer in the hotel to-night; he has asked for you."

Clinton took some time before replying. Marie was due in a few minutes—and he didn't want her seen by any one.

"A British officer?" he returned.

"Yes, monsieur."

The next words were as though he were speaking to himself: "I don't know any one in Paris who is likely to ask for me. Do you know his name?"

"Capitaine Mallory."

Relief came in an overwhelming flood. Clinton laughed. ("Peter Mallory," he told himself. "Well I'm damned!") And then, to the waiter: "Ask him to come up at once."

"*Oui, monsieur.*" The fellow was smiling as he turned away.

Chapter II

The Warning

Left alone, Clinton removed his Sam Browne belt and, after turning out the electric light, drew the curtains. A searchlight could be seen cutting a wide swathe across the night sky. He switched on the electric light again just as the door opened to admit a good-looking man of roughly his own age, wearing the uniform of a Captain in the Royal Field Artillery. The infantry officer darted across the room and the two friends cordially shook hands. Captain Peter Mallory sat himself down, and lit a cigarette with great relish.

"I say, Alan," he exclaimed, "this is simply great! Fancy meeting you here! I just dropped in on the off-chance—you remember telling me about this place after your last leave?"

"Yes—of course." (If there was one man he knew he could trust, it was Mallory. All his former hesitancy disappeared at the consoling remembrance.) "Marvellous, isn't it? But where the devil have you sprung from?"

"I'm direct from the line on five days' leave—slipping across to Dover to-morrow."

"Good man. I expect you're glad to get out of the shambles for a bit?"

Mallory's face hardened.

"It's been hell with the lid off, this last week. The Boche has had a battery of those bloody flying pigs directly opposite us. I tell you, I'm eternally dodging the blasted things, even in my sleep." He shook himself. "Nerves all shot to hell."

"Never mind, old boy," returned his friend consolingly. "You're out of it for five days; make the best of them."

"You bet I will!" But even the thought of his prospective good time in England could not shake the other's fear from off his shoulders. As though excusing himself, he continued: "You see, I've been in an advanced bit of trench, with just a handful of other blokes. It was pretty awful. Jerry bunged them over as though he was working some devilish piece of clockwork. *One—two—three—four! One—two—three—four!* A couple of seconds in between each, with all of us haring up and down, dodging them all the time. If they'd altered the sequence once, they'd have had the lot of us. And it went on all day. *One—two—three—four!!!*—until there wasn't a bit of that blasted trench left to hold." He shuddered.

Clinton did his best to impart some much-needed cheerfulness.

"Well, you'll be in London in a few hours." Then, as though anxious to change the subject: "Let's see, Peter,—the last time I heard of your crush, they were near La Bassée."

"Yes; we moved to the Somme six weeks ago. By the way, I haven't asked you yet, Alan—what are you doing here?"

"Oh, I'm just over from London with some secret dispatches for Major-General Bentley—the wallah in charge of R.E."

Mallory grinned—for the first time.

"Good for you! Seconded for special duty, eh?"

"Something like that. I don't suppose I'd tell any one else in the wide world, Peter; but I don't know myself out of those bloody trenches."

The other nodded.

"Don't I understand? Have you got the dispatches here?"

"Yes, and in the safest place." The speaker looked at the attaché case on the chair by his side. "There they are—and there they stay. I'm never going to take my eyes off them."

His visitor rose, went to the door, opened it, looked out, and shut it again. Then he returned.

"Look here, Alan, old boy," he said seriously, "let me drop you a hint. If you've got secret stuff about, look after it very, very carefully. Paris is alive with German spies. You may not believe it; but I know it's true. I've heard stories—perfectly appalling stories, too. You can't trust *anybody*. Why, even behind our lines it's been simply awful. Some peasants—supposed peasants, that is—were shot the very day I came away."

"What were they doing?"

"Directing Boche guns."

"I thought the spy mania was being overdone?"

Mallory was decisive.

"Not a bit of it. Paris is thick with the vermin. The whole war area, come to that, is infested with the enemy 'agents.' Watch your step while you're here, Alan, especially"—pointing to the attaché case—"with that dynamite stuff hanging about."

The other, although impressed, felt obliged to laugh.

"Oh, I'll be all right; don't you worry," he said with every confidence.

Mallory looked at him fixedly.

"I still think you believe I'm pulling your leg," he remarked.

"Not a bit of it," returned his friend. "I was only going to say that the Boche seems to be spending a hell of a lot of money on spies—and the better part of it must go to waste."

"All the same, their General Staff has got some damned fine tips now and again. One good coup is worth spending a few thousands to get."

"Oh, I agree." Clinton's tone was apparently indifferent. "You're fresh from the line, Peter; what's the feeling up there?"

"Well, according to what I've heard, Germany's beginning to flag. She's getting pretty desperate. The Army are becoming disheartened; that's why they are so anxious to catch us on the hop again and ram home a good old uppercut. It's the moral effect they're after; they want to bolster up their men."

Clinton turned away. Good pal as Peter was, he didn't want him hanging about much longer.

"Well, thanks, old boy, for the tip," he remarked. "I'll watch my step, as you say."

He hoped that Mallory would take the hint; but the Artillery captain still remained in his chair.

"By the way," said the visitor, "I haven't asked you yet—how's Cynthia and the kid?"

His friend became evasive.

"Oh, they're all right. You'd better look 'em up when you're in town. They'll both be glad to see you."

"I will if I have time. Let's see, how old is the boy now?"

"Getting on for eight."

"Big chap?"

"Yes, he's growing."

"Good Lord!" said Mallory. "The last time I saw him he was just a babe in arms. How time flies! But then, we lose touch with everything out here—damn it!"

"Why aren't you crossing to-night?" Clinton now asked.

"Oh, I've got an appointment."

The other laughed.

"Well, live while you can, old man—that's my motto."

Mallory stared at him.

"But you're married—with a terribly nice girl as your wife."

"Oh, I know all about that—but still, live while you can. You may be dead to-morrow."

Mallory shrugged his shoulders as though he admitted the truth of the statement without subscribing to it.

"Heard from Jill Chester lately?" asked Clinton.

"Jill Chester?" repeated Mallory. "That's all off. I meant to write and tell you."

"All off? Really? But I saw the engagement in the *Times*—when was it, now?"

"Over seven months ago."

"As long as that? You're right, Peter—one does lose all touch with things out here. Nice kid, Jill. I'm sorry."

Mallory looked uncomfortable.

"Yes, she was a nice kid all right, but we didn't seem to go together as a team. Anyway, marriage is too serious if you aren't absolutely sure. She's married now, you know."

"Married—to another bloke?"

"Of course! Some Belgian chap—Baron de la Proube. Met him, from what I can make out, when she was doing hospital work in town."

"Rather quick, wasn't it?"

A short, hard laugh greeted the statement.

"Well, everything's quick nowadays. Life, death, marriage—every damned thing. She was infatuated, I suppose. He was quite good-looking—for a Belgian. Besides, he was a Baron; that counts—even in war."

"I suppose it does. Must have been rather a shock to you, old boy."

"I don't think about it any more. But it's had this effect: it's made me a fatalist; if I'm to stop one, I shall stop one—there's an end to it. And—"

Clinton broke in.

"Don't talk like that, old boy. This bloody war is bound to end sooner or later—"

Mallory sprang up, evidencing signs of shell-shock. "Later rather than sooner," he declared. "I'm beginning to think that life is hell—sheer, unmitigated hell. Oh, God!" He broke down, repeating the refrain: "*One—two—three—four!*" The next moment he had flung his face forward and had covered it with his hands.

"*Mallory!*" cried Clinton, in alarm.

The other looked up.

"Oh, I'm all right. Don't you worry. The fact is, we're all in a bad way in my part of the line. The Boche has plastered us until our nerves are raw—*raw*, I tell you!"

His listener was glad to hear a knock on the door.

"Come in," he called.

The waiter entered, carrying a tray on which was a bottle of wine and two glasses. Clinton greeted him with enthusiasm.

"Is that the new wine?"

"Yes, monsieur; it is something very special, and I have two glasses. I thought your friend—"

"Good for you." He flung a coin, which was dexterously caught.

"*Merci, monsieur.*"

When the two friends were alone again, Clinton, after filling the glasses, gave a toast. It was the motto of the school they had both attended. The words made Mallory laugh.

"Good God!" he said. "What memories that brings back!" He fell into reminiscence. "Do you remember how we made Foshy Thomas walk the plank into the swimming bath?"

"Good Lord, yes!" returned the other. "Bobby Corbett went through it for that." He refilled Mallory's glass. "Good old Repington! Not a bad show; wish I were back there now. Well, here we are—no heeltaps."

"Cheerio, Alan!" cried Mallory, and then drank.

"Happy days!"

The R.F.A. captain, after putting down the empty glass, again fell into reminiscence.

"Do you remember that dormitory feast we had in Number Seven, when Chunk Johnson upset the tin of sardines in bed?"

They both smiled at the memory.

"And how Mitchamore tried to clean up the muck with a sock?" supplied Clinton.

They laughed again.

"Poor little devil!" exclaimed Mallory. "I'll never forget Mitchamore. God, Alan! To think how happy we were as kids—and then to be in this!" He shuddered again, and Clinton, afraid that another attack of shell-shock was coming, went across and placed his arm about the shaking man's shoulders.

"It'll end one day—and now you're going on leave—isn't that something worth having?"

"Yes—but the subs are in the bloody Channel. They'll get me; I feel sure of it. I'll never see—my mother again."

"Nonsense! Of course you will. You'll be kissing her good-night in twenty-four hours." Searching about in his mind for a change of subject, he asked: "Did you finish up in Galloway's house? I forget."

To his joy, Mallory responded in a normal tone.

"No, in Eggie Beard's. I went there the term after you left. By the way, I met Eggie's son last week. He's a major now in the Army Service Corps—brought some stuff up the line. We were talking over old times, and he mentioned you."

"Nice of him."

"Funny, but a fellow can get quite sentimental out here. Have you noticed it? Tommy Beard said the same thing. We were talking about the old school motto."

"'Stand by'? Well, most old Repingtonians have lived up to that out here, I should say."

"Yes. I saw Jenkins about three months ago."

"Jenkins—the white mouse expert?"

"You know what a nasty, smelly little beast he used to be—always getting caned by Burnell for not washing his ears?"

"Oh, hell!" laughed Clinton. "Don't I? He was the one fellow who didn't mind fagging for that swine Chalker." He poured out some more wine. "Here, drink this down; didn't I say no heeltaps?"

Mallory drank.

"I'm better for that," he said when he put down the glass. "And it's great to see you and to talk over old times, Alan."

Clinton responded courteously, although he was desperately anxious, now, that the other should be off. Marie was late already—if she should come....

"Well, I think I'll be turning in," he announced.

Before Mallory could reply, there was the sound of a terrific whirring of engines. They both stiffened to listen.

"Zeppelins?" queried Clinton.

"I expect so," was the slow reply. "They get a raid here practically every night now when the moon isn't out. I must be shoving off," he added a second later. "My man hasn't turned up, or they would have let me know."

Again he paused.

"I dare say it's asking a lot, but you wouldn't like me to stay a little longer, old man, would you?" His tone was almost pathetic.

Clinton felt terribly embarrassed, and something of this unease showed itself in his voice.

"At any other time I should have asked you, Peter, but—"

"A woman?" put in the other.

The other responded to the challenge immediately.

"Suppose it is?"

"Oh, nothing"—showing plainly that he was disappointed. "Well, I'll be pushing along."

"Look in and see me to-morrow before you leave, if it's only to say chin-chin."

"Righto!" His eyes turned towards the attaché case.

"Oh"—answering the unspoken question—"don't you worry. I'll have to go before they do."

"You can't be too careful here."

"What—this hotel is all right, isn't it?"

"I meant in Paris. It always was a damned hot shop—and now it's ten million times worse than ever."

"Oh, don't you worry." Clinton held out his hand, and Mallory, after a moment's hesitation, took it.

"Good-night, old fellow," he said, walking through the door.

"Good-night."

There was a hint of coolness in Clinton's tone as he returned the salutation. Then, with the other gone, he bolted the door, walked across the room, took the attaché case from the chair and turned the key. Taking some papers out of the case, he assured himself that none were missing. Then, replacing them, he locked the case again just as a tap—which sounded very discreet—came to his ears. Crossing the room, he unlocked the door.

Outside was the sallow waiter.

"Mademoiselle Roget to see you, monsieur," he said in a sly whisper.

Disregarding the furtive smile of the man, Clinton asked: "Where is she?"

"Below, in the lounge—waiting, monsieur."

The man was about to turn away when Clinton stopped him.

"Have you got a key to this room, Pierre?"

"A key, monsieur?" The waiter seemed startled.

"You heard what I said, you fool—a key."

"Monsieur wants a key to the room." The words were repeated in the manner of a stupid child endeavouring to learn a difficult lesson.

"A key to this room—I want to lock it up. Now do you understand?"

"I will go, monsieur."

With the waiter departed on his errand, Clinton picked up the dispatch-case and stood in a thoughtful attitude for several minutes. He appeared to be pondering over some problem.

So it was that when Pierre returned with the required key, he found the officer still brooding.

"Here is the key, monsieur."

Clinton took it, drew the man outside, and locked the door.

"Now, tell Mademoiselle Roget that I shall be down in a minute—give her my apologies for having kept her waiting."

"*Oui, monsieur.*" The fellow hesitated for a moment and then put the question which was evidently uppermost in his mind. "Will not monsieur leave his case in the room?"

Clinton turned on him angrily.

"Mind your own business, damn you! Get on downstairs."

This time the waiter fairly scuttled away.

Although his heart was thumping like an excited schoolboy's, Clinton waited until he had tried the door again and thus made sure no one could enter the room without the key which was in his pocket. The words he had heard only a few minutes before from Mallory had returned to warn him. That was why he had picked up the dispatch-case instead of leaving it in the room. His suitcase was still standing by the side of the easy chair. He had not yet troubled to have it taken to his bedroom.

He snapped his fingers irritably. What a fool he was! Mallory's nerves were shattered by shell-fire; that was why he had panicked so. Boche spies! The shadow on his face disappeared as he thought of the girl waiting for him, below. Marie, bless her, would make him forget. Of course, from the ethical point of view, he was behaving like a cad—but this was war; and aren't women sent into the world to provide entertainment for weary soldiers? That had been the rule since the beginning of Time. Besides—and here he shrugged his shoulders—with an invalid wife....Oh, hell! He was getting soft. He wished Mallory had not spouted all that stuff, although in the beginning he had been glad enough to see him.

Turning, he walked quickly towards the lift.

Chapter III

The Trap

For the space of ten seconds after the British officer's footsteps had been heard walking down the corridor, the sitting-room he had just left remained undisturbed. Then the portrait of Napoleon slid aside like a shutter, and a man could have been observed looking into the room from behind it. After a careful survey, he stepped down, showing himself to belong to that unmistakable wartime class—a Prussian officer in mufti.

The intruder had not long to wait; a couple of minutes only had passed before the lock of the door clicked and the waiter Pierre entered, key in hand. At the sight of the other man, Pierre's manner underwent a startling transformation. He saluted and stood rigidly at attention. He had changed from a nondescript into something approaching a personality.

Lieutenant von Ritter snapped out a question.

"Is the fool gone?"

"Yes, Herr Lieutenant. We shall have at least five minutes."

The officer made a gesture of caution.

"Speak lower," he said. "You never know who may be out there in the corridor. Have you arranged everything?"

"Yes, Herr Lieutenant."

"When Marie comes up, wait for your opportunity, and give her this. She'll know what to do."

The waiter took the phial that was extended to him.

"Yes, Herr Lieutenant. Has the Englishman brought anything important?"

The officer glared at him as though resenting such impertinence. Then, excitement rising in his voice, he replied: "Something colossal, I am told. We mustn't miss it."

"*Himmel*, no! It is not every day we get such a chance. Were you cramped up there, Herr Lieutenant?"

The other made a grimace.

"Horribly. Still, it's worth some discomfort to do such work for the Fatherland." With youthful enthusiasm—he did not look more than twenty-six—he continued: "This fool Englishman has brought the formula of a new gas—at least, that is what they wired us from London. It is something big, without a doubt."

"We must hurry, Herr Lieutenant," stated the waiter, looking anxiously at the door.

For reply, von Ritter pointed to the phial.

"That is what you are to give to Marie," he said. "That will keep him quiet—while we deal with the contents of his case."

"But he has taken the case with him. We must wait until he returns."

"Never mind. See that Marie has that stuff."

"Won't he taste it, Herr Lieutenant?"

"No; it's practically tasteless. He'll be off like a log in a quarter of an hour."

The waiter smiled evilly.

"You'd better go now," observed the other; "he may be back any minute."

"Very well, Herr Lieutenant." Saluting, he turned and left the room.

Waiting only until he heard the key click in the lock again, von Ritter re-entered the spy trap, shut it, and the picture of Napoleon swung back into place.

◇◇◇

When, five minutes later, Alan Clinton entered the room by the side of a remarkably pretty girl of nineteen he looked as though he had cast all his cares aside. But he did not give Marie Roget the passionate embrace she expected until he had locked the door behind them and deposited the dispatch-case in a chair by the farther side of the room.

"Have I to wait so long?" plaintively inquired his companion.

He turned quickly.

"Darling!" he cried.

After kissing her passionately he held her at arm's length and looked long into her face.

"Do you know, you're prettier than ever, Marie."

The girl laughed.

"You say such nice things, Alan," she replied, with only a trace of accent. "That is perhaps one of the reasons why I love you so."

She yielded herself to his caressing hands.

"It is lovely to be with you again—it has seemed so long since you went away. Englishmen are so frank and charming," she added with a certain naïveté.

"Englishmen?"

She laughed at her mistake—"One Englishman, I should have said."

Still he was not quite satisfied.

"There's no one else?" he asked suspiciously. "My God, if I thought there was, Marie—"

She satisfied him with a kiss.

"Of course not. Don't be so silly. I love you—and you alone. Oh, Alan, how I do love you!"

He was mollified.

"If you hadn't told me that I think I should have gone mad." The suspicion passing, he became himself again.

The girl took off her hat and flung it gaily into a chair.

"Now tell me," she said, "why have I had to wait so long? Why have you not written to me before?"

"Darling child, you seem to forget that there's a war on. I've been terribly busy in London."

"Too busy to think of even love?" she provoked him.

"Once more, child, let me remind you that we're at war."

"But isn't that the time for love? The warrior and the woman, *n'est-ce-pas*?" Again she looked at him in a manner that made his heart melt.

"My God, Marie!" he cried, straining her to him again. "You're marvellous—just marvellous!"

"What do you do when I'm away?" asked Clinton after a moment.

"What do I do, Alan? Why, I spend all the time thinking of you—that is what I do. I am always thinking of you. Do you remember that garden at Amiens?"

"Shall I ever forget it?" he exclaimed. "The first time I saw you—" He stared at the wall above her head. "Looking back, it's all like a dream."

Her lips sought his mouth. "But this is real."

"Yes," he laughed, "there's no dream about this. Come here, you witch." He took a chair and pulled her down on to his knee.

With a slim finger she traced imaginary lines on his forehead and face.

"You look worried, Alan—troubled. Is there anything wrong with you?"

He sighed.

"Oh, life's just a nightmare—has been for me lately, anyway."

"A nightmare?" Her face expressed surprise. "But you are not in the trenches. You have been home to England—or is it that you have told me lies?"

"No, I haven't told you any lies. I've been back home all right. But"—breaking off—"look here, we mustn't talk about the war!—It's taboo—*verboten*."

She reproached him with a gesture.

"'*Verboten*'? That's a German word. I hate it."

He laughed.

"Well, come to that, 'Boche' sounds German too—but everybody's using it." A knock. "And here comes our champagne."

He unlocked the door.

"Those dreadful Boches!" She shuddered. "They are trying to blow my beautiful Paris to bits. But do not worry yourself; let us drink this wine"—turning away and busying herself with the champagne which the waiter Pierre had now brought.

"And don't you worry about that: they won't succeed, my dear." He raised the glass she gave him.

The words appeared to console her, for she placed her head on his shoulder while her arms crept round his neck.

The departing waiter discreetly shut the door.

"How much longer is this terrible war going to last, Alan? When can we be together for always?"

At that moment Clinton would have been prepared to sacrifice what remained of his marital honour; he would have liked nothing better than to escape with this enchantress to some distant part of the world, where they could spend the rest of their lives in peace. But this could not be thought of; it belonged to the realm of fantasy. With a jerk, he came back once again to reality. Once more he locked the door.

"Until we can get the Boche on the run, my dear," he said, answering her question.

"And when will that be?"

He shook his head.

"Ask me something easier." A note of asperity crept into his voice.

But she was not satisfied.

"You English are so wonderful. Even here in Paris they are relying on you to beat the Boche." She looked up at his face and her lips pressed themselves against his cheek. "Haven't your Generals anything—what you say?—up their sleeve?"

"Well, as a matter of fact—" He stopped suddenly. Good God! What had he been about to say? He must be more careful.

"What were you going to tell me, Alan?" she pressed.

He disengaged the arms that were clinging to him and spoke seriously.

"Look here, darling," he told her, "we've simply got to stop talking about the war."

She made a little grimace.

"Is it that you don't trust me?"

"Of course not."

"Then tell me what this new work is you're doing in London."

"You mustn't ask me that. It's a secret."

"Oh, I'm sorry."

"That's all right, but don't let's talk about the war. Time is far too precious. Oh, Marie, if you only knew how I have looked forward to seeing you again! It was because I felt I would go mad if I didn't hold you in my arms soon that I got them to send me across instead of another man."

"Another man? Who was he?"

"Oh, he was in the regular Intelligence."

"But how brave of you! You might have been murdered. This Paris, I am told, is full of enemy spies."

He laughed. With her bewitching body so near him, the thought of death was impossible. With a fresh wave of intoxication passing through him, he drew her to him again. For a time the world seemed to stand still. Then Marie disengaged herself.

"You English are so splendid," she said, lifting a beautifully moulded hand to stroke his face. "My eyes fill with tears when I think of your sacrifices for my beautiful France."

If any one else had said the grandiloquent words Clinton would have smiled. As it was, there was a certain curtness in his reply.

"We gave our word and we had to keep it."

She embraced him.

"Alan, you are so strong. How I love you when you speak like that!"

"Yes, yes, my dear. But now let's be practical. Going to stay here with me to-night? But of course you will—you promised."

She looked at him provocatively.

"Did I?"

"Of course you did. Oh, Marie, you're not going to disappoint me?"

"No, darling, I will not disappoint. I have been saving myself up for you. Yes, I will stay here to-night and we will make wonderful love. But I must return first thing to-morrow morning."

"Darling! I say," he went on, prompted by a feeling of generosity, "wouldn't you like to go out to a theatre or something? I hope you won't"—laughing in an ashamed sort of way—"but I had to ask you."

"You needn't have. No, I want to make the most of every minute with you. I can go to the theatre when you are away."

He looked at her.

"You speak wonderful English, Marie."

She met the half-uttered suspicion unafraid.

"Have I not told you?" she retorted. "I was so much in London."

"When was this?"

"When I was a child—just a little girl. Do you know Hampstead Heath?"

He laughed.

"Hampstead Heath? Yes, I know it very well. Good God! I can hardly imagine at this moment that such a place exists." He put a hand up to his head. "Does it strike you that this room is getting very hot?"

"Hot?" she repeated. "No, I had not thought so."

"Is the window open?"

"Yes—why?"

"Excuse me, darling." He rose unsteadily to his feet and walked across the room. His manner was that of a man who was afraid that something was going to happen to him.

She followed him.

"Sit down, my dear. You are not going to be ill?"

"I hope not. I was perfectly all right until I drank that wine."

"Oh," she said, "it could not have been the wine. I had a glass myself, if you remember—and, you see, I am perfectly all right. No, something must have upset you during the journey. Soon you will be perfectly all right—and I am here to look after you."

Thus urged, Clinton sat down and, fired by her beauty, patted his knee.

"*Marie!*"

The girl shook her head.

"No, no more love-making for the moment. You must recover yourself. Besides, the waiter may be coming back in a minute. Put your feet up and be comfortable."

His speech became slurred.

"The waiter....I—don't—know—anything—about—the waiter—coming—back. But, of course—if—you—want anything?"

"I'd like some coffee...."

"You—shall—have—some. And...chocolates, eh?" Getting to his feet again, he staggered across the room and pressed the electric bell.

"You are so kind to me, Alan."

If his unsteady gait had been remarked by her—as it must have been—she made no further comment.

"Kind?" he returned like a drunken man. "It's—dam'—good—of you—to come. What—about—your parents? Aren't—they—very strict?"

"Oh, yes, they are very strict." She emphasised the words by nodding her head. "But when your telegram came I just slipped out and left them a note."

He laughed—stupidly.

"Little—devil! What—did—you—tell—them?"

"Why, I just said that a friend of mine—a girl, of course—was very, very ill in Paris and that I had to go and see her."

"That's good—that's dam' good. Very—very—ill. Well—I'm ill—ill with—love—of you."

He lurched his way back to the chair, groping with his hands for support. As his head sank against the back of the chair, the girl came and stood over him.

"Happy?" she asked.

"Utterly."

There was a knock at the door.

"That must be the waiter," she announced. "Shall I do the talking? May I unlock the door?"

He nodded, for speech by now was becoming increasingly difficult.

"Don't you worry; I'll see to everything.... Come in. Oh, waiter"—as Pierre showed himself—"I should like some coffee, please; and is it possible for you to get me some chocolates?"

"I will try, mademoiselle."

She turned back to Clinton; but she did not return his key.

"There! You see, there is no need for you to do anything. Didn't I arrange it nicely?"

"Fine... this damned heat...." The speaker commenced to unbutton his tunic.

"Close your eyes, darling; soon you will be quite all right."

The drugged man had become stupid.

"You mustn't—use—lipstick—in front—of—Napoleon's— picture—with the—eyes—of France—upon—you."

"Ah, Napoleon!" She saluted the picture and laughed. "Napoleon wouldn't have minded. He loved pretty things."

"Yes—he'd have—been—after you—if—you'd—lived—in—his—time."

She stroked his hair.

"You look so tired."

"It's—this ghastly—heat."

"Why not take off your tunic?"

Clinton tried to stand up, but his legs proved incapable. It was the girl who helped him off with his uniform. Suddenly he cried out:

"I'm—feeling—damned—ill."

"You must try to sleep a little. I will sit here by your side and watch." She looked at him with apparent anxiety, lulling his suspicions. "Just have a little sleep for, say, an hour—and then I'll wake you. It's quite early—and we have the whole night."

"But I—don't want—"

"You must, darling; it will refresh you." She showed determination. "I shall go if you don't."

"Oh, very well."

She stroked his hair. He felt consciousness leaving him.

"Marie—your—hands," he murmured; "they are—so—cool. . . ."

Chapter IV

The Betrayal

The time was a quarter of an hour later. Any one looking into that room could have observed von Ritter, the girl Marie, and the waiter Pierre standing over Alan Clinton, whose heavy breathing told that he was still unconscious.

"The idiot never suspected a thing—he just went to sleep like an English pig," observed von Ritter with contempt. "Minna,"—smiling at the girl,—"you did well."

The compliment did not receive the response that might have been expected. Speaking with a crispness that she had not used before, the young German Secret Service agent said, with a certain authority:

"Hadn't you better get on with the job?"

"*Himmel!*" declared the Prussian officer. "Where's the hurry? This hotel is safe and the English swine-dog will be unconscious until the morning. I can guarantee that." He turned up Clinton's eyelids and motioned the others closer. "Look, he's practically dead."

"Herr Lieutenant—" observed Pierre.

"What is it?"

"May this drug not act variously on different subjects?"

"Yes, but there is no chance of this one recovering. There was too much put in his wine. You did it very cleverly, Marie. But we will hurry, all the same. Get his other keys."

"You heard what he told me?" remarked the girl.

"I heard every word," said von Ritter sharply. "He has brought over something colossal—something of the first importance. When we send von Jago what is in that dispatch-case he will laugh for a week."

"I hope it is good," said the girl. "To have to listen to his maudlin love-making. . . ." She made a gesture of contempt before facing von Ritter resolutely. "I shall want something to compensate for being pawed about by this English swine"—grimacing again.

Her superior took the words seriously.

"You make the sacrifice in the sacred cause of the Fatherland," he returned, with heavy gravity. "If this coup turns out as I think, news of it will reach the ears of His Imperial Majesty." Like a clockwork figure, he automatically stiffened and saluted. "And you know how generously the All Highest can reward merit."

In the meantime, the man Pierre had been going through Clinton's pockets.

"Here are the keys," he announced, handing them to the officer.

At the third attempt the dispatch-case clicked open. The man in the chair moved as though unexpectedly recovering consciousness.

"He's waking," snapped the girl.

"Waking?" Von Ritter crossed and looked down at the unconscious Englishman. "No, he's not waking—it's just a dream—perhaps of Hampstead!"—accompanying the words with a sarcastic laugh. "But all the same,"—turning away,—"we had better not lose any more time."

Examining closely the papers which he had taken from the case, he heard a voice over his right shoulder exclaim in annoyance:

"But they're in code!"

"What did you expect?" he retorted angrily. "Even the English are not quite such fools as to have important secrets written in block capitals!"

"Then—?"

For answer, von Ritter took a small red-covered book from his pocket.

"Here, I think, I shall find the key," he observed with a satisfied smile.

There was a long pause while he studied the book.

"Can you read it?" asked the girl impatiently.

"I hope so.... No, not that one," he muttered to himself, and then turned the pages hurriedly.

Pierre started to become agitated. Although his behaviour remained unnoticed by von Ritter, his irritability got on the girl's nerves.

"Control yourself," she said sharply; and then, to the officer: "Haven't you got it yet?"

"Wait," he told her, turning another page. "No—not yet." More pages were turned. "It's not that, either.... The code must have been altered."

"Altered?" The girl's hands were clenched, while the blood mounted to her cheeks.

Von Ritter disregarded her.

"Have you searched him as I ordered?" he said to Pierre.

"Yes, Herr Lieutenant."

Abstractedly, von Ritter turned still more pages. At last he made an exclamation.

"I've got it!" he cried.

"Is it the one that Lessing sent us from London?" inquired the girl.

"I think so. Be quiet, please, both of you, while I try to decode this."

Sitting at the table, he got to work. The others watched him with nervous impatience as he worked out a few words. After he had written a dozen or so, the girl, who had been looking over his shoulder, gave a cry.

"Colossal, as you say!"

Over the other shoulder Pierre leaned forward, muttering to himself disjointedly. Von Ritter turned to both of them. His face was avid with excitement.

"A triumph for the Fatherland!" he declared. "This will mean an Iron Cross of the First Class." Turning back to his task, he wrote eagerly.

"Yes, yes," remarked the girl; "but we do not gather all the spoils. The British Intelligence has been busy lately."

Von Ritter made an angry rejoinder.

"You talk like a fool, Minna." He sprang up at the words. "*Donnerwetter!* Do you see that? Do you understand what that means?" he demanded.

"Not exactly."

"It means that these," tapping the dispatches, "have averted a most terrible disaster. The British know that von Kramer's sector is the weak point of our line on the Somme. They have somehow found out that an Army Corps has been withdrawn for the offensive in the extreme west."

"But how?" asked Pierre.

"Treachery of some sort, or one of their cursed spies—that you"—glowering at the girl—"were praising just now. Von Kramer's sector is to be left practically unprotected for several days. The British must have found this out. Their chemists have been at work. This," pointing to one of the papers on the table, "proves that a new gas is to be used on that day by the Allies. If we hadn't found this, our line might have been irretrievably broken, and perhaps the enemy would have pushed their way through. There it is, you can see for yourself"—pointing to certain words. "'*Attack to be made on August* 7 *at* 6.30 *a.m.*'"

"But now we are safe!" declared Pierre fervently.

"Yes, the Fatherland will be safe," returned von Ritter with fanatical zeal. "But that fool must never know his precious dispatches have been tampered with. He will deliver them according to plan, and on the morning of the seventh the British attack will take place. There will be machine guns in the front line all ready for them, the artillery will be reinforced, and instead of finding a weak defence they'll run into a hell. They'll all be blown to pieces!"

"And this new gas?" queried Marie.

"Here is the formula"—taking up one of the papers. "This will be passed to our chemists, who will be certain to be able to find a neutralising agent. They always have, up to now"—with a laugh. "Our triumph will be complete."

But his enthusiasm was not completely shared by the girl.

"It will not do for us to crow too loudly. I know the British," she declared. "Let us get the news through before we indulge in any more ecstasy."

It seemed as though von Ritter might strike her. Indeed, his right hand was already raised.

Then: "Perhaps you're right, Minna," he returned, with a drawing-in of his breath. "But you must allow me some little exultation."

"We are wasting valuable time," was her curt rejoinder.

Again von Ritter conquered himself.

"I accept your reproof," he said. He picked up the papers. "These are all in the same code, I find."

"You will photograph them?"

"Of course."

"Be careful you don't get caught with the copy."

He stared at her coldly.

"That's your job. I mustn't leave Paris—didn't von Jago tell you that?"

"He merely said I must co-operate with you."

"As soon as I have taken the photographs, you must go straight to Schlasser—oh, I'm sorry, I forgot. Not Hans Schlasser, but the very respectable Monsieur Delaine. He'll make it easy for you to get back to Berlin."

She shrugged her beautiful shoulders.

"But I don't require his help."

"Fräulein, you must not be presumptuous. Already to-night you have shown far too many signs of it."

This time his manner—and words—cowed her.

"Haven't I done enough?" she inquired.

He almost spat the rejoinder at her.

"The cause of the Fatherland must be always the first consideration of any secret agent." He turned away as though his choler would master him if he carried on any further talk. "Have you got the camera?" he demanded of Pierre.

"It is here, Herr Lieutenant." The speaker took a tiny camera from a secret drawer which he had unlocked in the table.

"Good. Now, fix these papers against the wall, but don't mark them."

Pierre laughed.

"You can trust me, Herr Lieutenant. It is not the first time."

"I know; but in matters of this importance you can't be too careful."

The girl interposed: "Aren't you taking a big risk with photography? Supposing the pictures turned out no good?"

Von Ritter licked his lips.

"You need not worry; I have never failed to get a good picture yet."

While the two were talking, Pierre had fixed the first paper against the wall.

"Now the flash-powder."

Pierre filled a small flash apparatus.

"It will be an instantaneous exposure," continued von Ritter, "and then back go the papers into our friend's dispatch-case, where they are locked up all safe and sound exactly as they were when he left London. When he comes to he will consequently never know what has happened. Are you ready?"

"Ready, Herr Lieutenant," said Pierre.

Von Ritter pointed the camera at the paper.

"Go!" he called.

A flash of magnesium from the flash machine filled the room with glaring light. The girl put her hands over her eyes.

"Excellent," announced the Prussian. "That is the first one. Now for the others."

When the various papers had been photographed von Ritter superintended the disposal of them back into the dispatch-case.

"We must be careful to replace them exactly as they were," he said. "We don't want our friend the Englishman to suspect that they have been tampered with. There—they are exactly as in the beginning." Locking the dispatch-case, he placed it on the chair from which he had originally taken it. "Now put these keys back into his pocket and then we will go into my room and I'll write my report for Headquarters." Disregarding Pierre, he turned to the girl. "And after that you must get away quickly, Minna."

"But first I must write a note." Taking a fountain pen from her bag, she scribbled on a piece of paper, reading the words aloud as she wrote:

> "Darling, I hadn't the heart to waken you, you slept so peacefully. I have now gone to see my sick friend. I will ring you up in the morning."

The two men laughed.

"Is that all you wish to tell him?" observed von Ritter cynically.

"No. I will add a little more."

> "You need sleep so badly that I have broken my promise to wake you in an hour. With all my undying love,
>
> "Marie."

"There!" She placed the paper by the side of the empty wine bottle on the table. "He'll find this when he wakes up; it will help to console him, perhaps."

"Although he is such a fool, he is bound to be suspicious."

"What does it matter?" returned the girl. "I may never see him again. My work with him is done."

Chapter V

The Penalty

Whichever way the eye turned, it encountered nothing but desolation. From the shattered windows of the farmhouse which was being utilised as the temporary G.H.Q. of the Ninety-fifth Brigade, B.E.F., the visual prospect was unlovely in the extreme. Hutments, ammunition and R.E. dumps—with a pock-marked terrain which looked as though an army of devastating maniacs had passed over it, venting their awful rage against the once-fair surface of the earth; a terrible sight—but the two British generals, striding agitatedly up and down the big room which served as an office, had other things to think about besides the desolated landscape.

Major-General Bentley, a short, stocky man with a high colour, was speaking his mind in very forcible fashion.

"I tell you, Garside," he said, "it was awful—perfectly horrible. The casualties were shocking. I hate these cursed stunts—always have done. I'll tell you what the trouble is. —" (mentioning a very august name) "takes his idea of war from the time of Wellington. He's got about as much conception of modern tactics as one of those...."

Garside—tall, thin, hatchet-faced, whose only sign of emotion was the restless tapping of his fingers on the desk before him—shook his head.

"The stunt was all right," he declared. "It would have been a good idea if it had only come off."

Bentley, stopping in his walk, barked a remonstrance.

"That's just my argument: it *didn't* come off! The enemy were prepared, and when we went over the top, expecting that the barrage with those new gas shells had cleared the ground, we simply got blown to hell and back."

"From what you tell me, they must have had guns hidden flat in the front line."

"Yes, it was absolute point-blank range. Cost us over five thousand men, and God only knows how many officers. I tell you, Garside, I hate these unnecessary stunts; they're nothing but blood baths."

Again the other shook his head.

"I can see your point of view, but I must still stick to my idea: if this business had only come off, it would have been well worth it."

Bentley forgot himself.

"You don't want me to call you a bloody fool to your face, do you, Garside? The whole idea was wrong, I tell you! It was ill-considered and ill-timed."

"Keep your shirt on, Harry," replied the other. "I'll tell you what it was—information must have leaked out."

"How the devil could it have leaked out?"

"You've been here long enough to know that spies are everywhere."

Bentley considered the point. And, in the consideration, something of his former terrible rage vanished.

"Yes," he conceded. "It may have been that their aircraft spotted our troops moving up to the front line in mass."

"But that doesn't account for their preparation against our new gas. The barrage, as you have said, was an utter washout."

"Utter. Over five thousand casualties."

"Then it must have been the work of some spy."

"Well, how are we to prevent spies?"

"That's up to our Intelligence."

"Intelligence!" Bentley snorted. "A thing like that should have been most carefully guarded."

"Who knew about it?"

"The War Office, of course; the chap who brought the dispatches over—Clinton; myself, and my staff. Not another soul, as far as I am aware."

"Well," observed Garside, "the War Office and yourself can be counted out of it. That leaves just Clinton and your staff."

"Three of those poor devils went under yesterday. There's only Morton, Greensmith, Mocksley and Pugh left. I need scarcely tell you, I suppose, that they're all above suspicion—every man jack of them."

"What about this fellow Clinton?"

"Clinton?" Bentley looked at his questioner in surprise. "He's all right. A most decent fellow. Knew his father—was with him at Oxford. Eustace Clinton was one of the best blokes I ever knew—and his son takes after him."

"Have you sent for him?"

"I have, as a matter of fact. Not that he'll be able to tell us anything, I suppose. By the way," putting his hand into his pocket, "I've got his report here. It gives exact details of how he spent his time from the moment he left the War Office until he handed the dispatches over to me. He never left them for a moment—according to his report," taking a paper from his pocket.

"He stopped the night in Paris, didn't he?"

"Yes. What's that got to do with it?"

"It may have a great deal to do with it. I know these nights in Paris," went on General Garside. "Where did he stay?"

Bentley looked at the paper.

"He gives the name somewhere. Oh, here it is—the Lion d'Or Hotel."

"Never heard of it. I wonder if the dispatches were got at during the night? You can never tell, these days."

Bentley lowered his head again.

"No,"—reading from the report,—"he distinctly states that he didn't sleep at all that night."

"Why not?"

"His reason is that it was too hot."

"All the same—" started Garside, who gave no sign, yet, of being convinced.

"Hold your horses a minute, Garside. He's got some corroboration of that. He says he spent the night talking to an old school friend—Captain Mallory of the Gunners."

"Mallory? I know him. Thoroughly reliable chap. Is he coming here, too?"

"Yes; we had to recall him from leave. I'm expecting them both at any moment. Perhaps you'd like to stay?"

"Sorry, but I have to go along to see the Big Man."

"I don't wonder at it, after this ghastly business. Well, anyway, you can rely upon me to put these two fellows through it properly. I'm going to get at the truth somehow."

"It certainly must be cleared up. We can't have men's lives thrown away in this reckless fashion."

"You ought to talk to certain people higher up about that, Garside."

The other, more cautious, let the words go by. He had turned away when there was a knock at the door.

"Come in," called Bentley.

An orderly entered. He saluted both generals.

"Captain Clinton and Captain Mallory are waiting, sir," he stated.

"Well, I'll be off," said Garside. "Good-bye. See you at lunch?"

"I hope so."

As soon as Garside had left, Bentley gave the orderly his instructions.

"Tell the two officers to come in."

"Yes, sir."

Bentley was reading Clinton's report when they entered.

"Good-morning, gentlemen," started the General. "Please sit down. I've just been through your report, Captain Clinton." Both men, he noticed, appeared very ill at ease. "So far as it goes it seems very straightforward. But all the same I'd like to ask you a few questions, if you don't mind."

Clinton moved nervously in his chair.

"Very good, General. I shall be pleased to answer anything I possibly can."

"Now, according to this report," said Bentley, "General Hutchinson handed you those dispatches on the afternoon of August the third. Is that correct?"

"Yes, sir."

"At the War Office?"

"At the War Office, sir."

"You put them in a dispatch-case, of course?"

"Yes, sir."

"Was it locked?"

"Yes, sir. General Hutchinson gave me the key at the same time."

"Quite so. Then,"—examining the report again,—"as I understand it, you had tea and caught the four-thirty train for Dover?"

"Yes, sir."

"You crossed to Calais?"

"Yes, sir."

"According to this," pointing again to the report, "you put the dispatch-case into a bag?"

"Yes, sir, a locked suitcase."

"This bag never left your hands, either on the boat or on the train to Paris?"

"No, sir. As a matter of fact, it was on the seat by my side. You see, General, I was afraid of anything happening, and I wasn't going to take any chances."

"Very wise of you. You had to hand over the dispatches next day to me, and spent the night, I notice," once again examining the report, "at a hotel called the Lion d'Or. Is that correct?"

"Perfectly correct, sir."

"You also were staying there, I believe, Captain Mallory?"

Mallory took some time before replying.

"Well, I'm waiting for your answer," said General Bentley.

"I'm sorry, sir." The R.F.A. officer pulled himself together. His hesitation was noticeable. "Yes, sir," he finally said. "I stayed at the Lion d'Or as well."

His inquisitor frowned.

"What sort of place is this hotel? Well conducted?"

"Oh, quite, General. I have never heard anything against it."

"Do you know it well?"

"Not well, sir, but—"

"I know it very well, indeed, General," put in Clinton. "I've stayed there several times before."

"I see. Now, I understand, Captain Clinton, that you and Captain Mallory are old school friends?"

"Yes, sir; we were at Repington together."

"Really? Good school, Repington.... But to return. You two spent the evening together, I understand?"

"Yes, sir," replied Clinton.

"The whole evening?"

There was a momentary pause. Then:

"Yes, sir."

"Now, this is most important. You state in this report, Clinton, that you did not go to bed at all that night—that it was too hot for you to sleep. You and Mallory sat up all night talking about old times. Is that correct?"

"Quite correct, sir," but a flush had crept into the speaker's face.

"Do you agree with that statement, Captain Mallory?"

"Yes—sir." The words were almost inaudible.

"You give me your word that you spent the entire night in Captain Clinton's company—is that so?"

"Yes, sir."

"I'm sorry to put it this way—but I must ask you if that is the truth?"

"It is the truth, sir."

"Good. The bag containing the dispatches was with you the whole time, of course?"

Clinton could stand this no longer. He hated to see his friend lying on his behalf.

"Yes, sir," he replied for Mallory.

"The next day it was duly handed over to me?"

"Yes, sir."

"One last question: During your journey from England the bag never left your charge? There was no reason to suspect that it could, at any other time, have been tampered with?"

"No, sir. As I have said, the bag never left my care."

"Thank you, gentlemen," summed up the General. "I wanted to be quite sure in my own mind. But, nevertheless, there has been a leakage, and that leakage has accounted for our defeat yesterday, and the loss of over five thousand British lives." There was a knock on the door, but the speaker disregarded it. "But, of course," he continued, "now that I've—"

The knock was repeated.

"Come in," he said, raising his voice.

The orderly, entering, saluted.

"Major Wright is waiting, sir. He says it's rather urgent."

"Oh, very well, I'll come."

After the orderly had closed the door, he concluded his remarks to the two officers.

"As I was saying, now that I have seen you and gone into the matter thoroughly, I find that no blame can be attached to either of you. That is, of course, if you are both speaking the truth—which I hope is the case. Wait here, please; I'll be back soon." Walking purposefully to the door, he left them together.

Mallory turned on Clinton with such fury that the latter imagined he intended to knock him down.

"You bloody swine!" he cried between clenched teeth.

"Not so loud, for God's sake!" sent back the infantry officer.

"Not so loud! I don't wonder that you are afraid. You slept with a woman all that night."

Clinton, grey beneath his tan, endeavoured to excuse himself.

"Don't you see I had to say that? What else could I do? But the dispatches were all right; no one could have touched them."

"How do you know? That girl may have been a spy."

"Stop that, Mallory! Stop it, I say, or—"

"Or—what?"

The challenge was ignored. Clinton made a despairing gesture.

"I know what you're thinking—but it's wrong. *Wrong*, I tell you. Marie was straight; she's no more a spy than you are."

"Some one you met was a spy—and why not she? You say she's all right, but the Boche got the news, and she seems the most likely source."

Clinton's nerves were bringing him to the verge of hysteria.

"I tell you, the papers were untouched." Yet, try as he might, he was not able to fight down that unnerving fear. *Five thousand lives....*

Mallory persisted.

"How do you know they weren't photographed?"

The other, still trying to fight his fear, cried in a cracked voice: "Impossible!"

The accusing voice went on:

"If it's impossible, then why didn't you tell the truth? Why invent a pack of lies, and call me in to corroborate them? Is that why I've been brought back from leave? Good God!"

"I thought you'd be glad to help me."

"So I would, in any ordinary thing—but not in a case of this kind. I had to lie to save your blasted skin."

"No harm's been done, old man."

"Don't call me 'old man.' Don't you realise that five thousand lives—the lives of better men than you and I—have been absolutely flung away? Don't you realise that it may have been your fault—and all through sleeping with a woman?"

"You're talking rubbish."

"I'm talking what is probably the truth. I lied to save you; I lied because we were friends. But, damn you, I never want to see you again. I thought you were a man; I find you're a skunk."

In the same weak, unsteady voice—his nerves being all shot to pieces by this time—Clinton endeavoured to put up a further defence.

"You're shooting off just so much hot air," he said.

Mallory looked at him and read in his face what he believed to be the truth.

"When you can convince me that the Boche didn't get this news through your mistress—a temporary one, I expect—I'll talk to you again. Meantime, there's only one name I have for you, and that's 'outsider.' " He turned fiercely away and, disregarding the instructions he had received from Major General Bentley, left the room.

BOOK II

Chapter I

Kuhnreich Commands

In the huge, barely furnished room which he used as an office, Kuhnreich, the supreme dictator of Ronstadt, that mighty empire of over sixty million souls, faced the Chief of his Secret Police. Emil Crosber, with his mean, shrivelled, sallow face, was almost as much feared as the Iron Man himself. His nickname amongst the masses was unprintable.

"You have found the woman?" snapped Kuhnreich.

The other bowed his head in slavish homage.

"I have found her, Excellency. She is waiting outside."

The Dictator, never one to waste words, pressed a button on his desk. To the secretary who came in he gave the necessary order.

A couple of minutes later a woman, whose beauty of both face and figure was striking, walked through the door. Whatever her inmost feelings may have been as she caught the cold, implacable stare of the man seated at the desk, she gave no sign of either fear or confusion. Mentally Kuhnreich registered a grudging admiration of such courage. A person of steel nerves himself (although some said he was a hopeless neurotic), he esteemed bravery in others.

He came immediately to the point.

"Your name is Minna Braun?"

"Yes, your Excellency."

"Seventeen years ago—that is to say, during the last year of the war—you were employed by the German Intelligence?"

This time she did not answer in words, but inclined her head.

Crosber pushed over a file and with an elaborately manicured finger indicated some entries on a certain page. Kuhnreich glanced at the typewritten lines and then resumed his examination.

"You then posed as a French girl by name Marie Roget?"

A smile played around the shapely mouth.

"With some success, your Excellency."

"I agree, Fräulein," came the harsh retort; "but, if you please, we will leave the compliments to a later time.... Your age was then nineteen?"

"That is correct, Excellency."

He stared at her. To himself he said, "She does not look thirty-five." But to the woman: "A chance has come for you to serve Ronstadt with the same courage and efficiency as years ago you served Germany."

The manner in which the words were uttered left no doubt that the speaker expected an immediate affirmative response, but the woman kept silent. Working for the new State of Ronstadt was a very different thing from working for the Wilhelmstrasse. Her old taskmasters had exercised a cruel despotism, it was true, but at least they paid well. Kuhnreich, fired with a madman's fanaticism, expected, on the other hand, a selfless sacrifice to what he grandiloquently styled "the call of the State."

"You do not answer."

The words cut the air like so many sweeps of a sword. Crosber's yellow features twitched. Was the woman insane?

"Your Excellency," came the reply after a pause, "much as I should like to do what you ask, I regret my hands are tied. I am no longer a free agent."

The man who ruled arbitrarily over the destinies of sixty million human beings rose from his seat. His bull-like neck was out-thrust, his face swollen with the terrific inrush of blood to the veins.

"Is it because you are living as the mistress of the Jew Masalsky that you are no longer a free agent? Answer me!" he thundered, his clenched fists raised as though he were addressing a mass meeting of his intoxicated adherents.

The woman, afraid to meet his challenge, looked at Crosber. The Chief of Secret Police paid her no heed; he was directing all his attention to his freshly-manicured fingernails. Sophie certainly did her work very well....

Minna Braun felt her bones turning to water. Fear struck her like a fell disease. When she had entered that room a few minutes before, she had been sustained by the realisation that, in spite of her age, she was an exceedingly attractive woman—so attractive, indeed, that a month back she had gained the appreciative notice of Ferdor Masalsky, so many times a millionaire that he was said to be the richest man in the capital.

But he was also a Jew....And Kuhnreich, she knew, hated Jews with a virulence that bordered on the incredible.

"Masalsky, your protector, has been ordered to leave Ronstadt within forty-eight hours."

"Why?" The word was forced out of her inner consciousness before she realised what she was saying.

The Dictator looked as though he were about to have an epileptic paroxysm. He waved a hand at Crosber.

"It grieves me to say that Ferdor Masalsky has been found guilty of treasonable conduct against the State," the latter said in his high, squeaky voice. "It is therefore necessary that he should be deported immediately and"—a momentary pause—"his money confiscated."

Minna's knees trembled. It was a plot—the vilest kind of plot—against the man who had given her every conceivable luxury; and it was this which caused her even more consternation of soul; the action had been taken because these two had meant to trap her. They—the wolf, Crosber, and the man without mercy, Kuhnreich—had set such a snare that it was impossible for her to do anything but fall into it.

"You will work for Ronstadt as you worked for Germany.... Crosber will now give you your instructions."

With these words she was dismissed.

"You do not appear to appreciate the fact, but his Excellency has been very generous. He could have ordered you severe punishment for associating with that Jew. Aren't you ashamed, as a good citizeness of Ronstadt, to have had any dealings with such a traitor?"

She did not reply—not because she could find no words to say, but because she was afraid that if she once opened her lips she would say too much.

"As it is, you are to be given a great opportunity to serve the State. Instead of scowling there, you should be proud."

The atmosphere of this room—the most private of all the many private rooms occupied in that building by the Chief of the Pé Secret Police—seemed stifling. She remembered some of the many terrible things that people whispered this man Crosber had done—some almost too ghastly to be given human credence. What a fool she had been to come back! She had been happy enough in America; she should have stayed there. America was a country where one could be free: Ronstadt was nothing but one huge and horrible prison.

The voice of Crosber continued.

"Yes, proud," he was saying. "We could have selected many women to undertake this task, but I induced his Excellency to choose you. I have always had a preference for von Jago's former agents. The old fox certainly knew his work."

He leaned back in his padded chair and lit a thin cigarette. He looked at that moment like a decayed ogre, and Minna would have liked—if only she had dared!—to strike him across his yellow face with her clenched fist. If her former chief, Hermann von Jago, had known his job, so did her present taskmaster. He had reduced a once-great city to a state of terror; he had delivered its millions of inhabitants over to the bondage of fear, in which each man spied on his neighbour, and lived from hour to hour in voiceless dread.

"But you are anxious, no doubt, to hear exactly what task is to be allotted to you. Fräulein, war is coming. Yes, war is coming—and that means that our secret agents must get busy. Already the English newspapers are regaling their readers with sensational details." He chuckled dryly as he opened a drawer in his desk and pulled out a long clipping. "Read that for yourself," he ordered, passing it over.

The woman took it with reluctant fingers.

She read:

SECRETS OF THE NEW WAR

HOW MODERN SPIES RISK THEIR LIVES

Europe once again has become a battleground. Although actual hostilities have not yet broken out, the legions of spies are busily at work, endeavouring to wrest from each other the war secrets of other nations. Within the past nine months over a hundred men and women have been convicted of spying, and of these the greater number have suffered the extreme penalty and have been killed.

Let us, for the enlightenment of those ostrich-like pacifists who are so vehemently declaring that another war of any sort is impossible, throw aside for a few minutes the curtain which hides the activities of these spies. According to the best military and naval authorities, the secret agents of every country in the old and new worlds are at present feverishly engaged in endeavouring to find the answers to the following questions. Two, it will be noticed, deal with aerial warfare, while the other is of particular interest to the British Navy.

(1) Has Ronstadt, that powerful nation, whose preparations for another war are said, on reliable authority, to be already assuming gigantic proportions, a new naval range-finder superior to the one that Germany used in the last war?

(2) Is it true that certain Continental chemists have discovered, to the satisfaction of experts, how to lay a poison-gas barrage in the air which no aeroplane pilot could pierce or a carborundum cloud so dense that machines entering it would inevitably crash?

How efficient Germany's range-finder was our naval leaders learned when they received a demonstration of its deadly efficiency at the Battle of Jutland. We are not betraying any official secrets, we believe, when we state that the Admiralty to-day—many years later, it is true—know every detail of that powerful instrument of war. But nineteen years have passed since the Battle of Jutland, and it is feared in high quarters that Ronstadt, taking over Germany's former experts, is now in possession of a range-finder so infinitely superior to the one used at Jutland that the latter may be declared almost archaic.

Minna looked up.

"Is this correct?" she asked.

Crosber smiled.

"Read on, Fräulein. It is the next paragraph that you will find especially interesting."

The woman bent her head again.

```
(3) Has a famous electrical chemist in
    the North of England at last found
    a ray that will short-circuit a
    magneto?
```

"Is that what you want me to find out?" she asked.

He smiled at her through the smoke of his cigarette.

"You are to be congratulated on your perception," Crosber answered. "Yes, that is what we want you to discover. You will be sent to England almost immediately on that mission."

She tried to point out difficulties.

"But I am no longer so young; I may lose my nerve. It is years since I did any work of this description."

Crosber, drawing to him a file of papers, negatived her words by a shake of his head.

"Then it is time you got back into harness again. Here," he said in a voice that cut short any further attempt at argument, "is your complete *dossier*. We took it over from the Wilhelmstrasse people when Kuhnreich (whom God preserve!) saved this once-mighty nation from anarchy by becoming Dictator. From this I learn," he went on, "that in the last few months of the war you performed a great service for Germany by making the acquaintance of a young Captain Alan Clinton. It may interest you to know, Fräulein," a sudden glitter coming into his eyes, "that this same Alan Clinton is now Colonel Clinton and occupies a very important position in the British Military Intelligence—M.I.5. According to the statement here," touching the *dossier* with a thin finger, "many thousands of British lives were lost as the result of his spending a night with you in 1918 at a Paris hotel called the Lion d'Or. Is that correct, Fräulein?"

She did not answer, but the expression on her face was enough for Crosber's purpose.

"You will be provided with sufficient money and credentials. I do not know at the moment when you will be required to cross to London, but it may be at any time during the next two days. You will be given technical documents to peruse, which will explain the matter in more detail, but, as I have another ten minutes to spare, I will myself outline the problems which we wish solved.

"It was during the last few months of the war that a Dutch inventor discovered a ray which, when submitted to laboratory tests, was proved able to stop a motor-car or aeroplane magneto, so long as the magneto was not protected by lead. According to the information we have been able to gather, the inventor, pressed to do what he considered at the time was impossible, abandoned this research in disgust and concentrated his attention in another direction.

"But it was recognised even then by every air authority that it was of the most vital importance that this work should be carried on and developed. For, conceive the situation for yourself; if a way could be found which would put out of action the engine of an aeroplane, then all hostile aircraft—and these are bound to be the deciding factor in any new war—would be rendered powerless."

The speaker turned to his desk as though suddenly tired.

"Well, that is all," he said. "You shall hear from me at an early date. But I would warn you, Fräulein," as the woman stood up, "not to indulge in any foolish misapprehensions of any kind. It will be useless for you to return to the luxurious home of your past few weeks: the house of Ferdor Masalsky has been closed this afternoon by my orders."

Feeling faint, Minna staggered away.

Chapter II

Youth In Love

In the small drawing-room of the house at the corner of Chesham Place, two people—a woman of forty-five and a girl of twenty—were talking in low tones. 1935 is not a year in which girls of twenty parade their emotions, but Rosemary Allister was very desperately in earnest.

"Are you ashamed of me for talking like this?" she asked.

The woman smiled and patted the girl's arm.

"Ashamed? No, darling; I think it splendid of you to give me your confidence." She looked at the young, ordinarily radiant face, now ravaged by anxiety, and sighed secretly that the days when a man had talked about her, as this girl was talking about the adopted baby whom she had always regarded as her own son, were over; they had passed her by many, many years before. Alan, her husband, was a dear, but the war had seemed to change him irretrievably, as it had changed so many other men. He had never been quite the same since.... Ah, well, she still had Bobby—although, if this vehement but singularly attractive girl had her way, her adopted son would soon pass into the keeping of some one else.

"You do understand, don't you?" went on the girl. "I've kept this bottled up so long that I really must find some outlet. I'm crazy—just crazy about Bobby, but I don't think he cares a solitary single damn about me."

Mrs. Clinton professed to be shocked.

"Hush, Rosemary."

"Well, that's my conviction, and I believe I'm right. Take this present leave, for instance. Why couldn't he let me meet him at the station? And why is he going off abroad, when I had planned so many lovely things to do with him?" Tears threatened in the deep-blue eyes.

Mrs. Clinton tried to pacify her as best she could.

"Sit down, my dear. Bobby will be here any moment now, and he mustn't see you upset."

The girl allowed herself to be drawn to a chair facing the wide window, but as soon as she was seated she started off on a fresh outburst.

"In spite of your being so decent, I suppose it's all wrong my going on like this—but I can't help it. The thing is getting me down— I can't sleep and I can't eat.... Mrs. Clinton, were you ever in love with some one who"—a suspicion of a sob—"didn't care?"

"Not when I was your age, Rosemary. You see, Alan—my husband—came along before I had had much time...."

"Lucky for you," was the comment; "for let me tell you it's just plain hell."

"Doesn't Bobby write to you, darling?" asked the older woman.

"Oh, he writes—but he'll fill up pages with stuff that bores one stiff; all about his duties, and so on and so forth. Can't you imagine how infuriated that makes me when all the time I want him to—"

Mrs. Clinton, feeling that old enemy of hers—the pain in the spine which had kept her more or less of an invalid for so many years—asserting itself, stooped and kissed the girl's forehead.

"I shouldn't worry, dear," she said. "I'm quite sure that everything will come out all right. Remember, Bobby is still very young—he's only twenty-four—and at the moment he's so terribly keen on the Army that perhaps everything else has to take a second place."

"I wouldn't mind being placed second; it's being an also-ran that infuriates me," replied the girl. "Yes, I know Bobby's young—but that's when we should enjoy each other—later on we shall be too old."

She did not realise what cruel thrusts she was giving her listener—how was this possible when she was so closely concerned with her own affairs?—and Mrs. Clinton gave no sign of her hurt.

To what an astonishing generation this girl belonged! Its frankness was so disconcerting that one was apt to be appalled by it—at least, at first. Yet, no doubt, it was better so; at any rate, a girl like Rosemary knew what she wanted and was determined to get it if it was at all possible. And Bobby might do a great deal worse, she reflected; this girl belonged to a good family; her father was a prominent banker, and there was money there. In far too many cases nowadays good breeding and wealth did not go together, but she had no doubts concerning Rosemary. The girl was amazingly outspoken, but there could be no question about her being devoted to Bobby. And she was quite old enough to know her own mind: girls of twenty nowadays had developed a remarkable selective capacity, from what she had been able to observe.

Suddenly the girl gave a cry.

"Here he is!" She stood up. "Oh, Bobby!" Mrs. Clinton heard her mutter, and noticed that Rosemary's teeth were pressing tightly against her lower lip.

Standing by her, one hand holding on to the chair back—the pain was very bad now—the older woman watched a young officer, wearing the uniform of the Tank Corps, get out from a taxi, thrust a hand into his pocket and pay the driver off. That the tip had been a liberal one was proved by the man's smiling and touching his hat in a salute.

Mrs. Clinton felt her heart swell. This upstanding, handsome young man, who carried the pride of his calling so well and with so much distinction—could it be possible that he belonged to her? At that moment she forgot her pain; even if the physical agony had increased, she would have ignored it: she didn't wonder that the girl by her side had fallen in love with Bobby—how could any one help admiring him? Even the ridiculous bonnet which the military authorities had ordained that officers in this particular corps should wear did not militate against his appearance. Instead, it gave him a jaunty look which—at least to her mind—was irresistible.

With swimming eyes, she watched Hannah, the old servant who had acted as "Nanny" to the boy when he was a baby, rush out from the front door, throw both her arms around Bobby's neck, and hug him as though her faithful heart would break. Then the young officer looked up, saw them at the window, and waved a gloved hand.

"There you are—all for every one else; nothing for me!" complained Rosemary. "Usually I love old Hannah—but now I feel that I hate her."

"Hush, darling! He'll be up in a moment."

Bobby Wingate entered the room in a rush.

"Hullo, Mum!" he exclaimed, throwing his arms around his mother. "How's the poor old back?"

"Oh, it's better, Bobby," she lied.

As he was in the act of kissing her, his eyes caught the girl.

"Hallo, Rosemary!" he said abstractedly. "You're looking fit."

"It's more than I feel."

"Why, what's the matter?"

"Oh, nothing." She turned away, fiddling with the pages of a magazine.

Mrs. Clinton gently disengaged her boy's arms.

"Now I must rush away to see about things, dear," she said. "I'll leave you with Rosemary."

After the door had closed behind her, the boy seemed ill at ease.

"If you would prefer me to clear out—don't be afraid of saying so, Bobby." She faced him resolutely.

"Rot! Why do you say a thing like that?"

"Why do I say it?" she returned. "Why, my dear, dear fool, because you don't seem to care a damn whether I'm alive or not, and I'm—"

"Rosemary!"

"What is it?"

"Rosemary, look at me. You know that's not true, don't you?"

Her eyes shone, but her voice remained accusing.

"If I weren't certain in my own mind it's true, I shouldn't have said it. Have you given me any reason lately to think otherwise? Take your letters—all about your mouldy duty—and then, what about this leave? I'd planned so many things....Oh, Bobby! It would be far better for you to tell me straight out that you don't care a damn."

"But I do care—I care a lot." His voice was low, but it held a note of pain.

"You do care?"

"Yes."

"Then why....?"

"Look here, Rosemary," he said, taking her hand, "you know I always like to be frank, don't you?"

"Yes."

"Well, I'm going to be frank now. I believe in frankness, because I don't think that there can ever be any question of palship, especially between a man and a woman, unless both are frank with each other. I know your—well, I know how you feel about me; and it makes me very proud."

"Proud!" she interjected. "I just want you to throw your arms round me, hug me like the devil and kiss me like hell. Proud!"

"Wait a minute," he cautioned; "just listen to what I've got to say. Oh, don't think I don't want to kiss you, darling."

"Say that again, Bobby," she pleaded.

"Say what again?"

"Call me 'darling' again."

Her face was so close to his that by reaching out a few inches he could have kissed her mouth. But he kept control of himself for a little while longer.

"I couldn't put this very well in a letter—it would have seemed a sort of cowardly thing to do. I had to tell it to you face to face."

"Tell me what?"

"That—well, that we'd just better be pals, Rosemary. You see, my dear," he went on in a voice that carried conviction, "I shall never have anything but my pay—and what's the pay of an Army officer?"

"I've got plenty—or shall have once I'm married."

He shook his head.

"It wouldn't do, darling. I couldn't live on my wife's money. That's why—well, I haven't been letting myself go in my letters. Oh, my dear, tell me you understand."

Although only twenty-four, he looked in that moment at least ten years older. His speech was that of a middle-aged man. The girl looked at him resolutely.

"You believe in frankness, don't you, Bobby?"

"Yes—of course."

"Then be frank with me now. Answer me one question truthfully. Will you promise?"

"Yes, but—"

"Never mind. I've only got one thing to ask you, and that is: Do you love me, Bobby?"

"My dear, I worship you." The words were out before he could check them.

"Then, you blasted fool, what else matters?"

The next moment they were in each other's arms.

Repentance came ten minutes later.

"I ought not to have done that," he said, as they sat together on the couch. "I ought not to be kissing you when—"

"When—what?"

"When I shall never be able to ask you to marry me."

She rippled with laughter.

"Marriage! Oh, that can wait—"

He looked at her queerly.

"The only thing that matters in this wide, wide world, my dear, darling ass, is that you've told me you love me. I'm crazy about you, so—" She sprang up, catching him by the arm. "Oh, Bobby, darling, isn't the world a marvellous place? Now let's talk about your leave."

His face fell.

"I've got to go abroad, dear."

"Abroad?"

"Yes—Paris?"

He seemed to be hiding something from her, and her feminine intuition became instantly alert.

"Paris?" she repeated. "Well, that's all right. We ought to have a wonderful time."

"I can't take you, Rosemary; I've got to go alone."

"Why?" She flung the question red-hot at him.

"I can't tell you that, darling; I've just got to go alone."

There was a silence.

"After what you told me just now?"

"Yes. You see—" But he was not allowed to finish.

"I think I see too well," she said, and flung herself out of the room.

Chapter III

Shadows

The pain had beaten even Cynthia Clinton's courage, and her husband and the boy he regarded as his own son had consequently dined alone that night.

Conversation had dealt with more or less commonplace matters until the port had circulated twice.

Then:

"What's this about your spending your leave on the Continent, Bobby?" asked Clinton.

"Well, governor," was the somewhat hesitant reply, "I thought I'd like to see Paris before it's too late."

"Too late?"

"According to the talk in Mess down at Woolvington, war between France and Ronstadt may break out at any moment—and then Paris will be very much off the map, so far as spending any leave there is concerned, at any rate."

He felt rather a cur. Certainly something of a coward. It wasn't playing the game to deceive the old boy like this. But, then, he knew very well what would happen if he told the truth: the governor would order him not to be such a damned fool.

The prophecy was fulfilled, for this was exactly what the Colonel did the next moment.

"I think it's damned foolhardy for a British officer to go running round the Continent at a time like this. Look here, Bobby, I'm being serious now; I know far more than any one down at your Mess can hope to know—and I shouldn't be surprised if Ronstadt declared war both on France and England at any minute. And if it does come it will come quickly. Now, if you were on the Continent.... Well, I leave it to your own imagination. The only consolation is that it will be quickly over; but while it lasts the popular conception of hell will be a fleabite compared with it."

The listener realised that the speaker knew what he was talking about. Colonel Clinton occupied a very prominent position in Military Intelligence, and consequently knew far more of what was going on behind the scenes than he could be allowed to pass on even to his adopted son.

"We are living on a volcano that may blow up at any moment," continued the Intelligence officer, "and I don't want you to be included in the débris before your time, my boy." The face of the man with the prematurely grey hair was grave.

"Oh, but Paris would be all right—why, it's only a couple of hours' hop away."

"I've told you I don't like the idea of your going on the Continent at all just now, Bobby."

The young officer shrugged his shoulders.

"Don't let's talk about it any more, then, sir." He changed the subject abruptly. "Isn't that fool of a doctor doing Mums any good?" he asked sharply.

Clinton sighed. A memory—a memory that went back seventeen years—returned to him as he looked across the table; and it was a memory that seared.

"He tells me he's doing everything he possibly can."

"Well, it doesn't appear to be worth much."

Clinton sighed. Again his memory went back over the years. He saw himself in that sitting-room in the Lion d'Or Hotel—was it because of this recollection that he did not wish the boy, whom he had adopted when a comrade was killed at Ypres, to go to Paris for leave?

Five thousand men killed! That was the memory that had haunted him all through the years. Never had he been able to forget it. The memory stabbed him at the oddest moments: he would wake up in the middle of the night, wet with perspiration; in the midst of a meal at a crowded restaurant, the spectre would stalk. Always he had to carry that intolerable load.

It had been useless for him to tell himself that the average man would have acted in much the same way. He had carried in his breast a cancer that had never ceased to gnaw. Never to be able to forget....

He had done what he could to make reparation: that was why, when, after the war, he was offered a permanent post in Military Intelligence, he had taken it without hesitation. And how he had worked! Day and night, slaving at languages and endeavouring to equip himself in every possible way for the life work that stretched in front of him. There was that much to be said for his credit: he had never spared himself.

Marie Roget! What had happened to her? He had never heard a word, and so had supposed that this girl, who, he was convinced, had trapped him, had become lost among the countless millions swallowed up by the Peace. Perhaps she was dead—or married. An ironical thought, to reflect that she had become an honest married woman!

Many times during the past seventeen years he had found himself praying that she might be dead. For, as long as she lived, she represented a danger. That seems fantastic after so long a period, but there was always the risk. One consoling feature was that she alone represented this stalking terror.

Major-General Bentley had died a fortnight after that harrowing interview at his Brigade Headquarters. A sniper's bullet had put an end to an illustrious military career as Bentley went on a tour of inspection in the front-line trenches.

Yes, there was only this woman left. Of course, he did not include Mallory. The man who had become "Uncle Peter" to his boy had long since held out the hand of friendship again, and, although no words had been said on the subject since, he knew that he could trust his old comrade as he could trust no other living soul. It had taken some time for Mallory to come round, but eventually he had wiped the slate clean. There was no longer any misunderstanding between them—and there had not been for over fourteen years.

Mallory had left the service after the Armistice and had gone into the insurance business. He was now quite a "big pot" in the City. He had never married, being, presumably, one of those men who never try their luck a second time. When Jill Chester had turned him down for the more spectacular prospect of becoming a Baroness, he had apparently forsworn all women.

As the years went by Mallory, always rather reserved, had developed a kind of queer introspective habit which enabled him to shut himself off from the rest of the world. Perhaps that piece of shrapnel, which had caused him to spend six months in a war hospital after the guns had roared for the last time, had had something to do with it. But he never mentioned the subject, and those few of his friends who stood nearest to him had taken him for what he had become—and had left it at that. He was still the best of good fellows.

Clinton's reflections were interrupted by a remark from the young officer.

"Well, governor, let's go into the fug hole," Robert suggested. This combined den, library, and smoking-room had always been a favourite of his.

Comfortably seated in two leather chairs, father and son fell again to talking. But this time all controversial subjects were barred. They concentrated on Bobby's work in the Tank Corps and his daily routine of duties. In every other sentence, young Bobby Wingate evidenced his unmistakable keenness as a soldier.

"You're glad you went into the Army, then, Bobby?" asked the Colonel, sipping his whisky and soda.

"Glad!" The rejoinder left no possible doubt in the listener's mind. "The only snag about it, though, is that one can never hope to make any money—any real money, I mean."

"What do you want money for?"

A shadow passed over the buoyant face.

"I turned down the best girl in the world to-night, sir, through that very same reason."

Colonel Clinton leaned forward.

"Do you mean—?"

"Yes, Rosemary Allister. We're desperately in love with each other—but I simply couldn't go on with it. Damn it, sir, a man can't live on his wife's money. So...." The hand which lifted the glass shook a little.

The older man felt genuinely sorry for him.

"I think that was a very silly thing to do, my boy. Both your mother and I like Rosemary, and we were hoping that—"

He was interrupted.

"Don't let's talk about it, governor—please."

The Colonel smiled.

"If I know anything of Rosemary, she won't let you off as easily as all that."

The boy flushed.

"But hang it, sir, I've got no money—and never shall have. All I've got is my job—and I shall concentrate on that. But," running his hands through his crisp, wavy hair, "just at this particular moment I feel that I'd do almost anything to put my hand on some coin."

"As you know, Bobby, I've only got my pay—but if a hundred or so would help...."

"No." The boy shook his head. "That wouldn't be any use....Well, what about a game of pills?"

"Good idea." The Colonel was anxious to divert his thoughts into another channel. It was a pity about Rosemary, but perhaps the lad—modern youth was exceptionally keen-sighted—had the right angle after all. When all the money was on one side, difficulties were apt to crop up at the most unexpected times.

At the other end of the long room there was a three-quarter-size billiard table—somewhat rickety, one of its legs having had to be wedged underneath, and with the cloth worn and stained. But too many close-fought battles had been waged on its ancient surface for it not to occupy a proud position in the hearts of both.

"Owe you twenty-five, as usual?" suggested the Colonel.

"Oh, not to-night, sir—I've improved a bit. Let's play level."

"All right. What is it?" spinning a coin.

"Heads."

"It's a woman. I'll break."

◇◇◇

The scores were standing at 75–69 in Bobby's favour when a visitor was announced.

The young officer gave a shout as the man walked into the room.

"Uncle Pete!" he exclaimed, holding out a hand.

There was genuine warmth in Mallory's voice as he replied to this spirited greeting.

"I thought I'd look in to wish you a good leave, Bobby," he said.

"Awfully good of you, sir."

"Don't let me interrupt the game. We can talk afterwards."

As though urged on to greater efforts by the words, Bobby ran out with a couple of useful twenty breaks. Putting up his cue, he turned with a smile to the visitor.

"You'll have a drink?"

"Well…a small one."

Within a few minutes the three were grouped round the fire.

"And now, what do you intend to do with yourself for the next ten days?"

It was Colonel Clinton who answered.

"Bobby wants to go to Paris," he started in a deprecatory tone.

"Well, why not?" was the comment. "There's a lot to be learned in Paris if one goes the right way about it."

The words evidently did not please Clinton.

"I was telling him that, with this threat of war, he'd better stay at home."

"War?" scoffed Mallory. "Why, you're talking nonsense, Alan. You've been paying too much attention to the spy-mania stories in the sensational newspapers."

"Very well." The Intelligence officer clipped his words.

Mallory paid no attention to the rebuke.

"Yes, go to Paris by all means, Bobby," he said. "Why, when we were your age…." He shut up quickly and there was an awkward silence. Turning, Bobby Wingate noticed that the Colonel was staring at Mallory as though regarding an enemy. What the deuce had happened?

He smoothed out the uneasiness of the atmosphere with a laugh.

"Oh, well, I don't suppose the governor was any worse than the average fellow when he was my age. You know the old saying—you're never young twice. And, talking about Paris, have you heard that yarn about the bishop and his nephew?" Without waiting for permission, he plunged into a story that the night before had sent his Mess into paroxysms of ribald laughter.

"Damned good," commented Mallory, wiping the tears from his eyes. He accompanied the words by an affectionate pat on his old friend's shoulder.

Bobby stood up.

"Sorry to leave you chaps, but I must go up and see how Mums is—you won't be going yet, Uncle Peter?"

"No, not yet."

Directly they were alone, Mallory made his apologies.

"Sorry for that slip, Alan—you know I didn't mean anything by it."

Clinton slowly lit a cigarette.

"That's all right, old man," he answered, "but you flicked me on the raw all the same. I can't get that beastly business out of my mind," he went on to confide. "And seeing the boy there…"—pointing to the chair which Bobby had recently vacated—"made it all the worse."

Mallory became a friend in need.

"That's all rubbish," he countered energetically. "That business of seventeen years ago has long since been finished and done with. What's the use of brooding? You were no worse than the average man, although I must confess I did go off the deep end at the time. Seventeen years!" he repeated. "Why, it's a lifetime. And if you're thinking of those poor devils—" He stopped to find some suitable words. "Look what the papers are now printing about the hundreds of thousands of lives lost by so-called generals. It was just the luck of the game. It's dead and forgotten, and my advice to you is to wipe it clean out of your mind."

"I wish I could, Peter."

"You *must*! I'm the only living person who knows anything about it—and you can trust me, surely?"

"Of course I can trust you."

◇◇◇

But late that night, as he sat alone, Alan Clinton wondered if his sin, like so many other men's, were destined to live after him. It seemed ridiculous, after so long a lapse of time, to speculate in this way....But still, he wondered.

Chapter IV

The New Von Ritter

The Prime Minister had had only one guest at dinner that night. The person honoured in this fashion was a very old friend.

Now that the two were seated one on each side of the fire in the library, Sir Brian Fordinghame, Chief of that important branch of the British Secret Service known as Y.1, looked across at his host and smiled.

"You go from triumph to triumph, Tommy," he said. "Your speech in the House this afternoon will make history."

The Right Honourable Thomas Devenish grinned like a mischievous schoolboy. For that was his way when receiving compliments.

"You're talking like a *Times* leading article. Come off your perch," he adjured.

Fordinghame puffed slowly at his excellent cigar. The speaker had interested him for the last thirty years—but he found him more of an absorbing human study now than ever before.

The mental stature of any man cannot be judged wholly in his lifetime. But shrewd political appraisers had already said of Thomas Devenish that he was the greatest British Premier of the last fifty years. Certainly he provided a very vivid contrast to his immediate predecessor, the Scotsman McTaggart, who—to the combined relief of friends and foes alike—had six months before departed to the House of Lords.

Devenish's had been known as a remarkable brain for the previous twenty-five years, but in the past his very brilliance had been a handicap. Impatient of delay, he had often acted precipitately, and, as the result of a bad error of judgment due to this trait, he had once left politics altogether for the space of five years. During that time he had won distinction in various other fields—as a big game shot, as a war correspondent, even as a soldier of fortune. Returning to the House of Commons at the age of forty, he had shown a mellowness of judgment that had been lacking before. This, combined with extraordinary energy and corresponding ability, had carried him, at the early age of fifty-two, to the highest honour that the British Constitution could bestow. His active adventuring days were over, but the courage which had been such a marked characteristic all through his life remained. Under his shrewd and brilliant leadership, England was once again taking her place among the leading nations of the world.

"Like that cigar?" Devenish now asked in his sharp, staccato manner.

"It's quite up to your standard, Tommy," was the reply.

The Premier lit a fresh cigar from the stub of his old one and flung the latter into the grate.

"I asked you here to-night, Brian, because I want to know exactly how things stand from a counter-espionage point of view. Personally, I don't like the look of things at all. That speech of Kuhnreich's yesterday afternoon—well, you know what it means, yourself. It means open defiance to the rest of Europe. It means—*war!* Have you seen what Radford has written in the *Sunday Messenger* to-day?"

"Yes," slowly replied the Intelligence chief.

"Well, it's true down to the last syllable. He was the man, remember, who warned us that Germany intended to make war, twenty-odd years ago. But who listened? No one. Who's going to listen now?" He broke off, in his characteristically quick manner, to ask another question. "Well, are you keeping tabs on the Ronstadt agents over here?"

Fordinghame nodded.

"That's the least that can be done," he said. "We know all the chief men and women and they are being watched. They could be rounded up at a moment's notice."

"You're also keeping an eye, I hope, on that inventor fellow—what's his name?"

"Milligan."

"Milligan," repeated Devenish. "It seems a curious name to belong to a man who possibly will revolutionise all future warfare. You know what progress he's making?"

"I saw him myself only yesterday, and he told me that he was certain he would be able to perfect his idea within the next few weeks."

"That may be too late; war may break out at any moment. See him again, Brian, and urge him to put more steam into it. You realise, of course, what an extraordinary thing would happen if he is successful?"

"Of course. It would mean that every enemy aeroplane could be driven out of the sky."

The Prime Minister remained silent for a few moments. Then:

"By the way, how's Mallory?"

Fordinghame smiled.

"There's a queer cuss if you like.... Oh, he's all right," he added hastily.

"Why queer?" asked Devenish.

The visitor proceeded to tell him—in a low tone.

At the end the Prime Minister blew cigar-smoke reflectively.

"It was a pity about Jill Chester," he remarked.

While this conversation was proceeding, some hundreds of miles away a man rolled out of a frowsy bed in a side-street off the Friedrichstrasse in Pé. Since the arrival in power of Kuhnreich, the perfervid propagandists of Ronstadt had blared incessantly that the former unsavoury night-life—which for some years after the end of the late war had made Pé the most notorious capital in Europe—had been completely cleaned up.

The man who now sat yawning on the side of his bed always smiled when he heard that. It is true he never allowed any one to see him smiling—but still he smiled.

Seventeen years had wrought a great change in Adolf von Ritter. To begin with, he had dropped the aristocratic *von*, and was now known simply as Ritter. Then, he had lost much, if not all, of his former offensive arrogance: the old Prussian jackbootery had gone out of fashion, even it if had been replaced by something even more ruthless and terrible.

After the war von Ritter, like thousands of his class, had found his occupation gone. A new world had come and it was a world in which he found he had no place. The different revolutions preceding the upheaval that had led to Kuhnreich's being enthroned as the first Dictator Ronstadt had ever known had scattered his class and sent the majority penniless into the outside world. A great many had fled to other countries, especially America; those who remained found themselves performing strangely menial jobs in order to get the means to live. Only a few tried to put up a show against the amazing new conditions.

Adolf von Ritter was not included in their category. In spite of undoubted personal courage, he had a very strong sense of self-protection. As a former Intelligence officer, he knew that his services would have a certain value to the new régime.

And he was right: before long he was summoned to a certain room hidden discreetly away at the back of the Unter den Linden; there he was put through an exhausting examination by a huge man dressed in a brown shirt and military breeches, who kept a hand on his revolver holster throughout the talk. Von Ritter recognised his inquisitor; years before, this man had been running errands for the butcher who supplied the von Ritter family with meat....

After two hours' searching examination, he had been passed on to another Storm-trooper, and finally he had found himself in the presence of the man whose very name caused a shudder to pass through any community in which it was uttered.

Emil Crosber was a stoop-shouldered man of fifty-eight. Some said he was consumptive, and his hollow chest and sallow complexion certainly seemed to indicate within his spare frame some deadly disease waiting to pounce. But whether his body was tainted or healthy, there could be no question about his mind being malignant.

Crosber had been reared in the traditions of the Secret Police in the deposed Emperor's time—and he knew how to hunt rats. It did not matter to him what type the rats belonged; as long as his superiors declared them to be rats, and that they had to be hunted, he was prepared to seek them out and apply a painful system of extermination.

Experience had taught him that renegades—and here was a very good specimen standing before him now, unless he was mistaken—often made the best hirelings. For one thing, they were so mortally afraid of their own skins, while for another they generally sought to win favour with superiors by being especially zealous.

In short, the former proud Prussian officer, Captain Adolf von Ritter, was placed in a minor capacity in Emil Crosber's "National Guard"—as his hand-picked Secret Police were called. Like the rest, he was detailed to hunt rats—or, rather, those men and women who, according to Crosber's reckoning, came under that heading.

He had proved successful. There had been no trick so foul that he had not played it. Posing as a degenerate, he had slunk through the underworld, listening and prying. Every now and then he would retire to a quiet corner and there, unobserved, make an entry in a small book...and that same night, or, at the latest, within a few hours, the man or woman who had been so rash as to criticise any ruling of the wise, beneficent, and all-powerful Kuhnreich, or those of any of his chief myrmidons, disappeared.

No one asked any questions—at least, not in public. By this time men's minds were so blurred that the fantastic and the incredible were accepted as the ordinary and commonplace.

Of course, Ritter had escapes. He was suspected, and attempts were made to silence this *agent provocateur*; but after two men had died (horribly) as the result, he was allowed to go his filthy way more or less in peace.

Walking across the small room, Ritter scowled at himself in the spotty mirror hanging on the wall. He was sick of his present life. Blast Crosber! Although he had been a success, his pay wouldn't have served him for tips in the old days. He could no longer afford to buy decent clothes, smokable cigarettes, or drinkable liquor. And now he had to go on duty again—prowling, listening, reporting....

His discontented musings were interrupted by a knock on the door. It was a low, stealthy sound and, instinctively, he reached for the revolver placed on the small table by the side of the camp bed.

The man who entered after he had turned the key in the lock wasted no words. He merely said a name:

"*Crosber!*"

"What does he want?"

"He wants to see you."

"Now?"

"At once—you are to come with me."

Ritter speculated momentarily—would it not be better if he turned the revolver he still held on himself? He knew of other men who had been asked, with equal unexpectedness, to go to Crosber—and had never come back. Crosber had his whims; and he never required very much of an excuse if he thought that an underling had outlived his usefulness.

"Come on—what are you wasting time for?"

Ritter got a grip on himself. He became more or less reassured. He could think of nothing that he had left undone; he had been a zealous agent to Crosber ever since the Chief of Secret Police had engaged him for special duties.

He dressed himself quickly.

The wheel had turned in the most unexpected manner. Ritter listened almost incredulously.

"Here is sufficient money to turn you into a gentleman," Crosber repeated; "you will buy what clothes are necessary. In this envelope you will find your full instructions. After you have committed them to memory, burn the paper. That is all—except"—as the other turned to leave—"don't fail me. If you do, I shall listen to no excuses."

Adolf Ritter became, for the space of exactly thirty seconds, Adolf *von* Ritter.

"Whatever it is—I shall succeed," he said stiffly.

Emil Crosber smiled at him sardonically.

"None of your theatricals here," he retorted.

Chapter V

Rosemary Is Provocative

"Rosemary!"

Her usually reliable heart commenced to do the most absurd things as she looked into Bobby's face. There could be no possible doubt that he was unfeignedly glad to see her. The sweet, sweet fool!

"My dear, I never thought that you'd take the trouble," he said, and flushed most delightfully.

She had to pretend, although she wanted nothing quite so much as to throw her arms around his neck.

"My dear, good ass, there's no need for you to hang so many bouquets on me. I had to come down this way, and, remembering you were going by the nine o'clock plane, I thought I'd look in. That's all," she added, with a puzzling smile.

Bobby Wingate felt bewildered. What extraordinary creatures girls were! Only a couple of nights before, Rosemary had been sportsman enough to give her feelings completely away. And now here she was, resolutely cutting out every possible suggestion of sentiment, and treating him as though he were merely one of a crowd! It made him feel sick; but in the circumstances there was nothing else to do but fall in with her suggestion and follow her lead. It was he who had applied the closure so far as love was concerned, and therefore he had no possible cause for complaint.

"How soon before she goes?" asked the girl, pointing to the giant passenger plane.

"Five minutes, I think. I say, Rosemary,"—unable to control his voice, although he tried hard enough—"it was terribly decent of you to come—really."

She lit a cigarette with a little defiant gesture.

"Stop swinging the incense, old man—and think of the good time you're going to have on leave." If there was a little bitterness in her voice was she to be blamed? Not used to feeling frustrated Rosemary now had an inclination to damn the whole world.

Bobby bit his lip. Watching that momentary twitch of pain pass over the face of the girl he was sorely tempted to say: "To hell with Paris—I'm going to spend my leave in town with you." But, as this would have been a direct contradiction to all the plans he had made, he kept silent. There was an awkward pause. Both felt there was so much to say—and yet they did not know how to start. It was during this silence that Bobby turned at a touch on his shoulder.

"Why, Uncle Peter!" he exclaimed. For there, smiling at him, was Mallory.

"Thought I'd come to wish you *bon voyage*, my boy," was the excuse the older man made. "As a matter of fact," he went on, "I may be running across you somewhere or other later on. I'm going over to Pé next week to see about some insurance business in connection with the exhibition of agricultural machinery."

Bobby for the moment was nonplussed. Then he quickly recovered himself.

"Why, that'll be fine," he declared. "Oh, by the way, let me introduce Miss Rosemary Allister—this is Mr. Peter Mallory, a great pal of my father's."

"And of yours, I hope, Bobby?"

"Well, yes, of course—awfully good of you to put it that way."

Rosemary, taking the proffered hand, looked at the older man keenly. She had heard a great deal about Peter Mallory in one way or another—especially from Mrs. Clinton—and, keenly interested in human character, she was now giving him what she would have termed the "once-over."

She saw a tall, rather gaunt man of latish middle-age, who appeared to have grown old before his time. She did not know exactly why this impression formed itself in her mind; it may have been the lined face, or the somewhat nervous mannerisms which the man appeared to have. But there was the conviction. Mallory addressed her in a pleasant voice slightly tinged with an Irish accent. "I feel I know you already," he said.

"You do?"

"Yes. You see, Bobby has been talking…."

"Oh! He has, has he?"

"And I don't wonder at it." The words were no doubt intended as a compliment, but somehow she found herself resenting them. A little storm of anger broke inside her.

"Well, he'll have plenty of other things to talk about during the next ten days—won't you, Bobby?"

He looked at her wonderingly. "I don't know about that," he muttered, feeling ill at ease.

It was Mallory who helped him out.

"But I'll wager that when he comes back he'll swear that the French girls aren't to be compared with—"

"Oh, you needn't trouble to say asinine things, Mr. Mallory," was Rosemary's crisp comment.

The tension grew instead of lessening. Bobby felt angry with himself and angry with the world. He recalled a remark made by his O.C. at Mess on the last night he was at Woolvington.

"Say what you like, you fellows," the Colonel had declared, "but men have a natural antipathy towards women. Oh, I know that the sexes call to each other—who better?"—with a slight chuckle—"but, nevertheless, I maintain that what I'm saying is right. When men want to have a good time—a good time with no subsequent worries, that is—they go to their club or foregather as we are doing now. Being in love"—turning to Captain Holliday, who had brought the subject up—"is the very devil. It upsets and disturbs a man no end. I ought to know,"—with another chuckle—"I've had sufficient experience in my time."

Bobby remembered that he had listened aghast to what at the time he considered was rank blasphemy. But now that he felt his nerves fretted, he was not so sure but what the Old Man was right. Yet, all the same when he looked at Rosemary's face....

A warning for the passengers to take their places broke up the little group. Rosemary, living up to the compact she had made with herself to cut out any sentiment, held out her hand to be shaken instead of proffering her lips to be kissed, while Mallory clapped the young man heartily on the shoulder as Robert stepped into the plane. The two watched the giant sky bird take off, and then Rosemary made a suggestion.

"Going back to town, Mr. Mallory?"

"Yes."

"Then perhaps you'd like me to give you a lift?"

There was something about this man which interested her. She didn't quite know yet what it was—but she meant to find out.

"It's very good of you—thanks very much."

Once the two-seater was humming its way through the streets, the girl decided to waste no further time.

"I suppose I shall be seeing something of you in the future, Mr. Mallory?"

He turned to look at her.

"Oh, you mustn't think that I'm asking you to invite me out to dinner—"

"Much as I should like to," he put in.

She disregarded the words.

"No, I didn't mean that," she went on to explain. "But aren't you a friend of Sir Brian Fordinghame?"

"Yes—a great friend. We've known each other for years. Why?" His tone had sharpened and his manner became taut.

"Oh, nothing—only I've just got a job with Sir Brian."

"A job? You?"

"Yes, as assistant personal secretary. You see, Daddy—you know he's a banker, I suppose?—wanted me to 'try to fulfil some useful purpose in life,' as he put it, and so I actually learned typing and shorthand. The idea was, I believe, that I should go into the bank—but I found it terribly dull. Life with Sir Brian promises a good deal more."

"Funny Fordinghame hasn't mentioned anything to me about this."

"Funny?" She seized on the word. "Why should it be funny? Are you as much in his confidence as all that?"

He turned the question aside.

"I'm afraid that was rather an absurd thing for me to say—forgive me," he returned.

"Of course. Give a man time enough and he generally finds something absurd to say—at least, that's my experience."

"Surely you're not a cynic at your age, Miss Allister?"

"I don't know about being a cynic—but I know quite a lot about men," was the succinct answer.

Conversation flagged after that. Rosemary, concentrating on driving, asked herself one question: was it possible that this man, who seemed so queerly introspective, was one of the secret agents attached to Sir Brian Fordinghame's Y.1 staff? She would have to find out. Funny that he should have made that remark about going to Pé—especially when tension between the two countries was so acute. Ten minutes or so had passed when Mallory renewed the conversation. "I was quite serious about the dinner."

"Dinner?" she repeated. "I don't remember anything about a dinner."

"Very well; I'll put it in a different way: would you honour me, Miss Allister, by dining with me one night?"

She prevaricated, desiring time to make up her mind.

"Well," she compromised, "you can always give me a ring. I'm in the book."

"Thanks—I will."

◇◇◇

She dropped him in Knightsbridge, Mallory saying he had a call to make. During the remainder of the drive to Clarges Square, Rosemary was thoughtful. Did she like this man—or did she dislike him? There was no question of sex, of course: for one thing, he was old enough to be her father, and, for another, so long as she had anything to give, for just so long would only one man—Bobby Wingate—exercise sufficient attraction.... No, it certainly wasn't sex. It was something which she could not yet define. No doubt, at a later date, some clearer perception would arise, but, in the meantime, she had to content herself with the knowledge that Peter Mallory was a man who was going to claim a good deal of her close attention during the next few weeks.

Her thoughts switched.

It was a wonderful stroke of luck, getting that job with Sir Brian Fordinghame. Of course, her father had helped, using a certain amount of influence, but all the same she knew herself to be jolly fortunate.

Fordinghame had been very honest with her.

"I don't know that I could have taken you into the office at all, Miss Allister, but for this recent stringent economy campaign of the Government. But, as you have been so frank with me and said that you will not require anything in the way of a salary, I shall be delighted to oblige both you and your father."

She was to start her duties the following morning, September seventeenth. She hoped it would prove an auspicious date.

Chapter VI

The Courteous Hungarian

Although he never once considered turning back—for that was not his habit—Bobby was thinking hard as he got into the Pé express, nine hours after leaving England. He knew that, having been granted leave to visit Paris only, he was guilty of a technical offence in going on to the Ronstadt capital. Under Section 40 of the Army Act—concerning "conduct to the prejudice of good order and military discipline"—he was transgressing. But he had made up his mind, and that was an end to it.

It has been mentioned that Lieutenant Robert Wingate was a very keen soldier. Very well; it was this same keenness which was, possibly, leading him into extremely hot water (not to mention grave personal danger) now. He realised that, but there it was....

While at Woolvington, he had heard considerable discussion of the new track-ways of the latest model of the tank which, according to gossip, would be used by Ronstadt in the next war. Of course, much of this, as he knew full well, was just the merest surmise, for, as might be supposed, the great military nation over which Kuhnreich, the Dictator, now held such undisputed sway was likely to guard her secrets very effectively. Still, when he read in a technical journal that these same new track-ways were likely to be on view at the great Agricultural Machinery Exhibition to be held at Pé, he decided that at least one officer in his Majesty's forces was going to be on hand to take a look-see. As an alibi, he had the excuse that being a keen lover of music—which did not happen to be the case—he was tempted to slip over the frontier from France and attend the great Pé Musical Festival, which was held annually, attracting from every part of the world devotees of the dead-and-gone masters.

He would have told his governor the complete truth had he not felt certain that Colonel Clinton of M.I.5 would have strongly disapproved of the whole scheme.

Looking up from the novel he had been pretending to read, Bobby frowned. It would be awkward if he met Mallory in Pé. But the next moment he consoled himself with the reflection that he did not think he would have much difficulty in inducing "Uncle Peter" to keep his mouth shut. In spite of his sometimes forbidding expression, Mallory was a thoroughly good sportsman; no doubt it was the Irishman in him which prompted him to treat life far more as a lark than his own father did. But, then, the governor had a very responsible and worrying job.

How queer Rosemary had been! The thought of her provocatively challenging face at Croydon that morning when he had stepped into the plane came back, while the conductor rushed past in the corridor outside, shouting "*Premier service!*"

Dinner! Well, he was jolly hungry. Food—as long as it was decently cooked—generally struck him as being a sound idea.

Walking down the fast-travelling train, which swayed alarmingly as it took a curve on the line, he collided with a man, who apologised instantly.

"It is rather like a Rugby scrum," he heard the other say; "you must please forgive me."

Although the speaker used excellent English, Bobby placed him as a foreigner of some sort. A Czech, perhaps.

"Have you ever played Rugby?" he asked.

"Yes. Perhaps that surprises you? But, you see, I am a doctor—and I studied for a time at your London Guy's Hospital."

"Really?" Bobby smiled. He had the true insularity of his race, and the statement put this stranger well inside the fold.

"Are you alone?" he found himself saying; why, Heaven only knew.

"Quite alone."

"Well—" and then, after a slight hesitation, for he hated to appear too effusive: "What about bagging a table together?"

"Nothing would give me quite so much pleasure. Of all the cities I have known I love none like your London."

In spite of the doctor's tendency to become mushy in his speech, especially when referring to England, Bobby took rather a fancy to the fellow. He looked hard-bitten, but that could be accounted for by the fact that people in mid-Europe (Dr. Emeric Sandor announced himself to be a Hungarian, journeying to Budapest *via* Pé) had been going through a pretty fierce time in recent years, and a man—any man, even a doctor of medicine—had to be able to look after himself.

After dinner they sat drinking coffee and smoking cigarettes.

"Do you in England realise that Europe is standing on the very brink of another war?" the Hungarian doctor suddenly asked.

"We realise that things look pretty bad between Ronstadt and France," cautiously returned the young officer.

"Listen, and I will give you a confidence," returned the other. "I have many friends in Ronstadt—my wife is a native of Echlen—"

"Echlen!" repeated Wingate. Mention of that town in mid-Ronstadt, given over entirely to Kluck's great munition factories, had made him prick up his ears.

"Echlen," repeated Sandor. If he had noticed the other's interest, he did not openly comment on it.

"Kluck's are now engaged in the manufacture of agricultural implements. At least, that is the story which is being spread in the outside world; but I could tell any one sufficiently interested" (here the Hungarian medical man stopped to contort his face) "some very funny stories about the new kinds of tractors that have recently been developed. They will be used for tanks in the next war," the speaker added.

Although he was tempted, Wingate kept his curiosity in check.

"Really?" he contented himself with replying, following the words with a slight yawn.

But this Hungarian would not be daunted.

"My brother-in-law is one of the managers at Kluck's," he continued. "It would be an easy matter for me to give any one a look around. My friend, you do not deceive me: you are a British officer, in—what do you say?—muffins?"

"Don't be a fool," exclaimed Wingate.

His companion laughed.

"You say 'Don't be a fool,' but I have lived long enough in England to know your class. But I beg pardon," he went on quickly, in an apologetic tone. "I talk too much. Forgive me."

The man appeared so sincere, and so anxious to remove any awkwardness that might have arisen through his recent disclosure, that Bobby was appeased. With the sensitiveness of the young, he hated to think that he had hurt the other's feelings in any way, and consequently, when, after hearing that his companion intended to stay at the Hotel Poste upon reaching Pé, the Hungarian offered his card, on which he had scribbled a few words, Bobby accepted the kindness in the same spirit in which he believed it was offered.

"The manager of the Poste is a personal friend of mine. I once operated on him for acute appendicitis—and if you make yourself known he will himself see to your comfort. Have you telegraphed for accommodation?"

"No—I did not think it was necessary."

The listener flung up his hands.

"Not necessary—with a great Musical Festival being held!....But never mind: Franz Aschelmann will see that you are put right, or I will never speak to him again. Tell him that from me—Emeric Sandor." The speaker laughed as though he were already chastising the man whose life he had saved. "And now I must leave you....I have some medical papers to read before I turn in. If ever you come my way, be sure to look me up; you will see the address on my card."

"Thanks, doctor."

His companion of the dining car bowed and turned away. Wingate watched him go with some regret. The other had beguiled him for a couple of hours, and, moreover, had done his best to be of service.

An hour later he was asleep.

Chapter VII

Through the Wall

The manager was profoundly apologetic—but there was the situation.

"I regret it is entirely impossible," he stated again. "The complete accommodation of the hotel was booked up weeks ago. You should have telegraphed, Herr Wingate. It is the influx of visitors for the Musical Festival, you know."

Bobby stood, frowning. He had heard so much about the Poste—easily the best hotel in Pé—that he felt reluctant to try elsewhere; and it was while he was standing irresolute that the manager made a suggestion.

"We have a guest-house that belongs to the hotel—it is not more than three hundred yards away—where we accommodate overflow visitors at such times as this. If you will pardon me a moment, I will telephone."

When the manager returned a couple of minutes later, his face was smiling.

"There is one room vacant. It is an excellent room, and you will be very comfortable. The head porter will take you across himself."

"Thanks very much."

The house—which was of the large villa type and evidently a private residence that had been taken over by the hotel management—was spotlessly clean and extremely well furnished; it looked eminently comfortable. Bobby congratulated himself on his good luck, as a valet offered to unpack his bags.

"You needn't trouble."

The man bowed.

"I am entirely at your service," he stated.

Within the three-quarters of an hour that was left to him after spending the day sight-seeing, Bobby had bathed, shaved, and got into his evening kit. He went down in the lift to find a group of twenty or so men and women drinking cocktails in the large room that served as a lounge. Somewhat to his surprise, the manager of the Poste was there in person, effecting introductions.

Among those to whom Bobby was presented was an extremely personable woman who was introduced as Fräulein Minna Braun. She smiled at Bobby after the manager had left them together.

"As you are on your own, I feel I must take you under my wing, Mr. Wingate. Oh, no," she went on with a merry laugh, "that isn't nearly such a sacrifice on my part as you might imagine—I was feeling very lonely and was looking for some one with whom I might talk. Shall we go in?" A gong had sounded.

The young British officer found his companion a brilliant conversationalist. This woman was evidently widely travelled and had seen a good deal of life. She left him far behind in her knowledge of men and countries.

"Tell me something about London," she pleaded, after Bobby had confessed that he had never visited any of the American cities. "I have always loved London—but have not been there for many years. I read the English newspapers, and try to keep track of your most interesting books and plays—but it is not like being on the spot."

This extremely attractive woman, who looked only a few years older than himself, placed Bobby under something of a spell during the rest of the evening. She seemed so *understandable*. She had the gift of making him feel, not merely at his ease, but as though he were something of a personage! With an artistry that was very deft, she brought him out of his shell to such an extent that he felt himself shining in unaccustomed repartee.

There was some talk, of course, of the Musical Festival, scheduled to begin on the following day; and Bobby, in a burst of confidence, confessed that he scarcely knew one note of music from another. The admission was greeted by a sympathetic smile on the part of his companion.

"If you have nothing better to do, we might play truant together," she whispered. "You see, I am just as naughty as yourself! I had arranged to take a party of cousins from Echlen to the different performances; but at the last moment they sent me a telegram to say that two of them were ill and so their visit had to be postponed. Not that I am overcome with grief," she went on, her eyes shining; "they are both heavy in the mind as well as in the body, and I was not looking forward at all to spending a week in their company. Perhaps that sounds very ungracious—but"—sighing—"I have devoted a good deal of time during my life to looking after relations, and I am now glorying in my freedom."

Bobby was quite frank with himself. If it had not been for Rosemary, back in London, he would have been considerably attracted by this woman. She was *soignée*, she had a sophistication which appealed to him enormously, and the evening sped quickly in her company.

Altogether, the people gathered at this guest-house seemed a very agreeable crowd. They were, in the main, well dressed, and, while one or two struck Bobby as being possible outsiders, the average level was pretty high. Some of them, he gathered from scraps of conversation that he heard around him, occupied quite decent social positions in various provincial towns of Ronstadt. There were two visitors from Holland, three from France, and quite a number from the countries forming the Little Entente.

◇◇◇

As eleven o'clock struck, Minna Braun pressed the stub of her cigarette into the ash tray and picked up her gold mesh vanity bag.

"Bedtime," she announced. "No doubt I shall see you in the morning."

"Of course. And—"

"Yes?" she prompted.

"I was going to thank you for a very jolly evening."

She made him a mock curtsey.

"But you are too kind," she replied, smiling into his eyes. "It is I who should be expressing the gratitude. For haven't you kept a tiresome old woman from being bored all night?"

She turned away before he could think of a worthy retort.

Bobby himself went up shortly afterwards. The long train journey, followed by sight-seeing, had been very tiring, and, now that he was left alone, he felt he might fall to sleep at any moment.

The weather had turned cold, although it was only mid-September, and the sight of a fire burning in the old-fashioned hearth was very comforting. He undressed by its cheerful warmth and got into bed.

◇◇◇

He awoke with something like a start. Some one was making

an awful racket—pounding on the door, it sounded like. Had a fire broken out?

He sat up and groped with his right hand for the electric light switch; but the noise, whatever it might have been, ceased directly he recovered consciousness. Had he merely dreamed it?

But, because the shock had been so considerable, he continued to train his ears to listen. And, after twenty seconds or so, he heard something which was unmistakably real: it was the sound of two men talking. Their voices could be distinctly heard, coming from the wall at the back of his bed. Evidently there was a very thin partition between the two rooms.

The first voice was angry.

"What did you want to make such a devil of a row for?—Just as likely as not you woke him up."

"Not a chance," returned a second voice, also speaking in English. "If you hadn't kept your door locked, I shouldn't have needed to make any noise at all."

The other seemed appeased.

"Well," Bobby heard him declare, "it may be all right, of course. Now, what is it you want to tell me?"

"Just this: that boy in the next room is the adopted son of Colonel Clinton, who's got a big job in M.I.5."

"British Military Intelligence?" gasped the other.

"Yes." The affirmation was followed by a short, harsh laugh. "I wonder what the British authorities would say if they knew the truth about Colonel Clinton."

"What do you mean by that?" asked the first voice, after a pause.

The reply was very confident.

"You can take it from me that I'm telling the truth. It happened seventeen years ago—during the last year of the war, that was—in August, 1918, as a matter of fact. Clinton—he was then just a Captain—was sent over from London with some very special dispatches. The British were going to try out a new gas, among other things. But something went wrong"—again a short, harsh, unpleasant laugh racked the listening boy's ears. "Clinton spent the night with a supposed French girl, named Marie Roget. She was a German decoy. She doped his wine, and a Prussian Secret Service officer named von Ritter was able to get at the dispatches and take photographic copies. As a result, the British got it in the neck and lost five thousand men when they attacked."

"What happened to Clinton? Wasn't he court-martialled?"

"Nothing happened to him. He swore that no one had got at the dispatches, and he had the support of another English officer named Mallory, an intimate friend, who lied like fury to save him."

"How do you know all this, Johann?"

"I got it from a waiter named Pierre, who was in the German Secret Service. All this happened at a little hotel called the Lion d'Or, just off the Rue Caumartin."

"I know it. Well, what does it all amount to? Why wake me up in the middle of the night to tell me something which happened seventeen years ago?"

"Because we are both hard up; and I thought perhaps, if we told the young man in the next room, he might be inclined to fork out a little money. These British officers are very sensitive about their honour, don't forget."

There was the sound of a yawn.

"Well, I'll think about it. As you say, it might be worth something. But what proof have you got? If we told this story to young Wingate, he'd just laugh in our faces."

The reply was sinister.

"I can get plenty of proof."

After that there was the sound of a whispered good-night and then—silence.

Bobby felt as if he had been turned into stone. It simply could not be true. His own governor! And yet, what was it Mallory had said the night he had arrived home from leave? Hadn't Uncle Peter made a jesting reference to some Paris sex exploit of Alan Clinton's when the latter was a young man? Had he had this very incident in mind?

Bobby's thoughts continued to race.

But if Mallory had been referring to this particular affair, he surely wouldn't have joked about it? On the contrary, he wouldn't have mentioned it at all. He couldn't have mentioned it, for the thing was far too horrible—too utterly horrible ever to be raised between two friends.

And Colonel Clinton had served in the trenches for two-and-a-half years on end.

Five thousand lives lost. The words kept repeating themselves in his brain, hammering out a devil's refrain. And he had been given special dispatches....

When he got back he'd ask Mallory. He'd put him on his honour. But would he tell the truth? Could he be expected to tell the truth—that was, if the truth was damning? As he had lied seventeen years before, so would he lie now. It wasn't likely that he was going to give his old friend away—more especially to the man's own boy.

Bobby's thoughts took another twist. Who were these men; and why had they had that talk that night? On the surface the answer appeared simple enough: they were a couple of crooks come to Pé to see whom they could pluck among the great crowds gathered for the Musical Festival. And their object, so far as he was concerned, was blackmail.

Blackmail! But that meant money—and he had no money! At least, nothing beyond the few pounds he had brought with him to cover his expenses.

Did this thing go deeper than ordinary crime? Had these men a more dangerous intention than mere crookery?

He suddenly realised that he, a British officer, was in a country which might declare war on England at any moment—and that if hostilities did so swiftly break out, he would be in an extremely awkward position.

The thought came—and persisted: Had that conversation been carefully planned? *Had he, in other words, been meant to listen to it? If so, what was the object?*

For the rest of the night Bobby debated the most important question which had ever occupied his attention. Should he do the sensible thing and return to Paris the next day, or should he stay on in the hope of discovering what lay at the back of the plot?

Long before dawn, he had arrived at his decision.

He would stay.

Chapter VIII

Drama

Morning brought merely a strengthening of this resolve. It was foolhardy, perhaps, but he was going to see this thing through. He simply had to get at what was behind the plot—for of the fact that it was a plot, every moment's further thought brought added confirmation.

As he lay in his bath, he endeavoured to piece together the different bits of the puzzle: Seventeen years before, if those men were to be believed, Colonel Clinton had committed an indiscretion which had been attended by disastrous consequences out of all proportion to his offence. Providentially, it had been hushed up, and nothing had been heard of it until—once again, war threatened. Was the governor to be blackmailed in some way? Was he to be threatened now because of his lapse seventeen years before? That was what Bobby had to discover. That was the reason why he had to stay on in Pé instead of doing what the average person, he supposed, would have termed "the sensible thing" and returning to Paris.

◇◇◇

At twenty-four, risk is the very salt of life, and the thought of possible danger merely gives a tang to existence. Bobby made an excellent breakfast that morning and, when he heard that the manager of the Hotel Poste would like to see him in his private office he sprang up from his chair in the lounge immediately.

The man whose life Dr. Emeric Sandor had said he had saved smiled at the visitor.

"I hope you have been quite comfortable, Herr Wingate?" was his opening question.

"Very, thank you."

"You slept well?"

"Very well."

Was this fellow in the plot, too? Of course, it was a completely conventional question for the average hotel manager to ask a guest for whose comfort he had made himself personally responsible; but....

"I ask because my friend Dr. Sandor has just telephoned. He wished to be remembered to you."

"Very kind of him."

The manager hitched his chair closer.

"He asked me to give you a message. He said that his brother-in-law—now, wait a moment," he broke off to rummage among the papers on his desk. "I have his name here somewhere....Ah, here it is: Ernst Schroder. Well, as I was saying, Dr. Sandor asked me to say that if you would like to pay a visit to Echlen, his brother-in-law would be very pleased to see you and show you round the works."

There was an intensity in the last few words which caused Bobby to be on his guard. But the next moment he was completely staggered. The manager, after going to the door and locking it, returned to stand by the young officer's side.

"I place Lieutenant Robert Wingate on his honour," he said.

Bobby stared at him.

"I don't follow you," he said. How the deuce did this fellow know who he was?

The man bent forward to whisper.

"I am of the British Intelligence—you can trust me. Dr. Sandor works under my direction; he is a thoroughly reliable agent."

"Honestly, I haven't the faintest idea what you are talking about." He had no means of checking this amazing information, and in the circumstances the only thing he could do was to play safe. It was just possible, of course, that the speaker—Aschelmann—was Swiss, and therefore he might be telling the truth; but Wingate was not taking any risks.

The manager smiled.

"In the absence of documentary proof you are wise to be cautious—but if you wish to visit Kluck's works, here is the opportunity."

"Why should I wish to visit Kluck's works? I am a civilian, and I'm in Pé to attend the Musical Festival."

The manager shrugged.

"You must please yourself," he returned. "I have done everything possible for you."

"You've made me very comfortable, and I'm very grateful," was the young officer's response. He pondered for a moment whether he should tell of the eavesdropping he had been forced to do during the night, but decided against it; it would involve too much explanation.

Returning to the guest-house, he felt himself in a quandary. If he did not go to Kluck's works at Echlen, he would miss the opportunity of a lifetime—but if he did go, he would be laying himself open to grave suspicion. Suppose the talk he had recently had with the hotel manager was nothing but a snare set to trap him?

He compromised by reminding himself that the big Agricultural Exhibition would have its opening on the next day. Any one was free to visit it, and if he kept his eyes and ears open he would probably be able to pick up almost as much as if he had paid a visit to Echlen, and certainly he would not place himself in anything like the same danger. Running a legitimate risk was one thing, but behaving like a damned fool was another. He assumed the worst for the moment: supposing the hotel manager had lied when he said he was working for the British Intelligence? Then, with his identity known, a visit to the famous Kluck works would give the Ronstadtian authorities every excuse to arrest him on a charge of "attempted espionage." He recalled, with a fervent sense of thankfulness, that he had not given himself away in any one detail either to the talkative Sandor or the equally loquacious Aschelmann.

He was still in a state of suspense, wondering what exactly he should do, when he heard a woman's laugh.

"Well, are you going to keep to your promise and play truant to-day, Mr. Wingate?"

It was Minna Braun, her face dimpled, the shapely lips drawn back in a smile showing dazzlingly white teeth. She made a supremely attractive picture—a companion, here, whom any man must have delighted to accompany on an adventure, amorous or otherwise.

Bobby responded to her lure. He would not have been true to his age or sex had he not done so.

"You don't really mean to say, Fräulein, that you were serious last night?"

"About playing truant with you?"

He nodded.

"But of course. In the whole of Pé I could not have found a more charming playmate.... The whole day is ours," she went on quickly; "we will do whatever you like."

"I'll leave it to you. I know I could not be in better hands."

"You are very sweet," Bobby heard her exclaim softly. And then, very unaccountably, she sighed. A shadow crossed her face, which a second before had been so radiant.

Just as quickly her mood changed once again; she became almost boisterously happy.

"Come," she said, "we will enjoy ourselves—and you shall make me forget, for a few hours at least, that I am an old woman."

"Old woman!" he returned scoffingly. "That's absurd! I think you're marvellous."

For the second time the transformation took place in the woman's face. It became drained of colour; a haunted expression showed in the eyes that had been so brilliant, shining with what had seemed high-spirited but innocent mischief. It was as if she were looking at a ghost.

"What's the matter?" asked Bobby, alarmed. "Are you ill?"

She recovered herself quickly.

"No, of course not. I am never ill. I was thinking of my cousins.... Oh, it was nothing—nothing at all," she ended with a trace of irritability. "Are you ready? If so, we will go."

They had had a wonderful time. Bobby, as he smoked a final pipe before the bedroom fire, decided that he had never more enjoyed a day. Sight-seeing had taken up the morning, then lunch—and what a lunch!—at a little select restaurant which his cicerone stated she had discovered the last time she had come to Pé.

After the coffee and cigarettes—a testing-time for the young officer, who realised that, but for the memory of

Rosemary, he would certainly have fallen in love with this extremely fascinating woman of the world—his companion had suggested a cinema.

"I admit I have a craving for films," she said, with a frankness that appealed to Wingate. "A deplorable taste, perhaps, but"—waving the manicured hand that held the cigarette as though the praise or censure of the world did not bother her in the least—"there it is! How does it appeal to my new—what is it you say in England?—boy friend, is it not?"

"I think it's a very sound scheme—but all your ideas are so good."

"You are beginning to spoil me," she protested.

"Then I'm merely in the fashion," he replied. "I can't imagine any one not spoiling you."

There must be some reason why this woman had never married, Bobby told himself—and started to speculate on what it might be.

She picked up her fox fur from the adjoining chair and signalled the waiter.

"If I stay here any longer listening to your nice words, I shall end by falling in love with you—and that would never do. The bill, if you please," she added to the waiter, who had now arrived.

Bobby, confused already by the remarks she had made, became more embarrassed.

"I say, you can't do that, you know—" he expostulated.

"But it is already done. Apart from that man over there—and I had a very good mind to tell him to keep his eyes to himself—no one knows that you have honoured me by taking lunch with me to-day.... Silly boy," she added, patting his hand. "What use is money except to bring one happiness?"

The words were puzzling. He couldn't understand this woman. Surely, with her attractions of mind and body, she could get any man she liked—and yet, here she was, saying things which…Oh, it was absurd. She couldn't possibly have fallen for him. Yet the emotion he experienced as her hand closed over his for the second time, and she told him that it was her determination to pay the bill, was very agreeable.

They then visited the latest monster cinema to be opened in Pé.

"Can you see?" his companion whispered as they entered. "Let me have your hand."

So it was that, with her fingers touching his own, Bobby walked down the carpeted aisle and presently sank into a seat at the end of a gangway.

The scent of violets came to him as Minna Braun leaned sideways to whisper: "It is said to be a good film—you will enjoy it."

Looking back, he realised that he had but the most hazy notion of what the thing was about. In straightening his legs, his knee brushed the dress of his companion; he felt the outline of the woman's thigh. Immediately her fingers pressed his hand.

The story of the film remained unheeded. Why not? he asked himself. If this woman—this marvellously attractive woman—offered herself, as she seemed on the point of doing, why should he refuse such a gift from the gods? Such offerings came but seldom. Young as he was, he knew that. Another man would not have hesitated—he would be a fool if he held back.

◇◇◇

The temptation he had gone through returned with added ardour as he tapped his pipe out on the bars of the grate and prepared for bed. The very fact that he had kept himself so rigorously under control—it was the thought of Rosemary Allister that had been largely responsible for this in the past—now came as an enemy to attack him.

The woman had been kind—too kind. Apart from what she had actually said, she had promised so much—it seemed, everything—with her eyes, that day. They had smiled at him as she wished him good-night.

"Sleep well—Robert," she whispered.

Gripped by a temptation infinitely stronger than anything he had ever known before, he turned to the bed. In doing so, his mind did a complete volte-face. He realised, with a sense of something approaching horror, that for the space of nearly twelve hours the thought of the danger and disgrace which threatened to close in on his father had been obliterated from his mind. Fascinated, almost in spite of himself, by Minna Braun, he had forgotten the one vital reason for his decision to stay on in Pé. The knowledge was humiliating and staggering.

The fact sobered him. It caused him to remember that there was a girl in England who still had complete trust in him. True, he could never marry her—it wouldn't be fair, as he had already done his best to explain—but, all the same, he couldn't let her down. He wasn't a prig, but Rosemary *believed* in him.

Sleep would not come. He tried to banish from his thoughts the woman with whom he had spent the day, but the face of Minna Braun would not be dismissed; her personality had taken too strong a hold on him.

He tried strenuously, and then desperately, to switch his thoughts. His first duty was to his governor: everything came back to that. He must, by some means or other, get to the bottom of the plot, which perhaps by this time had developed another stage. He ought, he supposed (his mind a jumble of conflict now) to have tried to get into touch with Colonel Clinton the first thing that morning. Yes, that was what he should have done, instead of wasting a whole precious day gallivanting about with a woman. He could have telephoned or telegraphed. There would have been no need to tell the whole story: just a hint that a blackmail plot of some kind was being prepared against him in Pé, and that these two men, who claimed to know a certain Marie Roget, were in it, would have been sufficient. The governor would have known what to do—he could trust him for that.

But now, perhaps, it was too late. Practically twenty-four hours had passed—and how much might not be done by unscrupulous enemies within twenty-four hours!

◊◊◊

He continued to toss from side to side.

Half-expecting and yet half-dreading it, he waited to hear another talk between the two men in the adjoining room. But no sound came; there was only silence on the other side of the wall.

Had he turned his eyes towards the ceiling, however, he might—had he been quick enough—have observed a face peering down at him.

As it was, he waited for—he scarcely knew what: his usually reliable nerves were at full stretch; the slightest further call and he felt they would snap.

And, presently, they did snap: with a bound he was out of bed and rushing across the room! Some one was outside his door, clamouring to get in—some one whose voice was shaking with terror. And that some one, unless all his faculties had played him false, was Minna Braun.

He turned the key quickly and the next moment the woman was clinging to him with all the desperation that fear can give. She was wearing such a thin négligé that she might have been naked. Her firm, full breasts pressed against his body.

"Bobby!" she moaned. "*Bobby…!*"

"Wait a minute," he told her. There was the door to be shut, and not merely shut, but locked, before he could hope to restore her to any state of normal behaviour. That she had recently been badly frightened—she, this sophisticated woman of the world!—was evident. What had happened to scare her so that her eyes were glassy, her voice faltering and her lips dry and trembling?

It was not until he had set her down in the easy-chair by the fire that she recovered sufficiently to smile. And even then her face was white and her whole body shook as though she had a fever.

"You're cold," he said, uttering the fatuity that a man does when his wits are scattered and he has not yet had time to gather them together again.

"I'm afraid," she replied faintly.

"Of what?"

"I will tell you in a minute.... You don't mind my coming to you? You're not cross—or ashamed of me?"

"Of course not. We're friends, aren't we?"

She took his right hand and pressed it to her lips.

"I knew I could trust you," she said; "that was why I came—and, besides, there was no one else."

She started trembling again and, cursing himself for his neglect, Bobby fetched first his dressing-gown and then a travelling brandy-flask. Pouring out some of the spirit, he held it to her mouth. She swallowed—and shuddered.

"Oh...how it burns!" Then, with his Jaeger dressing-gown round her shoulders, she looked up and smiled her thanks.

"You will look after me, Bobby?" she asked.

He nodded—mainly because he did not know what else to do.

"Of course—but what's it all about?"

"Have you a cigarette?" she asked. "My nerves are still shaky," and, indeed, her hand as she raised it was still trembling. "Put something round you, my dear—you will catch cold," she said, branching off with what struck the listener as amazing inconsequence.

"I shall be all right; I want to hear your story. What frightened you?"

She blew cigarette smoke slowly.

"Some men tried to get into my room," she said at length.

"Who were they?"

"I don't know. At least, I couldn't give them any names, but I believe I know who they were all the same."

"Then?"

"They belonged to the Ronstadt Secret Service." As she whispered the words, she cast a frightened look round the room as though expecting enemies to spring out from every side.

"The Ronstadt Secret Service?" he repeated, amazed.

She nodded, and reached for his hand again.

"Listen, Bobby," she said in a low, soft tone that thrilled him. "I am a Frenchwoman, not a native of Ronstadt. Does that surprise you?"

"Not altogether." Now that he came to remember, there were several things about the speaker that reconciled him to her statement.

"My name I must not tell you—it would be too dangerous for you to know—but for the last five years I have been in the French Intelligence Service. I know languages, I have travelled, I—well, according to the authorities, I possess many of the qualities which would make a good agent."

"Including the ability to make men fall in love with you." He had to say it.

"My dear," she returned quickly, "you should not have said that, because it is not true—not in your case, at any rate. Won't you believe me when I tell you this?"

"I believe you," he said—and wondered the next moment whether he was being a fool. But it seemed impossible to doubt this woman: she was either sincere or the most marvellous actress in the world.

"Tell me the rest," he said.

"I must be quick." Again she cast that hurried glance round. "I was sent to Pé on a special mission. I was forced to do—no, I must not tell you; it might make you lose any respect you have for me. Yes, although I did it for my country," she added proudly. "Let it suffice that I was successful in this mission, that I gained what I had been sent to get. Here it is." She thrust a hand into her breast and withdrew a small package, the outer covering of which was oiled silk.

"I want you to keep that for me, Bobby. They would never suspect you; but they have begun to suspect me. You are my only hope. I may be arrested at any moment. I would not ask you to do this if you were not an Englishman—but our countries are united in a common cause. The information contained in these papers," tapping the package, "will be found to be of the utmost value to our two nations."

"What is the information?"

She shook her head.

"I cannot tell you—it would be too dangerous for you to know. Besides, it is all written in code. Will you do this for me?"

He looked at her and she met his gaze fearlessly.

"Yes," he said, "I will."

"You will keep the package until a messenger calls for it?"

"How shall I know the messenger?"

"In the first place, he will show you this." She took a ring off her finger and let him examine it. It was a plain signet ring with the initials "R.F." engraved on it. "R.F.," she said—"Republic of France. Will you remember that?"

"Of course."

"The messenger will also give you a password—it will be the English word 'Reliance.' Now repeat that, Bobby."

"'Reliance,'" he said, like a child learning a lesson.

"The ring first,"—showing it to him again—"and then the word, 'Reliance.' And now I must go."

"Let me see you back to your room."

She shook her head.

"No, that might involve you in some risk. Besides, the package.... Where will you put it?"

He pointed to his suitcase.

"In my luggage."

"These men might search it."

"I shall keep it locked."

She seemed on the point of demurring, and then turned to the door.

"I am relying on you, Bobby," she said; "remember, we work for the same cause. And, my dear, I shall never forget to-night." Taking off the dressing-gown, she flung her arms round his neck and kissed him with passion on the lips.

He was reluctant to let her go. The sex-urge which she had awakened earlier in the day returned with such force as almost to overwhelm him. But some power which he could not analyse made him release himself after a while and open the door.

"You are sure you will be all right?"

She smiled at him.

"Yes, I shall be all right," and with that she went.

For the rest of the night Bobby remained on guard. The package was locked in his suitcase, as he had promised, but there could be no question of sleep. He felt too perturbed. He had pledged himself to help the woman—but he could not disguise the fact that, in helping her, he was running a very grave risk. With his identity known, if the package was found in his possession he would be in just as much danger as the supposed Minna Braun—probably more. Yet he had to remain true to the trust she had put in him.

When he went down to breakfast the package was in the breast pocket of his coat.

On his plate was an envelope with "Herr R. Wingate" written on it in pencil. Guessing that it was a message from the woman, he put it into his pocket without reading it.

The other people staying at the guest-house dribbled into the dining-room. He began to speculate on the identity of each man who entered. Were the members of the Ronstadt Secret Service who had tried to get into Minna Braun's room the night before included in that gathering? Were the men he had heard talking about Colonel Clinton's indiscretion, the night before last, also present? He ate his breakfast quickly and then walked out into the garden at the back of the house. Making sure that no one could be watching him, he opened the envelope, drew out the single sheet of paper within and read:

> MY DEAREST BOBBY,—This is just a line to tell you that I have left Pé. It was too dangerous for me to remain. If ever you want to communicate with me, write to this address: 12 *bis, rue Danou, Paris*. Even if I am not there, the letter will be forwarded.
>
> I can tell you now what perhaps you have already guessed: I love you.

Below was a signature: "Adrienne Grandin."

During the time that it took him to smoke a cigarette, Bobby gave very earnest thought to the problem that now confronted him. How long was he to wait for the woman's messenger? She had said nothing about this in her note. And, even if the messenger came, he might be working for Ronstadt instead of for France. Why had she left so secretly? Obviously, because she was afraid of being placed under arrest.

The more he thought about it, the more he disliked the situation. Then, out of the murk, there flashed a thought which seemed to supply some sort of solution. Not altogether a satisfactory one—but the best that offered itself in the circumstances.

He remembered what the governor had so often told him—namely, that the censorship of the newspaper post was not nearly so rigidly carried out as it might have been. What was there to prevent him from sending this package to some one else, by newspaper post, and writing to Adrienne Grandin telling her what he had done? He could explain that he had decided that this was the best thing he could do. And then he must leave the guest-house himself. Oh, he knew that he had intended to remain until he was able to get some sort of clue about the plot against the man whom he had always regarded as his father—but this unexpected happening had put a very different complexion on the position. With the Frenchwoman suspected by the Ronstadt Secret Service people, it could not have escaped their notice that he had been very friendly with her. They would put two and two together....

On the way from the guest-house to the Hotel Poste, where he intended to give notice that he would be leaving Pé the next day—that was the idea, he suddenly decided: he would return to Paris, call at the address in the rue Danou, and leave a message for the woman— He turned off and bought a copy of that day's *Tageblatt*. Going into a stationer's, he placed the package carefully inside the newspaper, tied it securely with string; and then, walking into a post office, he addressed the newspaper to Rosemary Allister. Hearing the packet drop into the wide letter-box gave him a sense of relief greater than he would have thought possible.

Then he turned again in the direction of the Hotel Poste.

Chapter IX

Startling News

Rosemary had been working at the office of Y.1 for only a couple of days when she knew that she would like this post. It gave her a sense of satisfaction—not to mention a thrill—to realise that she was actually behind the scenes during big events.

The only blot on the landscape was Horatio Brander. The latter, who was acting as principal private secretary to Sir Brian Fordinghame, had viewed her with suspicion from the start—and not only with suspicion, but with positive dislike. So much was plain. But, then, she deduced that Brander—a raw-boned individual, prematurely bald, gaunt-featured, and possessing no sense of humour whatever—disliked all women on principle, especially any of the sex who by some unfortunate mischance has been allowed to stray into the work of Intelligence. She wondered why Fordinghame had selected such a man to have always at his elbow, and then quickly decided that it must have been because such an individual would remain impervious to any possible scheme of seduction by a female.

Seduction! She would like to see Brander's face while the process was going on....

At this particular moment she was listening, with what patience she could summon to her aid, to a lecture by the man himself.

"You must realise, Miss Allister," the secretary was saying, "that in work of this description the utmost secrecy is necessary."

She yawned prettily, touching her lips with immaculately kept fingertips.

"Really? I rather gathered something of the sort from Sir Brian when he engaged me. You needn't bother, Mr. Brander; I'm not exactly a fool, and you can take it from me that I can be trusted. I know you don't like my being here—"

"Miss Allister!"

"Well, that's the truth, so why trouble to deny it?"

A tongue was passed over dry lips. She rather fancied, from the contortions of Brander's face, that the man was possibly attracted to her physically, but hated himself for being so weak....

◇◇◇

The next day she arrived at the office to hear that Brander had been stricken down with influenza and would not be turning up in the building in the cul-de-sac off Whitehall for at least another week.

"I'm afraid, Miss Allister," said Sir Brian, when she went into his room in answer to the bell, "that this will mean putting a good deal of extra work on your shoulders."

"I shall like it, Sir Brian," she told him promptly.

He looked at the attractive face, brimming over with enthusiasm, and motioned her to a chair.

"Very well. Now, will you take some dictation? You mustn't be offended at what I am going to say—but this matter, like everything else transacted in this office, is in the highest degree confidential."

"You can rely upon me, Sir Brian."

"I know I can. But many years at this game have forced me to be doubly cautious. Are you ready?"

For the next ten minutes the Chief of Y.1 dictated rapidly but clearly in his pleasant voice. This contained a more than usually serious note, and when Rosemary began to get a glimmering of what the thing was about, she did not wonder at it.

Retiring to her own private room, she pieced the puzzle together while typing Fordinghame's voluminous notes, and this was the result:

Y. 1, which was really the civilian branch of Military Intelligence, had been asked through the War Office by the Military Attaché at the British Legation in Pé for particulars as to the identity of a young man whose initials were "R.W.," who lived in London, and who was the bearer of passport Number 235467X. Further inquiry, which had been made to the Passport Control Office twenty-four hours before, had resulted in notice to Y.1 that morning that the passport in question had been issued to R—W—of 71, Chesham Place, S.W.3, occupation shown as "gentleman," together with the further information that the owner of this passport had been shown, on the return of the Paris Control Bureau, to have visited that city. Subsequent inquiries established that R—W—was identical with Lieutenant R—W—, of the Royal Tank Corps, now on annual leave from his unit. The Director of Personal Services, War Office, was asked for a report, and sent information to the effect that the said Lieutenant R—W—was granted ten days' privilege leave commencing September 15, 1935, with permission to visit Paris. No application for a visa to visit Pé had been made—also, in view of the tension existing between the two countries, permission would not have been granted at this juncture in any case.

This was the kernel of the situation—and when Rosemary realised the truth, she had such an overwhelming sense of dismay that she was forced to stop typing to try to readjust her thoughts.

Why she had not identified Robert Wingate with the Lieutenant R—W—mentioned in the secret report, she could not decide; it must have been that her wits had been temporarily scattered. But, now that she went on to read her later shorthand notes, and discovered that Y. 1 had the further information that Bobby had obtained a visa to visit Pé at the British Embassy in Paris, without making any mention of being a serving soldier, she realised something of the serious situation that the information represented.

For some reason which he had kept to himself, Bobby had run a grave risk. Although there was no definite charge made against him, he must have given the Secret Service agents in Paris and Pé sufficient excuse to have him watched. Why?

Later in the day she was to learn the answer. Called again into Fordinghame's room, she found the Chief of Y.1 sitting, grave-faced, at his desk.

"This business is turning out to be far more serious than I could have believed," he told her. "This young officer, Wingate, is playing the fool—why, I can't tell, and I don't even like to guess. What makes it all the worse is the fact that he is the son of an important official at the War Office. Good God! A boy of Colonel Clinton's a traitor!" the speaker added, as though addressing himself.

She would have protested had not she felt that all the breath in her body had been driven out by the revelation. But—Bobby a traitor! It was utterly and completely preposterous.

And yet, as Fordinghame commenced to dictate further matter to her—this being an epitome of subsequent reports received from the agents of Y.1 in Pé—she felt even her own confidence wavering. According to these statements, Bobby had been seen consorting with well-known agents of the Ronstadt Secret Service at Pé. These agents included a notorious woman spy who had worked for the Germans in the Great War under the name of Marie Roget.

One report ended:

> I can only conclude that Lieutenant R—W— is mixing with these people for some definite purpose of his own. He is being kept under constant observation.

She looked up from her notebook when Fordinghame stopped talking.

"What does this actually mean, Sir Brian?"

"I scarcely like to think. But you have intelligence, Miss Allister; you know the facts now. This young officer goes to Pé under what amounts to false pretences, and while he is there he meets a woman who is, or has been, a notorious agent for an enemy Power. Nothing so serious as this has come under my observation during the whole twenty-five years I have been in the Intelligence Service."

Dismissed, she was glad to have the privacy of her own room. What should she do? On the one hand, she was bound to secrecy—but, on the other, she felt that Bobby's father should be told. In the ordinary way, the information might not come through to him for some time, as it was a matter which was to be dealt with exclusively by Y.1.

Why, oh, why, had Bobby been such a fool? But it was too late to mourn over the fact that he had played the infernal ass. She must try to do what she could to help him, and the first step in that direction, according to her present reckoning, was to see Colonel Clinton and acquaint him with the terrible facts.

◇◇◇

As it happened, she was forestalled. Distasteful as he found the task, Fordinghame decided it was his plain duty to let Clinton in on this as quickly as possible. Perhaps—although it seemed a forlorn hope—the boy's stepfather might be able to give some explanation of the lad's apparently inexplicable conduct.

He picked up the telephone and made a call.

Within five minutes the visitor was announced. The two men shook hands with the informality of people who are attracted to each other. In the course of their daily work Fordinghame and Clinton often came into contact.

"Good of you to come over, Colonel," started the Chief of Y.1. "As a matter of fact, I'm very worried about something."

"If I can help, of course—"

"I don't know whether you can. Cigarette? Perhaps I ought to start by saying that this chat is in the nature of a little private talk between our two selves. Is that quite clear?"

"Perfectly."

"Then I can go on. Heard from your boy lately?"

Clinton finished lighting his cigarette before replying.

"Do you mean Robert?"

"Yes."

"I had a line from Paris. He's over there on leave." Fordinghame swung round in his chair.

"Did he say anything to you before leaving England about going on to Pé?"

The Colonel stared. His face hardened.

"Before we go any further, Fordinghame, suppose you tell me exactly what is in your mind?"

"I will. We've had reports through from our agents at Pé to the effect that your boy has been associating with a notorious Ronstadt woman agent called Minna Braun."

"What nonsense! I don't believe a word of it."

"I'm afraid the evidence is pretty circumstantial. Read that." He pushed over the typewritten notes which Rosemary Allister had placed on his desk a half-hour before, and watched the M.I.5 man read with incredulity growing on his face. "I thought I ought to let you know as quickly as possible," he wound up.

"Thanks." The reply was curt. "But I can't believe it—I simply can't credit that Bobby could be such an almighty fool. If he has been seen with this woman, rest assured, Fordinghame, he has some purpose of his own in mind."

"What purpose?"

"I don't know," conceded the other frankly. "But I'll tell you this: he did say something to me about going on to Pé from Paris, and I strongly advised him not to do so. If I'd only known what was likely to happen, I should have seen that his leave was cancelled."

"Why did he want to go to Pé?"

"There was an Agricultural Exhibition or something, and he was keen to have a look at the new tractors. He thought that they would be interesting."

"They're used in connection with tanks, aren't they?"

"Yes; that was why he was so keen—he's an enthusiastic soldier, you know."

"But somewhat indiscreet, it would seem."

"Perhaps. But, good God, Fordinghame, it's no worse than that—thank God! Who is this Minna Braun?"

For reply, Fordinghame pulled out a drawer of his desk and took from it a file.

"I have had her looked up. Listen." He started to read:

> Minna Braun, or Marie Roget—the child of a German father and a Swiss mother—was born in the fortress city of Strassburg, in Alsace-Lorraine. At the outbreak of the Great War Minna Braun was employed as a typist in the office of the City Treasurer and while thus engaged she came into close personal contact with von Reinhardt, at that time the Chief of the German Secret Service in that sector. Being an accomplished linguist, her services were at times made use of for translations, and later she became more and more in touch with Secret Service work, so that she was in due course regarded as a member of that Service and duly sworn in as an accredited agent. Subsequently, when a French-speaking female agent was required for special work in Paris, Minna Braun was instructed to adopt the guise of a French-born Alsace-Lorrainian, and she took the name of Marie Roget. In Paris she worked under the direction of an agent named Adolf von Ritter.

He broke off to inquire:

"What's the matter, Clinton?" For he noticed that his listener had become deathly pale.

"Nothing...never felt better," was the evasive answer. "It's this news about my boy. If you had a son, you'd understand, too."

"I understand fully as it is, my dear fellow. I'll keep you posted with whatever else comes in. Can't you communicate with him direct?"

"I don't know where he is. The only address I had was his hotel in Paris—the Meurice. I'll telephone there directly I get back on the off-chance that they know."

The two shook hands and Clinton left.

Back in his own room at the War Office, he tried to pull himself together. This was a crushing blow—so devastating, in fact, that he wondered he had not collapsed entirely at Y.1. Certain words kept ringing in his ears. "*I'd do practically anything to lay my hands on some coin.*" Was that what Bobby had said?

And his own predictions had come true. A man's sins *did* return home to him, even after the lapse of seventeen years! But the cruel part was that his own boy had fallen into the same trap that had ensnared him in 1918! Bobby! In the grip of that woman!

He looked with lack-lustre eyes at a letter placed on his writing-pad. He had not noticed it before, but now he picked it up and read the typewritten address. The postmark bore the significant name of "Pé."

Hoping against hope that it might be a communication from Robert, he slit the envelope.

The typewritten words danced before his eyes:

> DEAR COLONEL CLINTON,—After so long a time you have probably forgotten all about me. But don't you ever recall those happy times we spent in Paris in 1918?
>
> There is a little favour I want you to do me, but more about that anon.
>
> In the meantime, I am sure you will be interested in the accompanying photograph.
> Yours very sincerely,
>
> MARIE ROGET.

There was a snapshot, as the woman had said, and when he looked at it Clinton felt the blood draining from his heart.

It showed Robert, wearing pyjamas, with his arms round a woman dressed in a very seductive and scanty négligé.

He had no difficulty in recognising the seductress as the woman who had betrayed him seventeen years before.

Chapter X

The Poker Party

Bobby continued his walk to the Hotel Poste in a reflective mood. There had been no way out of the difficulty so far as he could see—but that did not alter the fact that he had plunged himself into what might prove very turbulent waters. If Minna Braun—he still thought of her by that name—had laid herself open to direct suspicion, as she had said, then he, too, as her constant companion for many hours, was quite likely to be trailed. Had any one seen him post that newspaper to Rosemary Allister, for instance?

Well, there was no sense in working himself up into a sweat; what had been done could not be undone, and there was an end of it. Only a rank outsider would have refused to help a woman who had been so up against it as this French agent, and, besides....

This momentarily swept his thoughts away into a side channel. Now that Minna Braun was no longer near him, now that he could not see her face, be conscious of her beauty of figure, smell the perfume she used, her influence had lessened. Was it true what she had said—that last line in her letter, the bit about loving him? He didn't suppose so for a minute. Wasn't she French? And didn't the French make a habit of saying charming, insincere things? They had had a thundering good time together, and had got on splendidly—perhaps this was merely the feminine way of saying "Thank you." Although why she should trouble to thank *him* when all the obligation (apart from the package, of course) had been on his side, he couldn't imagine. Women were queer.

Was all this fair to Rosemary? His conscience troubled him as the thought came. Then, quite quickly, he felt a certain relief; his affection for the girl he had left behind in London was the genuine article, whereas he had been merely infatuated with this Frenchwoman. True, it had been pretty thick while it lasted—but, compared with real love, it was just a passing fancy. It might have happened to any man at any time; it was only one of those things that happened every now and then.

Getting what satisfaction was possible out of this reflection, he now found himself outside the imposing entrance to the Hotel Poste. During breakfast he had made up his mind: he would leave Pé the next morning, going by air from the great aerodrome on the outskirts of the city to Le Bourget. Arrived in Paris, he would call at the address in the rue Danou which Minna Braun had mentioned in her note, tell her what he had done, and then return to England. Because he did not like the idea of its being imagined that he had bunked, and because Aschelmann had gone out of his way to make him so comfortable, he was now going into the hotel to say that he would be leaving the following morning.

But before he could reach the reception clerk, whose small office was on the other side of the huge hall, he noticed Aschelmann himself. The manager was talking to another man—and the faces of both, Bobby quickly noticed, were very serious.

While he continued to watch, wondering whether, now that Aschelmann was available, he should not speak to him personally, the second man turned. Bobby was able to understand now why, even from behind, this individual had seemed vaguely familiar: the manager's companion was the very agreeable man he had met in the Pé express, Dr. Emeric Sandor.

Recognition was mutual. Whether Aschelmann nudged the other, Bobby could not decide, but after the two had exchanged a fleeting look of understanding, Sandor came forward quickly, his hand outstretched.

"Well, this is a great pleasure, Mr. Wingate—you don't know how glad I am to see you again!"

Bobby took a little time to recover from his surprise.

"But I thought you were in Budapest?" he exclaimed. Even while his hand was still being held by the other, he was endeavouring to find the answer to two questions: What was this man doing in Pé, when he was supposed to be so many miles away? And could he be trusted?

Sandor might have been expecting the questions, so ready was his tongue.

"I had to change my plans. Yesterday I was telegraphed for to attend a consultation here in Pé—and I am very glad, because it has enabled me to run across you, my very good friend, again. I was just asking Aschelmann how you were getting on. Have you been comfortable?"

"Very."

"He tells me that you did not go to Echlen." The speaker lowered his voice as though afraid of being overheard. "But we can't talk about that here—there are too many people about, and some of them would give a great deal, I have no doubt, to overhear what we two are discussing, *hein*? Come up to my room."

Bobby hesitated. He had no great desire to stay jawing to the voluble-tongued doctor, and, besides, he did not know what they could talk about: certainly he wasn't going to be drawn into any discussion of the reasons why he had chosen not to visit the Kluck works at Echlen, or why he had made up his mind to leave Pé within twenty-four hours. A grave doubt as to the truth of what the smiling-faced manager of the Poste had told him—namely, that both he and Sandor were accredited members of the Foreign Branch of British Intelligence—remained in his mind. Of course, it might be so; agents were recruited from all ranks and oftentimes the most unlikely persons were chosen; but, as he could not make sure, he must still pretend to be "dumb."

Consequently he did not accept the invitation with the enthusiasm which Sandor evidently expected him to show.

"Well, as a matter of fact," he said, "I'm rather pressed for time at the moment. I wanted to have a word with Aschelmann."

The listener changed countenance.

"But this is important—vitally important," he returned. "Aschelmann can wait. You weren't thinking of leaving Pé?" he went on to inquire sharply.

"Why do you want to know?"

"I have plenty of reasons—when we get up to my room I shall be pleased to tell you them. In the meantime, let me just say that you mustn't go to-day. Your father—" And then the speaker closed his mouth as though determined not to say another word until he had had his own way.

Puzzled and irritated, Bobby allowed himself to be led towards the lift. On the third floor Sandor stepped out, walked along a carpeted corridor until he came to the end room on the right, pushed the door open, beckoned his companion inside, and then promptly turned the key in the lock.

"That is to make sure we shall not be disturbed," he explained. "Sit down," pointing to a chair, "because I want to talk to you very seriously. It concerns your father, Colonel Clinton, I mean"—he paused—"and the woman who calls herself Fräulein Minna Braun."

Because he had to play for time, and, while doing so, felt that it was necessary he should have adequate control over his features, Bobby took a cigarette from his case and lit it.

"How is it you know my governor?" he inquired. That was safe enough, at any rate. Any fellow in his position might very well have asked the same question.

"Because, as Aschelmann told you yesterday, both he and I work for Colonel Clinton. You did not appear to believe him, but we are both members of the Foreign Branch of M.I.5."

Bobby controlled himself. There were a hundred questions he wanted to ask, but he kept on smoking without making any comment. He was still determined to play "dumb."

"The reason I have come back to Pé was to get into touch with you and this woman Minna Braun, who, actually, is a French Secret Service agent."

Bobby tried to look surprised.

"Is she really? Still, I don't quite see—"

"You will in a minute," he was patiently informed. "I should not be talking to you like this, of course," he went on, "but for the fact that I have assured myself you are the adopted son of Colonel Clinton. If you know anything about Intelligence work at all—if your father has given you the slightest confidence—you will know that many Secret Service agents follow a genuine occupation, because it is necessary for them to have a cast-iron alibi in case of trouble. That is why I am a doctor."

Bobby began to feel a little more reassured. He knew enough to be aware that this statement might be true. Many agents did their Secret Service work as a side line.

"I am a resident agent in Budapest, but I am often called to Pé," continued his informant. "No doubt you are aware that there is tremendous activity in every European capital among Intelligence men at the present time. With war threatening to break out at any moment, so much is obvious, of course." He waved a hand as though anxious to push on and not waste any further time in dealing with trivialities.

"It was while I was in Paris that I received at the local Headquarters a coded message from your father to the effect that I was to look you up on the way to Pé and do everything I possibly could to ensure your comfort—and safety"—adding the last two words significantly—"while you were in this city. According to this message, Colonel Clinton was rather worried about you—you had not, I believe, told him definitely that you were going on to Pé from Paris—and that was why, no doubt, he sent me my instructions. That was also why," sinking his voice, "I was able to get you the opportunity to visit Kluck's works at Echlen—a chance which apparently you were reluctant to accept."

A note of asperity had crept into the speaker's voice. Looking at him, Bobby felt some of his former doubts return. This chap, when viewed critically, was not quite satisfactory. He was rather shifty-eyed. Naturally, the British Intelligence people had to find helpers where they could; but he had always understood that only men of decent character were put on the payroll.

Suddenly the young officer realised that he was stepping on quicksands and that these might engulf him at any moment. If Sandor had not been so glib with his references to his father, he would have risen immediately and demanded to be let out of the room.

As it was:

"Colonel Clinton has not communicated with me in any way," he returned.

The other was ready with a reply.

"For the very simple reason that he did not know your exact address. Have I not already said that he was not sure whether you were going on to Pé, and, if so, where you would be staying. He knows now," were the added words.

"Then no doubt I shall be hearing from him."

"No doubt. But meanwhile time presses, and I want to talk to you about Minna Braun. You made good friends with that very attractive lady yesterday, I believe?"

With difficulty Bobby kept his temper. He loathed this talk—every word of it—and he was in no mood to discuss the woman who had placed such confidence in him.

"I don't know that I care to discuss Fräulein Braun even with you, Dr. Sandor," he said stiffly.

"But I am afraid it is necessary. Let me explain," the other continued. "As I have already told you, Minna Braun is actually a French secret agent stationed in Pé. She is a very clever and talented woman and has been highly successful at her work. Both the French people and the British think a great deal of her. It was because she knew that you could be trusted, and because Ronstadt agents were pressing her very close, that she handed you that package last night."

Something prompted Bobby to remain "dumb."

"Package?" he repeated, like a man who has heard an astonishing and puzzling fact for the first time.

"You heard what I said. Minna Braun handed you a package last night for safe custody. It is vitally important that I should know what you have done with it."

Wingate rose. He had made up his mind. Whether this fellow was honest or a bluffing liar, he did not care; he was not going to give him his confidence.

"I'm sorry, Sandor," he said, "but I haven't the least idea what you're talking about. And now, if you don't mind, I'll go downstairs again."

For a moment it looked as though there would be an explosion. Then, surprisingly, Sandor shrugged his shoulders.

"I see you still don't trust me. Well"—without waiting for the younger man to reply—"I do not know that I blame you entirely. After all, you have only my word. Of course, it would be simple enough for you to telephone through to London—but even then I doubt if your father would convince you. Very well, we will leave it at that. But when I tell you that the package which Minna Braun handed you last night contains information so valuable to the British authorities that your father's Department has been working night and day for months, scouring Europe for these very same facts, you will perhaps understand why I have been so persistent. But I have done everything possible; the further responsibility must rest with you. And now," with a change of tone, "perhaps you would be kind enough to let me know when you intend to return to London? I have a letter for your father which I should be pleased if you would undertake to deliver. There is a certain risk attached to your carrying it—but I do not suppose you will think twice about that?"

If the last few words had not constituted in his mind a direct challenge, Bobby might have acted differently. As it was, he came to a fresh resolve: already very suspicious in his mind about Sandor, and with the knowledge that the package was now safely on its way to London, he determined to stick to this fellow with one definite purpose: he was going to try to ascertain if Sandor was in the plot against his father. It seemed quite likely; to begin with, he had a lot of information about the governor, and, for another thing, he was much too glib.

It was because of this that, forcing himself to do a little prospective double-dealing in return, he now adopted a change of front.

"I'm sorry, Sandor," he said, "but you can quite understand that I had to make sure before I could talk frankly with you."

The other was quick to respond.

"That's quite all right, Mr. Wingate; I should not have thought so well of you as I do if you had behaved differently. And now—what did you do with the package that the Frenchwoman handed to you?"

Bobby, smiling, shook his head. He had to lie; there was no other way out.

"I'm quite willing to believe that you work for my father, Dr. Sandor—but the lady you call Minna Braun did not hand me any package."

"What?"

"I say she did not hand me any package. She certainly came to my room last night in a highly terrified condition, explaining that two men had endeavoured to break down her door—but after a while I induced her to go back to her room. That is all."

The statement, although not appearing to satisfy the man, was allowed to pass without comment. Sandor, it was very evident, was endeavouring to overcome an attack of intense irritability. At last he appeared to have succeeded.

Taking out his handkerchief and blowing his nose violently, he said: "Then, if she did not hand you the package, my information is wrong. But let us forget our worries. When did you say you intended to return to England?"

Bobby thought for a moment and then decided on the truth this time. Why not?

"I thought of going back to-morrow *via* Paris."

"By train?"

"No—air."

Sandor broke into a smile.

"Then I must make your last day's stay enjoyable. Would you care to visit a small club of which I am a member? I promise you will meet some very interesting people. But not, of course, if you have any remaining doubt about my *bona fides*."

It was the second challenge, and Bobby felt compelled to accept it.

"I'll come with pleasure," he said.

◇◇◇

The men to whom Sandor introduced him in the small but extremely comfortable club off the Unter den Linden were certainly agreeable, and, being of the true cosmopolitan type, they strove to make the visitor feel as much at home as though he were sitting down in the Junior Army and Navy in London. They were all civilians, and talk touched on many subjects dear to the hearts of men of the world: the latest fashionable members of the demi-monde, the different attractions of night life in Pé, Paris, and the various ports of the Far East. Such conversation, while it carried a distinct masculine tang, never became unnecessarily coarse, and Bobby, while he did far more listening than talking, could find no objection to it.

His host, he remarked, seemed fairly popular in this particular set of well-to-do men, and certainly no one could have looked after him with greater assiduity.

After lunch—and this was a meal which would have satisfied the tastes of any but the most exacting gourmet—some one in the smoking-room suggested cards.

Sandor touched his guest on the shoulder.

"Do you play poker, Wingate?" he inquired.

"Yes—but for small stakes. Remember, I'm anything but a millionaire. What's your limit here?"

"Oh, we play for various amounts."

Bobby, who liked the game, but who was very conscious of having only a few pounds on him, said:

"Perhaps I'd better watch—I haven't very much with me."

They would not listen to this. While Sandor offered to back him to any reasonable amount—a suggestion to which Wingate shook his head—the others said:

"Well, what about a five marks' limit?"

As he knew he could not lose a great deal—unless he lost his head—Bobby agreed, and they sat down to what Sandor described as "a quiet, friendly game" of five players.

After a couple of hours, Bobby's counters had grown to quite a respectable pile. He must be in, he thought, to the tune of about thirty pounds. The party was now showing signs of wishing to break up, but, just as one suggested another round of drinks, a man sitting on Sandor's right—that was two away from the Englishman— proposed a final round of jackpots with no limit.

Wingate looked at Sandor, who nodded reassuringly at him.

"Don't worry," the glance said.

It was not up to him to demur. He had no wish to appear a spoil-sport—as would undoubtedly have been the case if he had raised any objection. For one thing, he had been winning handsomely; for another, there was his natural pride.

"Is that all right, Wingate?" inquired his sponsor.

"Yes." He had only to keep his head, he told himself.

The luck of the cards was still with him; he could never remember having such a run—it was uncanny. Never once, for instance, did he find himself without the necessary "openers," and when he had filled in after discarding, he found himself with the very cards required to make his hands unbeatable. Bobby was not in a position to realise, of course, that the dealer on these occasions was Albrecht Ballin.

He would have been foolish in these circumstances not to have given his unexpected good fortune its head, and, although the amount of the "rise" caused him uneasiness at times, he went through with it, with the result that when the last jackpot had finished he found himself a winner of between 1,300 and 1,400 marks.

"You appear to have all the money in the world there," Sandor said with a laugh. "Now the question is: how are you going to get it out of Pé? You have heard of the recent restrictions prohibiting the removal of capital from Ronstadt, I dare say?"

Bobby, excited and not quite his usual self, imagined at first that the other was pulling his leg, but the confirmatory nods of the other players convinced him that Sandor was serious.

"The only way to get round it is to change your counters into English banknotes," one suggested.

"Good idea, Stürm," promptly replied Sandor. "As it happens, I've just got back from England and I have two £50 notes on me."

Still flushed, and somewhat out of control, Bobby thanked the speaker and placed the two notes in his pocket-book.

"I don't like taking this money, all the same, gentlemen," he said.

A roar of laughter greeted the remark. The listeners appeared to think it was the funniest thing they had heard for years.

"Well, I must be going," now announced Sandor, after the other necessary financial adjustments had been made; "I must see about earning some bread and butter."

Wingate parted from him on the steps of the Hotel Poste.

"I hope to see you again before long," the doctor said. "In the meantime, a safe return to dear old London. Don't forget to mention me to your father."

"I won't." It was only after the man had gone on his way that Bobby recalled Sandor's enigmatical smile.

But he decided to waste no further time in trying to solve *that* riddle: the quicker he was out of Pé the better. It was a pity that he had not been able to get any clue as to the plot against the governor, but against that he offset the fact that the governor would be ready with a full explanation when he talked to him. Trust a Colonel in M.I.5 to be able to look after himself!

Walking into the hotel, he told the office that he would be leaving in the morning, and returned to the guest-house.

Here he found drama awaiting him.

Chapter XI

The Inquisition

Meanwhile, the man known to Emil Crosber as Adolf Ritter was undergoing a stern cross-examination in the Headquarters of the Secret Police in the Wilhelmstrasse. With him, looking ashen-faced and trembling, was Aschelmann, the manager of the Hotel Poste.

Crosber's tone was venomous.

"Because I want you both to get the right angle on this, I propose to narrate the facts," he said, showing his teeth in a snarl. "Britain, with whom we shall shortly be at war, is known by us to possess the plans, and to be secretly manufacturing a new shoulder weapon, capable of being carried by any infantry soldier, which fires a small high-explosive, armour-piercing steel. Tests at Aldershot have proved this can put out of action any modern tank. These plans are being very jealously guarded, but, working through his old paramour, Marie Roget, this Department had hoped that sufficient pressure could be brought to bear on Colonel Clinton, to ensure that he, in his prominent position in M.I.5, would be able to place his hands on them.

"Before the woman I had commissioned to do this work left Pé, however, two rather surprising things happened. The first was that, by a queer stroke of luck, a certain friend of this country, long resident in England, was able to secure excellent prints of the plans of the anti-tank gun, and the second was that, out of the blue, as it were, Clinton's adopted son came to Pé—I have not the slightest doubt in the hope that he could do a little honest spying himself. At least, that is your belief," looking up at Ritter.

The latter person, whom Bobby Wingate would have had no difficulty in recognising as that very obliging medico, Dr. Emeric Sandor, nodded.

"That is the information which was given to me by—"

He was sharply interrupted.

"Don't mention that name, you fool—even here!" cried Crosber. "Don't you realise that when war breaks out that same person will be worth several army corps to us? Let it be sufficient that you were given this information."

"Yes," humbly agreed the other.

"With the son available, what more natural than that we should endeavour to improve on the position by compromising him so that we could exert a further hold on his father—even to two such crass idiots as you both have proved, that much is clear, I suppose?"

The listeners, looking like badly whipped dogs, gave murmurs of acquiescence.

"That was why I stopped Marie Roget, or, as we know her, Minna Braun, from going to London to interview the father, and instructed her to concentrate on the son.

"The plan—she is a clever woman—appears to have worked very well—up to a point." It was now that Crosber's face grew as black as a thundercloud. "In order that the hold Minna Braun had already obtained on the young man should be strengthened, she appealed to his sense of chivalry—always a good card to play with the British. She posed as a French agent who was being trailed by Ronstadt agents. Would the young Englishman with whom she had fallen in love help her by taking charge of the packet which contained the information she had been sent to Pé to get? He was quite willing to help her.

"Everything would have been all right," Crosber concluded, "but for your unpardonable mistake, Aschelmann." He glared at the hotel manager. "You had been handed the package by Ritter here, to be planted on young Wingate, and you had also received, for transmission to Ritter, a package from England. What do you do but get the two packages mixed up!

"But the package handed by Minna Braun to Wingate must be found if we have to search the whole of Ronstadt, and don't come back here, either of you, without it. That is all."

◇◇◇

Bobby had nearly finished dressing for dinner when the knock came on the door. He had been devoting considerable time to thinking of the events of the day. Then his mind turned to London—and Rosemary. What would she think when she got that newspaper? She would recognise his writing, no doubt, but would surely look inside for a message of some sort from him.

He was putting the finishing touches to his tie when knuckles rattled on the outside of the door.

"Yes?" he called, thinking it was the valet offering his services.

But when the door opened, a stranger showed himself. He was a thickset man of dominating appearance, and Bobby did not like the look on his face one little bit.

"Herr Wingate?" this fellow asked.

"Yes, that's my name. What do you want?"

The man scowled at him unpleasantly and ordered his two companions, who had been waiting outside in the corridor, into the room.

"I am from the Secret Police," he announced, "and I have authority to search your luggage."

Without waiting for any comment, he walked over to the two suitcases that stood on the luggage rest at the bottom of the bed.

He had his hands already on the first when Bobby recovered from his surprise.

"What's the idea?" he asked.

The leader of the raiding party gave him another unpleasant scowl.

"The idea is that you do not move from this room until we have gone right through it." He made a sign and his two underlings took up a position by the young Englishman.

Bobby realised it would be foolish to attempt to put up any kind of fight. What lay at the back of this he could not decide, unless—yes, that must be it: these men were after the package which Minna Braun had handed to him for custody. Well, that package was now safely on its way to London, so he had nothing to fear. Rosemary would readily understand his quickly pencilled note on the outside page of the newspaper: "*Keep this safe for me.*" The confidence he felt conquered his sense of rage.

"Do I understand that I am under suspicion of having committed some crime?"

"I am not here to answer questions."

"Then may I smoke?"

"You may not smoke."

A bully, this fellow, with his fleshy jowls and little, piglike eyes. A petty tyrant, rejoicing in his power that could instil fear into the hearts of all those he visited or even passed in the streets. The type was so new to the young Englishman that Bobby stared at him with the greatest interest.

It took fifteen minutes for the two suitcases to be examined. After that, the clothes hanging in the wardrobe, the drawers of the dressing-table, even the bedding—all these were gone through with the utmost care.

"If you'd only tell me what you are expecting to find, I might be able to help you."

"Shut your mouth."

Now was the time when Bobby felt he had to call upon all his reserves, but he managed to control himself. They were three against one, and all armed. Probably they were asking nothing better than to be given a chance to beat him into insensibility. He had heard sufficient of the methods of the Pé Secret Police, long before he had come to the city. For months the European newspapers had been devoting columns to the unsavoury subject.

Still, it was terribly galling to be insulted by this brute—and even more nauseating to feel the fellow's hands going over his clothes, as they did the next minute.

"Put on your hat and coat," Wingate was now ordered.

"Why?"

"Why?" roared the man. "Because I tell you to, that's why! You're coming for a drive with me, if you must know."

Bobby made a stand at this.

"I have been very patient with you so far," he said quietly, "but the time has come, I think, when I should remind you of certain important facts. I am a British subject—"

The emissary of the Secret Police spat.

"As though I didn't know that!" he returned, with infinite contempt.

"And, being a British subject, I demand to be treated with proper respect. I'm not a criminal."

Although he did not see that there was anything inherently humorous in the words, they were greeted with low, menacing laughter.

"Not a criminal! That's good, *hein*?" asked the leader of his two satellites.

The couple laughed again, as though savouring some private jest of their own.

Bobby boiled with anger. But mixed with his rage was a sense of—well, not exactly fear, but certainly uneasiness. Where were these men going to take him? What was the meaning of that "drive"? If he demanded to be taken to a lawyer or some responsible official at the British Embassy, they would rock with fresh scorning laughter, without a doubt. They recognised no law but their own wishes—and the commands of their superiors.

"Come along; we've wasted enough time. Besides, some one will be waiting."

◇◇◇

There were three men in this room to which he had been brought, and all of them were in uniform. The man seated at the desk, who was evidently going to take charge of the proceedings, was middle-aged, immaculately dressed in the uniform that fitted his slim figure like a glove, and had a face as hard as flint. He wore a monocle in his right eye.

He wasted no time.

"Good-evening, Lieutenant Wingate," he said in a chilling tone. "I regret the necessity for having you brought here—by the way, to relieve your mind of any further doubt, this is the Headquarters of the Ronstadt Secret Service—but I am afraid the necessity has arisen through your own actions."

Bobby took a cigarette from the box which was pushed towards him and slowly lit it.

"I shall be pleased to hear some further details."

"That request can quite easily be granted. Now, according to the information we have about you, you left London on ten days' leave on September sixteenth. You had a military pass entitling you to travel to Paris—but no farther. May I ask why you came to Pé?"

"Certainly." It was no use losing his head. He was on the brink of serious danger, but he must put the best face on it possible. "I came because I wished to attend the Musical Festival as well as the big Agricultural Exhibition."

"I see. You would go to the Festival as a civilian, I take it, and to the Agricultural Exhibition in—shall I say, another capacity?"

"I don't understand you."

"No? Then I will be more explicit. The evidence we have, Lieutenant Wingate, all goes to prove that you came to Pé with the determination to undertake a little spying work for your country."

"It's a lie!"

His interrogator shrugged his elegant shoulders.

"I should like to accept your word, Lieutenant, but I am afraid it is not possible for me to do so. Do you deny, for instance, that you spent practically the whole of yesterday in the company of a woman calling herself Minna Braun?"

"Yes, but—"

"Is it not equally true that this woman confessed to you in your bedroom last night that she was a French Secret Service agent?"

He kept silent. What reply could he give? His inquisitor continued.

"Is it not equally also correct that this woman, afraid that she was on the point of being discovered, handed to you a package—"

Bobby's brain, working quickly, made him interrupt. He knew what line of defence he must take: he must continue with the denial on this point that he had already given to Sandor.

"I am afraid I must give you the same answer as I gave a gentleman calling himself Dr. Emeric Sandor earlier in the day," he said with a smile. "I know nothing whatever about this very mysterious package. And I know nothing whatever about the lady calling herself Fräulein Minna Braun declaring herself to be a French Secret Service agent. She came to my room last night, it is true, and told me that she had been badly frightened by some men endeavouring to break down her door. I tried to reassure her, and after a short while she went back to her room. I do not see that that constitutes any crime, even in Ronstadt, Herr Major."

The cold blue eyes tried to outstare him. The man looked as though he knew Wingate was lying. He had put far too many poor devils through their paces in that same room to be deceived. And yet, hating himself as he did for the falsehoods, Bobby could not see any other line of conduct. It was impossible to go back on his word to the Frenchwoman—equally impossible, once he had started the denials, to tell what he had done with the package. If Minna Braun were to be believed, that package vitally concerned the future safety of both France and Great Britain. It was a dirty business in which he had become involved, but, once in, he had to make the best of it and fight with what weapons he could find.

The man in the middle chair lit a cigarette.

"So that is your story?" he inquired with a sneer.

"That is my story. The only other thing I have to say is to complain of the crude manners of the members of your Secret Police who brought me here. They appeared to think it very funny when I told them I was a British subject."

The other acted as though he had not heard; he was bending towards the older man on his left, listening intently to what the latter was saying. Presently he turned again to

Wingate, and now there was a suspicion of a smile on his flintlike face.

"We do not appear to be getting anywhere, Lieutenant. Perhaps we shall understand each other a little better if I tell you something that occurred seventeen years ago. A certain British officer, a few years older than yourself, was sent to Paris with secret dispatches. What those dispatches concerned does not matter greatly after this length of time. What does matter is that, owing to his association with a certain attractive young woman, then working for the German Secret Service, he proved false to his trust—with the result that the British were badly beaten back at a certain part of the line and lost over five thousand casualties in men and officers. That officer, Lieutenant Wingate, was your stepfather. He occupies now, I understand, quite a prominent position in the Military Intelligence Department of your War Office."

The listener laid down his cigarette.

"You don't expect me to believe that, of course?" he said.

For reply, the Major opened a drawer in his desk and placed a large envelope on the table before him.

"The story can best be substantiated by a number of photographs. You will no doubt be able to recognise your father here?" handing the first one over.

Bobby stared at the speaker before glancing towards the photograph. Strange that an enemy should be the means of providing the very evidence that Bobby himself had wanted to find!

He picked up the photograph. With a growing sense of dismay, he was able to recognise the man in British uniform: without any possible doubt, this man was the governor.

"Here is another," said the Major, passing over another photograph.

The blood flooded into Bobby's face. The scene now was a room in what was either a private house, or, more likely, a hotel.

"I can give you the name of the hotel—Lion d'Or, in Paris," supplied the Major.

An officer in British uniform—his father again—was embracing a girl whose face was so hidden that she could not be recognised.

"And, finally, here are photographs of your father's letters to this girl, Marie Roget, together with facsimiles of the secret dispatches he was supposed to deliver safely to Major-General Bentley of the Royal Engineers."

Bobby, after scanning the incriminating evidence quickly, thrust the documents aside.

"Why are you showing me these?" he demanded.

Another fleeting smile played over the grim lips.

"Because I wish you to understand that it would be politic of you to inform me what you did with the package handed to you by Minna Braun."

So that was it! Blackmail! If he didn't come through with the truth, they would put the screw on the poor old governor! But even that fear did not sway him. He could not allow it to do so.

"You can go to hell," he said very distinctly.

The Major's face stiffened into yet more formidable lines.

"I am not likely to forget that remark, Lieutenant Wingate," he said—and then the telephone by his side rang. Taking off the receiver, he listened carefully. Then, with a murmured "Very well," he hung up.

"You are at liberty to return to your hotel," he said surprisingly.

Chapter XII

Bobby Draws a Blank

During the taxi ride back to the guest-house, Bobby wondered at his escape. That this was entirely due to the mysterious telephone message he had no doubt; otherwise, the Secret Service authorities would have detained him until he came through with the truth.

But what did anything matter now that he was free? The only thing of consequence was his determination to get out of Pé as quickly as possible. Things generally were in a hell of a mess—not only was he suspected of being a British spy, but there was that horrible cloud hanging over his father's name.

Arrived at the guest-house, he was informed that his luggage had been transferred to the Hotel Poste.

"For what reason?"

The clerk shrugged his shoulders.

"We had orders," he said—and would not be drawn to any further extent.

Well, it didn't matter whether he stayed at the guest-house or the Poste for that one night. He would be off first thing in the morning, in any case.

The mental strain under which he had been labouring for the past two hours had given him an appetite, and he went into the dining-room determined to fortify his nerves with a good meal. Before he could sit down, however, he was accosted by a familiar voice.

"Hullo, Bobby! I've been waiting for you to show up."

Peter Mallory!

"Don't look so startled, my boy; I can easily explain everything. If you don't mind, I'll sit with you. I haven't dined myself yet."

Here was a bit of luck! But, nevertheless, after the first pleasant shock of surprise had passed, Bobby told himself that he must not give his confidence even to his old friend. The governor must not be exposed—and, for his own part, he did not wish to discuss his own foolhardy behaviour (for that was how any outside person would sum it up, he had no doubt).

Mallory was very tactful. It was not until the meal was well under way that he explained the reason for his unexpected appearance.

"I came over here at your father's request, Bobby," he said. "He didn't know you were going on to Pé, and has been very worried. You appear to have been rather playing the fool. Fordinghame, of Y.1, began to get reports about you—the things you were doing here—and so your father asked me to look you up and advise you to return home at once. Good God, my boy," he went on, speaking more seriously, "you really ought to have been more careful—especially at a time like this."

It was a direct invitation for confidence, but Bobby ignored him. It hurt him to do so, but he felt compelled to keep his tongue under control. All he permitted himself to say was this:

"I am leaving to-morrow morning for Paris."

◇◇◇

It was not until the great air liner had actually left the ground that Bobby felt safe. Till then he had been expecting to feel a hand fall on his shoulder at any moment.

Mallory, who had come to see him off, had rallied him on being so preoccupied.

"I am beginning to think that you must have fallen in love over here, my boy," he had said. "That won't do at all, you know, with a certain very charming girl waiting for you in London. By the way, she drove me back from Croydon; I hope you aren't jealous?"

"Jealous?" Bobby had laughed. "No, I'm not jealous." Why should he be jealous of a man old enough to be his father, even if there were any likelihood of Rosemary's being attracted? Uncle Peter was a damned good sort, of course, but with his gaunt face and general unprepossessing appearance he could not conceive of any woman, let alone a modern girl of twenty-two like Rosemary....Oh, it was ridiculous. He had been having his leg pulled.

"When are you coming back?" he had asked.

"Directly I have finished up the insurance business which brought me over. To-morrow, I hope. I must say I don't think the atmosphere in Pé just at the moment is particularly healthful to any Englishman. I shall be glad to get clear—and only wish I were going with you."

"Well, look after yourself. Don't forget the governor would be terribly upset if—"

"Oh, I shall be all right; they wouldn't dare to touch me; I'm a *bona fide* professional man—over here on perfectly straightforward business. It was rather different with you, young man; they knew you were an officer in the British Army, and, with the tension as it is between the two countries, they probably thought that you had come on from

Paris with the deliberate intention of doing a little amateur spying. And they were right, I take it?"

"I wanted to try to do the governor a bit of good," Bobby had replied.

"Dashed risky way of attempting it, if I may say so.... Well, a safe trip; my regards to Miss Allister."

Mallory then turned away. Just as Wingate had refused to give him his full confidence, so had he withheld a certain amount of the truth from the younger man. Within a half-hour of making his farewell remark to Bobby, he himself was on board an air liner—bound for London.

Bobby looked at the paper again. Yes, there was no doubt about this being the rue Danou—but although he had traversed the short street from end to end, there was no number corresponding to the one Minna Braun had written in that good-bye message to him.

She must have made some mistake—and yet, in an affair of such importance, how could she have made a mistake, even assuming that she was terribly agitated at the time she wrote the note?

Was the thing a blind—a trap? He had dismissed the idea immediately, annoyed with himself at the suggestion. That the woman who called herself "Minna Braun" was really working for the French Intelligence Service had been amply proved by the statements of that swine of a Major who had interrogated him.

Noticing a man on the other side of the street watching him with what appeared to be more than ordinary interest, Bobby tore the note into tiny fragments behind his back and scattered these to the winds. He had been rather clever about secreting that address, he considered; screwing up the paper, he had placed it at the bottom of his pipe and covered it with tobacco. At the time his luggage and person were being searched, the pipe, all ready for lighting, had been resting on the mantelpiece. That was why he had asked permission to smoke—a permission which had been so curtly refused. Perhaps that bullying leader of the Secret Police had thought that he had intended to commit suicide through the medium of a drugged cigarette!

Ronstadt had numerous agents in Paris, no doubt, and, with the thoughts that the sight of the possible watcher on the other side of the street had aroused filling his mind, he decided that it would be better to get a move on. He dared not run any further risks. When he reached London he would send a few words on a plain sheet of paper to the woman at the address she had given him—something like "Everything all right"—and chance its getting to her. That was all he *could* do, of course.

Chapter XIII

Rosemary Is Perplexed

Rosemary had been obliged to alter her decision. She felt, on reflection, that she could not abuse an office confidence, not even when Bobby Wingate was concerned. So she had not lived up to her original intention of going to his father and telling him all that she knew. A subsidiary reason was that she felt certain Sir Brian Fordinghame would communicate the information himself. The one person to whom she would have liked to talk was Bobby's mother, but here again the same condition ruled. Besides, it would be the height of cruelty to bring added pain to that sweet soul. No, all she could do, she decided, was to watch events in the office and be thankful that she was on the "inside" of what was happening. Of course, this was a mixed blessing, but she had to put up with that.

Events moved swiftly. Reports from the British Secret Service agents in Pé continued to come through every few hours. Word was received that Bobby had been taken to the Headquarters of the Ronstadt Secret Service and there interrogated.

She could not help questioning her chief on this point. The excuse she gave for her personal interest was that she knew Bobby Wingate intimately.

"Of course," returned Fordinghame; "I had forgotten that for the moment. No, Miss Allister, I confess," he went on, "that I cannot understand this new move—unless it is meant as a blind to throw our own people off the scent. Such things do happen."

She risked a great deal.

"It's impossible to imagine that Bobby Wingate is a traitor, Sir Brian."

"On the surface, yes. But these are very damning facts"—pointing to the papers on his desk.

It had been a very heavy day, with Brander away, and when she reached home she felt extremely tired.

At dinner that night her father had turned to the minor politician who had come to consult him on a point of banking rule which formed an important platform in a speech he was scheduled to make the following afternoon in the House of Commons.

"You mustn't mind Rosemary," he said, in part apology for the girl's preoccupation. "She's living a life of tremendous excitement just now. No, I cannot possibly tell you what it is—but the ordinary film star has nothing on her at the moment."

It pleased Matthew Allister, who actually was a pedant to the bottom of his soul, to pretend to be ultramodern on occasions. This was one of the occasions.

Knowing that her father was merely trying to make a mild joke, she forced herself to smile at the words. If only he knew the tumult that was in her heart....

It was when she was trying in vain to sleep that the dreadful thought came. Sir Brian Fordinghame, acting on the information he had received, strongly suspected Bobby of being a traitor. She didn't believe if for a moment—how could any one who knew the boy intimately give it one single moment's thought?—*but…*

It was then that she put a hand to her heart to try to stop its furious beats. Suppose—just suppose—that, in a fit of mad desperation, Bobby had attempted to sell some military secret. For what purpose? Why, in the frenzied craving to get some money so that he might be able to marry her.

As quickly as it came, she dismissed the suggestion. Even although she had moved for the last few days in an atmosphere of sheer melodrama, such an event was inconceivable. Besides, it would have to be something of tremendous and vital importance to bring him in any such sum. And how could he, a mere lieutenant in the Tanks, get hold of such information?

Yet, there was this certainty: he had run and was still running, probably, terrible risks. Why?

Out of the jumble of her thoughts she endeavoured to sort something that was clear and coherent. And this is what came: (1) she knew she loved Bobby Wingate more than ever, and (2) she was going to help him. It seemed preposterous, such a resolve, especially as at the moment she did not possess the slightest inkling of how she was going to set to work. But, strong in her faith and affection, she felt sure a means would be shown her.

◇◇◇

The next morning she found on the breakfast table a newspaper addressed to her in Bobby's handwriting—with the words "*Keep this safe for me*" on the outside page. It was not until she had cut the string and had smoothed out the pages that she realised the journal was a covering for another package. This crinkled as she touched it, and, tearing it open, she found—*just two blank sheets of paper.*

What was Bobby's idea? Was he playing some stupid prank? It certainly seemed like it. Why should he have scribbled on the outside page of the newspaper "*Keep this safe for me*"?

After a couple of minutes she calmed herself. Bobby was not the type to play the fool. He must have had some definite purpose in mind when he sent this to her. She would keep both the newspaper and the sheets of paper safely locked away until he returned.

Until he returned! Would he ever return? Would he join that grisly throng who, put into prison on a real or false charge of espionage, become lost in the shadows of a never-never land to which the ordinary person was not allowed to penetrate?

She was early at the office, and when Sir Brian entered to give her a courteous good-morning, she was tempted to confide what she knew to this man of knowledge and affairs. But she beat the temptation down; this was her own affair. Bobby had singled her out for his confidence—very well, she would respect it. If he had wanted to, he could have sent that package to his father. Why he had not done so, she was unable to understand—but the fact remained: he had given her his confidence. She would be a nice sort of rotter if she let him down. She was not going to let him down!

Late that afternoon there was an unexpected visitor—unexpected, at least, so far as Rosemary was concerned. Peter Mallory walked in; he smiled at Fordinghame, and gave her a slight bow. Never very slow on the uptake, Rosemary left, after a word or so of greeting to Mallory, for her small inner room.

The visitor stayed for about half an hour, and then Fordinghame recalled her to take some fresh dictation. When he had finished, he seemed inclined for a chat.

"Remarkable man, that, Miss Allister; he is one of our most reliable agents. He flew back from Pé to-day."

She stared at him, unable to control her surprise.

"That astonishes you, evidently."

"Well, Sir Brian, I—I confess it does. I always understood from the Clintons that Mr. Mallory was in the insurance business."

Fordinghame laughed.

"So he is, my dear young lady—but that is merely one side of his character. He is what the medical wallahs call a dual personality. By day—if I may put it that way—he is engaged in his insurance business, while by night (or the equivalent of night) he serves me as the ace of Y.1! But that, of course,"—becoming serious—"is a very close secret. You understand?"

"Perfectly, Sir Brian. And you can trust me to respect your confidence."

"I felt I could; otherwise I should not have told you." He opened his cigarette case and held it out. Rosemary declined the invitation to smoke; she still had a great deal of typing to do. Indeed, for a girl who had never had to think about any kind of work before, she was getting through an astonishing amount of labour.

It was half-past six before she had finished the final page. Sir Brian had been gone for nearly twenty minutes, and, apart from the couple of clerks, she had been alone in the building. It gave her an uncanny sensation to reflect what secrets could have been disclosed by that huge steel cabinet let into the wall on the opposite side of the room to Fordinghame's desk.

As she walked down the few steps to the pavement, a man stepped forward, raising his hat.

"I've been waiting for you, Miss Allister," said Peter Mallory.

Her first impression was one of resentment. No matter how much value Fordinghame put on this man's services, no matter how deeply he was in the personal esteem of Colonel Clinton and Bobby Wingate, she was unable to fight down the feeling of antagonism he inspired in her. Perhaps it was because, loving all beautiful things, she did not like his gaunt face and generally unprepossessing appearance. Mallory was a gentleman beyond any question or quibble. His manners were polished, his approach good. But—well, there it was!

It was because she kept silent, perhaps, that the man continued.

"I didn't like to ask you in the office just now—but may I ask if to-night is propitious for our little dinner-party?"

"Did I promise to come to a dinner-party?"

He raised his eyebrows in an almost comic look of bewilderment.

"But, of course, Miss Allister. Don't you remember? It was when you were driving me back from Croydon on the day that Bobby Wingate flew to Paris."

It was the mention of Bobby's name that did it.

"Oh, yes," she replied, as though suddenly remembering. "Well, to-night will do as well as any other night—perhaps better: I've had a frightfully thick time of it here to-day, and I must say I should not object to a little mild excitement. Do you feel awfully rich, Mr. Mallory?"

"Awfully rich?" he repeated, a little perplexed.

"Because," she went on quickly, "I'm in that mood: I feel like the Savoy Grill or the Berkeley, with orchids and lots of distinguished people about; a famous *maître d'hôtel* at my elbow, a fleet of soft-footed waiters, Pommery on ice—and all the rest of it."

He was quick to respond to her mood.

"Then I suggest the Savoy Grill. We will dine late—and dance."

"Eight-thirty will suit me. That will give me an hour for sleep before—"

"I call for you," he supplied.

The famous rendezvous was crowded to the last improvised table when Rosemary entered the Savoy Grill at 8.35 that evening.

"You booked a table?" she inquired.

Her escort regarded her quizzically.

"You surely don't think I should have asked for the company of the most charming young lady in London without taking such an elementary precaution?" Mallory replied. "Yes, I've booked a table."

Indeed, at that moment the *maître d'hôtel* approached. His professional smile looked as though it might slip out of place at any moment. The man was worried.

He recovered his poise when he recognised Rosemary's companion.

"Ah, Mr. Mallory—the table by the wall.... Will it suit?"

"Admirably. Don't you think so, my dear?"

Objecting to being addressed in this way, although Mallory probably did not mean anything beyond an avuncular interest, Rosemary nodded.

"Yes, quite well," she said.

Her escort proved to possess one quality: he could order a dinner, while his choice of wines was also to be commended. Enjoying her food and interested by the company around her, Rosemary began to feel that perhaps she had not made such a sacrifice after all. A couple of hours before, when resting in her bedroom, she had told herself that if it had not been for Bobby she would not have accepted this invitation. It had been for his sake—in the hope of learning something about what he had really been up to in Pé—that she had agreed to dine with Mallory that night.

"Did you go to Pé, Mr. Mallory?" she inquired, after declaring the fish delicious.

"Yes; I went on my usual business."

"Insurance, isn't it? Sir Brian told me," she added quickly.

"Yes—insurance. Are you willing to give me your confidence, Miss Allister?"

"My confidence? About what?"

"I'm worried about young Wingate—Bobby," he returned, without answering her question. "I suppose you know—working with Fordinghame, as you have done during the last few days—that Bobby has been behaving very indiscreetly in Pé?"

"Do you think I ought to answer that?"

"Answer it?" He laughed. "I admire your discretion, but surely you need not be so careful with me? Apart altogether from my association with Y.1—hasn't Fordinghame told you I work for him?—the fact that we're both such close friends of Bobby—"

"Yes, I know all about that, Mr. Mallory," she broke in sharply. "But tell me exactly in what way Bobby has been playing the fool?"

"Well, I hate to say it, but he has apparently laid himself open to suspicion by our own agents in the city."

She looked at him with a directness he appeared to find slightly amusing.

"You don't seriously think that Bobby is a traitor, do you?"

He glanced round cautiously.

"You never know who may be listening," he explained. "No, I do not think Bobby is a traitor," he continued; "the idea is absolutely ridiculous. I should very much like to know the numbers of the British agents who have communicated these reports."

Rosemary took some time before replying.

"Then if you don't think Bobby is a traitor, what has he done to place himself under such suspicion?"

"You are in a better position than I am to know that, Miss Allister. All I know is what I have heard from Fordinghame. Look here," he continued, "if you could let me have the numbers of the agents who have sent in these reports I could judge pretty well whether their information was likely to be true. Do you think you could get them for me—without, of course, letting Fordinghame know? He's a fanatic on some points."

"I must think about it," she replied.

It struck her as being curious that Mallory should have made this request. Being a trusted Y.1 agent himself, he must know that the concealment of the identity of any man or woman working for the British Intelligence was most strictly observed. So far as she had been able to ascertain, this rule was never broken. Then why should Mallory ask her to break it? Was it because he thought he could trade on her inexperience?

"I dare say you think that is an unusual request, Miss Allister?" he remarked.

"Well, frankly, I do."

"Then forget all about it," he said easily. "I was only anxious to help allay any suspicion you yourself might have had about Bobby."

"I have never had any suspicion of Bobby. When he gets back to town, I haven't the slightest doubt that he will be able to explain everything."

"I'm sure he will—and now suppose we talk of something else."

For the next half-hour Mallory proved such an agreeable companion that, in spite of the perhaps unfair prejudice she had against the man, she found herself almost liking him.

After that his talk lost its sparkle and the speaker became *distrait*. She wondered if some remark she had made could have caused this change, and then noticed that Mallory was staring with great concentration at a table on the opposite side of the room. Two men were occupying it. One was young, the other middle-aged.

The expression on Mallory's face was puzzling. His eyes were alight and his face was flushed. The rest of the world (herself included) might not have existed: all his attention and interest were focused on the other table. When she suggested they should have their coffee while watching the cabaret in the restaurant, he did not answer at first.

Then, like a person coming out of a trance, he said disjointedly: "I'm terribly sorry.... What was it you said?"

Her reply was slightly tart.

"I merely suggested that I should like to drink my coffee while watching the cabaret—but, of course, it doesn't matter."

"My dear, I am tremendously sorry—but I am afraid my mind was wandering."

"Exactly," she said dryly.

"But I will endeavour to make amends." Yet, still, for some as yet unexplained reason, his attention was not on her, but on the couple at the distant table.

She was forced to follow his gaze. What was it about these two men that Mallory found so absorbing? What attraction could they have for him?

At that moment the older man, who had been sitting with his back to her, rose—and Rosemary imagined that what before had been dark was now clear. Of course, she might possibly be wrong—she hoped she was. At any rate, she was completely satisfied on one point: her companion's interest had been drawn not to the older of the two men, but to the almost unnaturally good-looking youth who shared the table with him.

But as soon as she believed she had solved one puzzle, another one presented itself. The older man had risen with the direct purpose of speaking to Mallory. The latter's face had gone white when he recognised the other; he was labouring under some sense of apprehension—that was evident.

The stroller must have made some imperceptible sign, for Mallory whispered to her, "Will you excuse me for a moment?" and, without waiting for her permission, rose and walked towards the entrance. He had gone to join the other man, without a doubt.

◇◇◇

Rosemary found her father in the library when she got back.

"Hullo, pet!" he said, looking up from the book he was reading. "Have a good time?"

"I had rather an *interesting* time," was her reply.

The banker blinked behind his reading glasses.

"Well, isn't that the same thing?" he demanded.

"Not always.... What have you got there?" She looked over his shoulder. "Another of those horrible detective stories again?"

"This one isn't dreadful—it's written by A. E. W. Mason."

"Oh, well, that's different—then it's a work of art," agreed his daughter. "I want something to read, myself."

She drifted over to the well-stocked shelves. Like many a sedentary worker, Matthew Allister's tastes in literature ran strongly to tales of adventure and bloodshed, but he also fancied himself as a serious student of criminology, and dined solemnly on the third day of each month with a number of men of similar inclinations who had formed a club the title of which none of them ever seemed very clear about.

Absorbed in *The Prisoner in the Opal*, Allister did not pay any more attention to his daughter until she stooped to kiss him "good-night." Then, with perfunctory interest, he looked at the book she was carrying.

"I shouldn't have thought that would appeal to you, pet," he said. "Whatever makes you want to read it?"

Rosemary's face was inscrutable.

"I have a reason," she said.

Chapter XIV

At Woolvington

The joy of returning to London! It was this sense of delight that made Bobby Wingate smile instead of frown when, a short while after the air liner took off, homeward bound for Croydon, he was addressed by the man sitting in the seat behind.

"Excuse me, but aren't you Wingate?" said the voice.

Bobby looked at the speaker for a few moments before recognition came.

"Why, it's you—Stinker!"

The man who had laboured under this insalubrious nickname at Repington grinned as though he had received the choicest of compliments. Aubrey Dexter had never been one to put on side, and even now that he was an Under-Secretary at the British Legation at Sofia, he conformed to his school tradition.

"What are you doing so far away from your base?" asked Wingate.

Dexter's freckled face slipped into a fresh grin.

"Oh, I'm trotting back to attend the Annual Reunion dinner of the Old Boys' Association. Haven't you had a card?"

"It may be at home. I've been on leave in Paris," explained Bobby.

"Well, you ought to come, you know," said the other. "What will happen to the old school tie if you slack like this?"

"All right, don't rub it in. Where is the show?"

"Trocadero to-morrow night, seven-thirty. That gives you plenty of time to make up your mind. By the way, you're still in the Service, I suppose?"

"Yes—Tanks."

"Then you must wear uniform. The President (old 'Smiler' Bunty is the big noise this year) put it expressly in the notice that all members now with the Services should wear uniform, and that others who held decorations should flaunt them to the world."

"Damn!"

"Why, what's the matter?"

"Well, it will mean my going down to my unit at Woolvington and collecting my mess kit, which is in my quarters."

"That's not much of a hardship, surely?"

Bobby grimaced. He was thinking of Rosemary Allister and how delighted she would be when he turned up so unexpectedly. There were still three days of his leave to run, and he determined to spend as much of that time as possible with her. He'd been a bit of a fool, now that he came to look back—spouting all that stuff about her money being such a fatal obstacle. It had only needed a few days' absence from London to convince him of how deeply he was in love with this girl. Minna Braun? Well, that was entirely different; and, besides, she was—well, not the type to get married. An affair, yes: he couldn't imagine any one more attractive for a thing of that sort; but marriage—definitely, no.

The last words that Stinker said to him as they left the bus which had conveyed them from Croydon airport to Victoria Station were:

"Now, I'm relying on you, Bobby—you will come?"

"Yes, I'll come. But curse you, all the same—it will mean my spending a night in Mess instead of in town."

Parking his luggage in the left-luggage office at Victoria Station, he was fortunate to find that a train for Woolvington was leaving in twenty minutes' time. That would just allow him to ring up Rosemary and explain the position. But when he got through to the house in Clarges Square the butler told him that Miss Allister was out.

Oh, well, it didn't matter—she'd be back the next day. His greeting kiss could wait, and he hoped would taste all the sweeter for the delay.

◇◇◇

He arrived at the Mess about ten o'clock, to be greeted joyously by his fellow-officers when he entered the anteroom.

"Why, you old rotter," shouted Hollister, "I imagined you were up to no end of games in gay Paree. Why this thusness?"

Bobby explained as quickly as possible.

"What on earth made you cut short your leave, man? Weren't the girls the right shape, or did the money run out?"

"Both," he said succinctly, hoping that this would close the argument more quickly. But all the time he was conscious of those two fifty-pound notes nestling in his pocket-book. He would pay them into his bank the first thing in the morning, draw out a tenner and give Rosemary the best lunch the Berkeley could provide. Dear kid! she loved the Berkeley. Well, she should go there and have that favourite table of hers in the corner.

From the O.C. downwards every one appeared glad to see him, and very quickly he had plunged into "shop" talk, just as though he had never been away. Hollister, who was his particular pal, told him that the prize item in the latest news was the arrival from the experimental section of a new amphibious type of tank which was to undergo trials early the following morning.

"By the way, Wingate," went on Hollister, "did you hear much prospective war talk in Paris?"

"No. Everything seemed much the same as usual." Billy Hollister's eyes would have opened wide enough, he imagined, if he told him all that had happened since he had left the Mess.

Keenness was the dominating characteristic of his brother officers, and they all sat up late that night discussing the possibilities of this new type of amphibious tank. Bobby was on hand the next morning to witness the trials, but prior to this he had visited the bank and had taken the keenest interest in the construction of the new land fortress. It was not until the early afternoon that he was able to get away.

Arriving at Victoria about tea-time, he took a taxi to his club. Prompted more by habit than anything else, he asked for his letters and was handed a telegram.

Thinking it might be from Rosemary, he tore open the envelope eagerly. But what he read caused his eyes to open wide with astonishment:

> VITALLY IMPORTANT YOU SHOULD COME IMMEDIATELY HOTEL CONTINENTAL SCHUYLERSTRASSE THE HAGUE STOP BRING PACKAGE STOP DON'T FAIL STOP LIFE OR DEATH FOR ME

It was signed "Adrienne."

Conscious that he was probably behaving in a manner which was bound to attract attention, Bobby folded up the wire and walked away in the direction of the small smoking-room.

What was he to do? But, first of all, how had Adrienne Grandin known the name of his club? That was puzzling.

During the time they had spent together in Pé he had never once informed her that he was an army officer or that he was a member of the Junior Army and Navy. Still, being in the French Secret Service, she would have means of getting information denied to the ordinary person. That might account for it.

Should he ignore the message? No, he could not very well do that. He couldn't let the woman down.

He pulled out the telegram and read it again. And, as he did so, a thought came—a disturbing, stealthy, menacing thought.

Was this telegram a carefully planned plot? Had Adrienne Grandin been the sender or had her name been forged?

He must be calm, he told himself. Big issues were at stake. As he saw it, there were three things he could do: (1) ignore the wire altogether, or (2) get the package from Rosemary and post it with a covering note to the Frenchwoman, explaining that it was impossible for him to leave England again, or (3) go himself but take a dummy package.

The more he thought about it, the more he became convinced that the message was a snare of some kind. Was the woman herself in the plot? Suppose—just suppose that she was the same person who had seduced his father? It was possible: the woman who had called herself Minna Braun in Pé was cultured, refined, and possessed extreme physical attractions. Seventeen years before she would have been quite a girl, but....

He ought to go straight to the governor and lay all his cards on the table, he supposed. But, if he did, he would be the means of giving his father the cruellest blow of his life.

Out of the welter of conflicting emotions which surged through his mind, he finally came to a decision. It was his duty, as he saw it, to probe this mystery to the uttermost: he owed that to his father, if not to himself. He simply had to know what was behind that blackmail plot of which, perhaps quite soon, his father was destined to be the victim. The Hague was in Holland; he would be on Dutch, not Ronstadt, soil. If he kept his wits about him, nothing very much could happen. He would go armed to that rendezvous, and if there was any tricky business....

The package? Should he take it? No. He would keep to the plan which he had been considering a few minutes before. If the woman really turned up and everything seemed straightforward, he would explain; if some one else was at the Hotel Continental, then he would know it was a "plant." What might happen after that he must leave to chance.

After making a few inquiries, the club head porter was able to inform him that the boat train for Harwich and the Hook left Liverpool Street at 8 p.m.

Bobby's next anxiety was about money, but this quickly passed. He had paid in the two fifty-pound notes at the Woolvington branch of his bank that morning, and was now able to cash a cheque for fifteen pounds at the club, which he considered would carry him over on this Holland trip.

The night journey was uneventful, and, arriving at the Hook of Holland the following morning shortly after six o'clock, he breakfasted on the boat leisurely and caught a train which was due to arrive at The Hague shortly after 10 a.m. There were very few other people in the saloon, although he noticed a couple of men sitting at a table on his right.

Getting out of the station at The Hague, he called a taxi and gave the address mentioned in the telegram. The Hotel Continental reminded him somewhat of the Berners Hotel in Berners Street, off Oxford Street; it looked up-to-date, comfortable and well run. After a much-needed wash and brush up, he descended in the lift and took a seat in the hotel lounge. Now that the moment for actual confrontation was drawing near, he began to feel slightly nervous.

Lighting a cigarette, he waited. Was he to discover within the next few minutes that the fascinating woman he had met at Pé was really a decoy?

In any case, whether she was a straight dealer or a professional seductress for spy purposes, he would have to use all his guile to get her to accompany him back to London. He had thought this out on the boat coming over. That affair in which his father had played the most prominent part seventeen years before simply had to be cleared up. No doubt the governor had been exploited—and, in view of the present tension between Ronstadt and England, he simply had to know where he stood.

Bobby had not long to wait. The cigarette he had lit was only half-smoked when a page approached. The boy was carrying a salver, on which rested a sealed envelope. This, Bobby was able to see when he picked it up, was addressed to "Mr. R. Wingate."

"For me?" he asked the page.

The boy nodded.

Breaking the seal and opening the envelope, he read the following typewritten message:

> PLEASE COME TO ROOM NO. 127 AT THE EARLIEST POSSIBLE MOMENT.

Now for it! He must steel himself against the woman until she had convinced him that she was actually what she had claimed to be at Pé.

Preceded by the page, he went to the lift and was carried to the second floor. Here, in a large, comfortably furnished bedroom, he was greeted—not by Adrienne Grandin, but by a stranger. The latter looked like a Frenchman and spoke English with a Parisian accent.

"I am delighted to meet you, Monsieur Wingate," he started. "It is very good of you to come. No doubt you have been expecting to meet a certain very charming lady—walls have ears, you know," he added, looking round, "so I will not mention any names."

"Oh, that's all right," returned the Englishman, as though recognising the good sense of what the other was saying; "but this is a very important business, and I must be convinced that you are the right person."

The other smiled.

"Your caution does you credit, monsieur. This," taking a letter from his coat pocket, "will remove all doubts in your mind. As you will be able to see, it is in a certain person's handwriting."

Sure enough, the handwriting closely resembled that contained in the note he had received from Adrienne Grandin at Pé. But, still, he had to pretend to require more confirmation.

"There was to be some other form of identification," he said, handing the letter back.

The man looked confounded.

"Some other form of identification?" he repeated.

"Yes."

"But the person we both know said nothing of that."

"Oh, well—perhaps she forgot," conceded the Englishman, after a brief pause. "That letter's good enough. If you'll kindly wait here, I'll go to my room."

Once out in the corridor, Bobby felt he knew exactly where he stood: that message to The Hague *had* been a trap of some kind. What the Ronstadt people hoped to gain by it, he did not know—but the very fact that this messenger did not show him the *real* form of identification—the signet ring with R.F. engraved on it, which Adrienne Grandin had assured him was carried by every genuine French

Secret Service agent—was ample proof in his own mind of treachery of some kind.

All right! He had come prepared for that. In his room, to which he was now rushing, was a dud package—an exact replica, so far as he could remember, of the envelope which the woman had handed to him with so much melodramatic detail in his bedroom at the guest-house at Pé. He smiled to himself when he thought of the expression on this messenger's face when he opened the envelope and found nothing in it but two blank sheets of paper....

Within five minutes he had handed over the package and had received the emissary's fervent thanks.

Then he allowed the man to go; it would be foolish to attempt to probe him about the blackmail plot against Colonel Clinton—the fellow would first pretend to know nothing and then tell a string of lies.

He would have to wait.

Chapter XV

Under Arrest

Rosemary's face was clouded.

"What is the meaning of all this?" she asked.

"Meaning of all what?" he replied.

She became impatient.

"Don't think me the worst possible kind of fool, *please*, Bobby! Why did you go to Pé? Why did you cause yourself to be watched by our people?"

He looked at her sharply.

"How do you know I was being watched?"

"Mr. Mallory told me, the night we went to the Savoy Grill. It was he who said how indiscreet you had been.... Oh, my dear, why were you such an awful ass?"

He felt hurt, and showed it.

"I don't know that I *was* such an awful ass," he retorted with some heat.

The answer angered her. Was he going to brazen it out, even to the girl who loved him?

"Don't you?" she retorted. "Then I'm afraid you haven't very much sense of proportion." Should she tell him all she knew? She decided it was only fair to do so. "Bobby," she went on, and her face was now very serious, "you'll get to know this soon in any case, and I would much rather you heard it from me than from any one else: since you've been away I've been acting as assistant personal secretary to Sir Brian Fordinghame."

"The Intelligence man?"

She nodded.

"Yes. He's Chief of Y.1, the department which looks after counter-espionage among other things."

Looking at her, Bobby realised that she was in deadly earnest. But what on earth could she be getting at?

"You're suspected of being a traitor," she told him, straight out.

He laughed.

"Don't be a fool, my dear," he said. "You're trying to pull my leg."

"I only wish to God I was, Bobby! But I'm perfectly serious. Let me tell you this: from the moment you got to Pé—and even before, when you were on the Paris express—you were under the constant scrutiny of British Secret Service agents."

"But why?"

"Because you played the fool. Didn't you know that the man who called himself 'Dr. Emeric Sandor' was a Ronstadt agent?"

"No, of course I didn't."

Rosemary lit a cigarette but flung it into the grate almost immediately.

"I don't know that I can possibly help you—I want to, of course," she said. "But I can't help you unless you tell me the absolute truth. Why did you go to Pé?"

He wetted his lips with the tip of his tongue, which had become suddenly dry.

"Because I wanted to see the new tractors which I heard they were going to use for the latest model of tank."

"Is that the truth, Bobby?" Her eyes were very accusing.

"Of course it's the truth. Damn it, Rosemary, I'm getting tired of being called a liar."

"All right," she returned. "Then, if you're telling me the truth, where does the woman you spent so much time with in Pé come in?"

"She was a French Secret Service agent."

"She was *what*?"

"A French Secret Service agent."

"Oh, Bobby, what a fool you've been! She was nothing of the sort. She was a Ronstadt spy. She set out deliberately to trap you."

"That's nonsense."

"It's the truth—you can read it in the reports we received at Y.1. During the last war she worked for the Germans, posing as a French girl named Marie Roget."

"Marie Roget." He repeated the name quietly, but not so quietly that the girl was not able to hear it.

"Didn't you know that?"

"No, of course not. I never heard of the name before. We were staying at the same guest-house. One night she came to my room in an awful state—said that she was being trailed by Ronstadt agents and that she was terrified for her life. It was she who gave me the package I sent to you. She said that it contained something which was of vital importance to both France and Great Britain."

Rosemary laughed—and it was not pleasant to hear. "How do you know she wasn't fooling you, and that this precious package contained only blank papers?"

"I couldn't imagine anything so silly, and in any case she relied on me."

He sat down, his hands to his head. He was feeling dazed. He didn't want to talk about this thing any more—not even to Rosemary Allister. He wanted to get away quietly by himself.

"Haven't you anything else to tell me, Bobby?"

"Nothing," he said. But, because he kept his face averted, she believed that he was lying, and the knowledge was like a sword in her breast.

"I am sorry—but I am afraid you must consider yourself under close arrest, Lieutenant Wingate."

The young officer, his face drawn but under stern control, looked his Commanding Officer straight in the eyes.

"I think I am entitled to ask on what grounds, sir."

Colonel Harrison twisted the end of his closely clipped moustache.

"On the grounds of betraying military secrets—charges will be preferred against you," he said curtly. "That is all."

Bobby felt a hand touch his arm and he turned smartly. The whole thing was incredible—a living nightmare; he felt too stunned to be able to think clearly; a wave of physical nausea was rising up within him.

The officer by his side was—final ironical touch!—his own company commander. The latter's face was not good to look upon....

This ghastliness had started over two hours before. After the talk with Rosemary, he had rejoined his unit at Woolvington, and, directly after breakfast, had received a message to the effect that his company commander wished to see him.

Major Birtles, with whom he had always been on good terms, had looked at him in what he thought was a very peculiar manner, but said nothing, after an abrupt "Good-morning," until he had carefully knocked the ashes from his pipe.

Then:

"I have to take you along to the O.C., Wingate—word has just come through from the Orderly Room."

It was the tone the speaker used that had made Wingate ask, "Is there anything wrong?"

"Something damnably wrong, from what I can hear," had come the answer, explosively.

More than that, Birtles would not say; and the younger officer, after one other question, which remained unanswered, kept silent. But it was very puzzling....

Now, ten minutes later, the two were standing before the Commanding Officer.

The interview was short.

Looking as if Wingate were a complete stranger to him, and an unpleasant stranger at that, Colonel Harrison said:

"I have received instructions, Lieutenant Wingate, from the Southern Command Headquarters, to investigate a report that you, during the period of your recent leave, visited a foreign country other than that to which you were granted special permission to travel. Have you got anything to say to that?"

"Yes, sir; I certainly went to Ronstadt and stayed at Pé," he replied immediately.

The C.O. seemed surprised at the frankness shown. A glance passed between him and the company commander.

◇◇◇

The horror of the next twenty-four hours, he felt, would never pass from his mind; no matter how long he lived, the memory would be an unfailing torment to him.

After leaving the C.O.'s office, he was told that he was to be transferred and attached to the London District Command. The escorting officer—another supreme piece of irony!—turned out to be his own particular friend in the unit, Hollister.

"What on earth *is* all this?" the latter demanded when he could get a word with Wingate alone. "What in the name of hell have you been up to? They say you're going to be charged with selling secrets to Ronstadt. Tell me, Bobby—it simply isn't true!"

"Of course it isn't true."

"Thank God! Did you go to Ronstadt when you were on leave?"

"Yes, I went, but—"

"You needn't tell me any more. As long as you can clear yourself that's all I—any of us here—are troubling about at the moment. We all feel there's some ghastly mistake. It's going to create a terrible stink throughout the Corps, of course," the speaker added.

"You needn't have reminded me of that."

"Sorry."

Throughout the journey to London there was an almost unbroken silence between the two. Bobby was occupied with his own thoughts of the filthy trick that fate had played him, while his escort, having asked the one essential question and got what he considered a satisfactory answer, was hesitant to break in on his friend's reflections.

At the Headquarters of the London District Command, Hollister was instructed to take his prisoner to the Tower.

Here, the prisoner found that he was indeed under close arrest—a Lieutenant of the Guards was to sleep in the same room, and he was to be allowed liberty only when he took his daily exercise, and even then he would be accompanied by his escort officer.

The horror mounted. At ten o'clock on the morning after his arrival at the Tower, a visitor was announced. This proved to be a major who declared himself to be a member of the Judge-Advocate General's staff.

"I have come," he told the prisoner, when they were alone, "to ask you certain questions relative to your recent visit to Pé. Are you prepared to answer those questions?"

"Certainly. I have nothing to hide."

"That is excellent. Now—"

Throughout the searching interrogatory that followed—and which lasted for the better part of three hours—Wingate answered every question promptly and frankly. The only facts he did not disclose were those relating to Colonel Clinton's affair with Marie Roget seventeen years before.

"You did not know that the man calling himself 'Dr. Emeric Sandor' was a Ronstadt secret agent?"

"Certainly not. As a matter of fact, he told me he worked for our own Intelligence."

"Did you speak to him first?"

"No. If the people who sent you the reports about me had kept their eyes open, they would have told you that he bumped into me as I was going along to the dining-saloon. He apologised, and after that we talked."

"You sat at the same table?"

"Yes, of course."

"Why did you go to Pé?"

"I've already told you." He was keeping his temper well controlled. "I went to see if I could get a look at the new tractors which were being shown at the big Agricultural Exhibition."

"If you were so keen on seeing these tractors, why did you not apply for leave to go to Pé?"

"Because, with the present threat of war between the two countries, I did not think it would be granted. I told my father I thought of going as a civilian and he warned me against it."

"You are the adopted son, I believe, of Colonel Clinton of M.I.5?"

"Yes."

"He warned you against going to Pé?"

"Yes."

"You admit crossing to the Hook of Holland on the night of the twenty-second?"

"Yes."

"Why did you go?"

"Haven't I already explained? I received a telegram from the woman calling herself Adrienne Grandin and Minna Braun. She wanted me to bring her the package which she had given me in Pé."

"You say you did not know she was a Ronstadt agent?"

"No, of course not."

"Do you admit receiving in Pé, from the Ronstadt agent who called himself 'Emeric Sandor,' two fifty-pound notes?"

"Yes—but I won that money gambling."

And so on and on until he felt like screaming.

The visitor concluded:

"These charges are considered so serious that a summary of evidence will need to be taken, as I understand that you are to be tried by a General Court-Martial."

Bobby stared stupefiedly at the speaker. His knowledge of military legal procedure had warned him of this pending ordeal; but, even now that he had heard the words, he could scarcely bring himself to believe that such a fate was actually in store for *him*....

Chapter XVI

Fleet Street on the Job

Rosemary could see that her Chief was perturbed directly she entered the room that morning.

Her own nerves were so sharply on edge that she had to break through the usual etiquette and ask:

"Is there anything wrong, Sir Brian?"

Fordinghame nodded.

"Young Wingate has been arrested," he said.

"Arrested? On what charge?"

"Selling military secrets. Of course," he went on quickly, "it was to be expected; the evidence against him is overwhelming."

"But it's purely circumstantial evidence, Sir Brian. I was talking to him myself before he left for Woolvington, and he told me the whole thing was preposterous."

"That's all very well, but facts are facts, young lady. A mountain of evidence has been accumulated against him, and he will find it very difficult, I think, to persuade the court-martial—"

"Court-martial?"

"Yes, he is going to be tried by General Court-Martial.... Good God!" Fordinghame broke off to exclaim. "This will break his father's heart....He will be tried by General Court-Martial," he repeated; "and if he's found guilty he'll probably get several years' penal servitude. Naturally enough, the military authorities would not take such drastic action if they were not sure that he was guilty. And I must say, that's my own opinion. I can't think anything else."

She kept silent. For what was there to say? Although convinced in her own mind that the boy she loved was merely the victim of some malignant fate, what was her own opinion worth? Exactly nothing!

Sir Brian went on talking.

"This will create a most unholy scandal. And it couldn't have happened at a worse time. All kinds of war inventions are now being perfected, and these are causing no end of trouble. Throughout Europe nearly two hundred people have been convicted of spying during the past year. Every Government is at fever-heat about espionage—I'm afraid it is going to go very badly with this young man. But, at any rate, he has taught us a lesson. For instance, the man who is working on an invention for perfecting a ray which, it is believed, will stop the magneto of an aeroplane engine, is being so closely guarded that no one can possibly get either at him or his plans. Any leakage in that direction is now impossible—and thus, as this is probably the most important of all recent war implements, some good may possibly have come out of this dreadful affair. The person I am sorry for is Colonel Clinton. For an officer occupying a very important position in British Intelligence to have his adopted son arraigned as a traitor—well, it's unthinkable!"

Rosemary forced herself to speak.

"Have you seen the Colonel, Sir Brian?"

"Yes. I looked in on him early this morning. He was absolutely crushed."

"Apart from the authorities, does any one know yet?"

"No. But the Press won't be long in the dark—trust them for that. Wingate is a prisoner at the Tower, and information is bound to leak out. The modern reporter is a vulture for news—especially when it's of the sensational type."

"Will any one be allowed to see—Bobby?"

"Only privileged persons. And even then they will have to talk to him in the presence of the officer who is in charge of him."

◇◇◇

Rosemary worked throughout the rest of the day in a kind of dream state. Even now, she could scarcely bring herself to realise that this dreadful thing was really true. Bobby a traitor! It was fantastic, incredible, and—beastly.

The first thing she did, as she walked up Whitehall on her way home that night, was to buy a paper. With a hand that trembled she took the copy of the *Evening Sun* from the newsboy and quickly scanned the front page. Her eye immediately caught huge headlines:—

GRAVE CHARGES OF ALLEGED TREACHERY: MILITARY SECRETS SOLD TO FOREIGN POWER

The *Evening Sun* is in the position to state that an officer of junior rank belonging to the Tank Corps has been arrested on the grave charge of selling military secrets to a foreign Power, and is at present under close arrest.

It is believed that directly the summary of evidence dealing with the charges made against him has been completed, he will be brought before a General Court-Martial, to be held in London, and there placed on trial.

```
The affair has caused the utmost consterna-
tion in both military and political circles,
and a further sensational feature of the case
is that the father of the accused occupies a
very prominent position at the War Office.
```

Hastily folding up the paper, Rosemary signalled a passing taxicab. Her duty was plain: she had to see Colonel Clinton and tell him what was in her mind.

The old servant at Chesham Place looked as though she had been crying.

"You know who I am, Hannah?" the caller said. "I am Miss Allister. Is Colonel Clinton in?"

"Yes, miss." The words were scarcely above a whisper.

"Then tell him I must see him—Oh, go quickly, please; it's very important."

Within two minutes the servant had reappeared, saying that the Colonel would be pleased to see her.

Colonel Clinton looked like an old man as he rose to shake hands.

"It's very good of you to have taken this trouble, Rosemary," he said in a low tone. "We shall want all our friends. . . ."

She took his arm and led him back to the easy-chair.

"And they won't fail you—don't be afraid of that. This charge against Bobby is incredible. I know that the evidence is very strong—I've seen practically all of it in the office—but if we can only get him to be sensible, everything will be all right."

"Sensible? What do you mean, my dear?"

"Why," she said heatedly, "isn't it obvious that he's shielding some one?"

She noticed the Colonel start, while a fresh look of pain flashed over his face.

"Whom could he be shielding?" he asked.

"That's what we have to find out. It's Sir Brian's job, of course, to do his best to convict him—but nothing on earth will ever convince me that Bobby deliberately sold his country. He may have been a fool—a dupe—"

"Stop talking, Rosemary," pleaded her listener. "I have had just about enough to-day."

"You poor darling!" She did what she could to comfort him, and, after the Colonel had swallowed the whisky-and-soda which she poured out, she was able to ask the question which rose imperatively in her mind.

"Bobby will have some one to defend him, I suppose?"

The Colonel nodded.

"Yes—of course. I've already made up my mind about that."

"Whom are you going to get—Casson?" This was the name of the very successful K.C.

"No; I'm going to ask Peter Mallory to defend my boy."

She looked at him, stupefied.

"Mallory?" she repeated. "But he's not a barrister."

"You don't understand, Rosemary," he said, and she could see he was forcing himself to be patient with her. "The ordinary King's Counsel is of not much use at a military court-martial. They split hairs, are generally ignorant of the finer points of military law, and are apt to put the judges' backs up. Mallory used to be an officer, he is my closest friend, and—"

"Don't have him," burst from the girl's lips.

It was plain that Colonel Clinton was utterly nonplussed.

"Why do you say that? What do you know about Peter Mallory?"

She shook her head like some one utterly confused. It would be useless, she knew, to put into words her private feelings concerning Mallory.

"I don't know anything, of course," she said; "but I feel that you ought to get some one else—some one with more knowledge of law.... Oh, forgive me," she broke off quickly, "but all this has been hellishly difficult. I'm terribly fond of Bobby—"

This time it was the man who comforted the girl.

"I know you're fond of Bobby," Clinton said, "and both his mother and I were hoping that something would come of it."

"It would have—if he'd had any sense. He pretended that my money was an obstacle." She stopped as though some leering monster had raised its head to mock her. The dreadful suspicion that had come to her before now returned with added power. Suppose, after all, that *was* the secret! But it couldn't be—she had thrashed it out before, and had come to the conclusion that it was impossible—what money could Ronstadt possibly have paid Bobby to compensate him for his loss of honour, or to lead him to think that it was sufficient to make him change his views about marrying her?

It was because she wanted to thrust this out of her mind that she exclaimed vehemently: "Don't you see for yourself, Colonel, that Bobby either must be shielding some one or is being used as a cat's-paw for the real traitor?"

At that moment Hannah announced a visitor.

"Mr. Peter Mallory."

Rosemary felt confused. She did not want to meet the man. He had rung her up two or three times since the night at the Savoy, but she had always pleaded prior engagements.

"I must go," she said. "Do you think it would be too much for me to see Mrs. Clinton?"

The Colonel shook his head.

"We are keeping it from her," he said.

"I understand. Well, good-night, Colonel. Don't let this thing get you down—Bobby's innocent."

"Of course he's innocent," was the reply, but there was no animation in his voice.

Outside in the hall, the girl passed Peter Mallory. The latter would have engaged her in conversation, but she pleaded an urgent excuse to get away.

"My father is expecting me home," she said, and rushed past him.

It was strange that this man, of whom both Fordinghame and Colonel Clinton thought so highly that they had given him their close personal friendship, could inspire in her so much distrust. She was glad when the front door closed between them.

Chapter XVII

Mallory Accepts

Frowning to himself, Peter Mallory went on to join his friend. Alan Clinton shook his hand warmly.

"My God! Peter, old man, I'm glad to see you," he said fervently. "I was just telling Miss Allister that I shall know now who are my real friends."

Mallory patted him on the shoulder.

"Well, you've no doubt about this particular specimen, I hope?"

"None whatever. In fact, I'm going to give you the best possible proof of that."

"Yes?"

"Peter, I want you to act as the Accused's Friend if there is a General Court-Martial."

Mallory whistled.

"But I'm not a barrister, old man."

"I realise that. But you know as well as I do the feeling against professional lawyers at courts-martial. You were an officer, and you are now in the Intelligence—"

"I'll do it like a shot if you think I am the best man. But it's a very important job, you know. I shouldn't like to have the responsibility of Bobby being found guilty through any fault of mine. I must say, Alan, that, so far as I can judge, it looks pretty bad against your boy. You know what Fordinghame is—a good friend, but he'll press this thing relentlessly, even though you are one of his pals."

"I know that," was the gloomy response, "and that's why I want you to defend Bobby. You'll be able to put forward things in his defence that the ordinary professional lawyer would know nothing whatever about."

"All right, old man. If you've got that amount of confidence in me, I'll do my best."

"I knew you would."

The two shook hands.

It was after Clinton had finished another whisky-and-soda that he made his impulsive outburst.

"That girl who was here just now—Rosemary Allister. She's in love with my boy. Well, she said something in which there may be a certain amount of truth. She said that the mystery at the back of the business could be solved in two directions: one, that Bobby was shielding some one, and the other, that he had been made a cat's-paw for the real traitor. I've got something on my mind, and I simply must get it off," he added quickly. "Peter, you've been to Ronstadt; have you ever heard of Marie Roget since....?"

"Never," was the immediate answer.

"And yet, she's still alive. I had a letter signed by her only the other day."

"You did? What did she say?"

The other man groaned.

"It was more or less a threat of blackmail. She spoke about the 'happy times' we spent together seventeen years ago, and hinted that she would be getting into touch with me again. Why?"

"That's obvious, surely," was the answer. "She's gone back to her old job, and intends to make use of you in some way. With another war likely to break out at any moment, she thinks you will be valuable—especially in your present post. Blackmail is right, Alan.... But what's this got to do with Bobby?" Mallory broke off.

"I'll tell you. Although Bobby went to Pé for a perfectly legitimate reason (at least, from his point of view), I feel certain somehow that he was trapped by this woman, working in conjunction no doubt with some one else, that the Ronstadt Secret Service worked him into a false position, told him about—" The speaker paused. "Well, what happened to me seventeen years ago, and held that over his head as a threat. You must ask him about it."

Mallory leaned forward.

"Then is it your opinion, Alan, that Bobby did give some valuable information to these people?"

"I don't know. But it's possible—when you think of what I've just told you. The point is this: I feel inclined to go to Fordinghame and make a bargain with him."

"What kind of bargain could you make?"

"I'd tell him that—Well, he knows that the plans of the new anti-tank shoulder weapon have been stolen. I'd confess to—"

"You wouldn't be such a damned fool, surely! Why, it would be your ruin—besides, you'd get years of penal servitude."

"I'm an old man—at least, I feel old; and it would be better for me to be a sacrifice than for my boy...."

Mallory stood up.

"You're talking nonsense! I won't listen to another word. If Bobby has played the fool he must face up to it. I'm not going to let an old friend like you make such a preposterous offer. Besides, Fordinghame wouldn't believe you—it would be useless."

"Not even if he knew about Marie Roget?"

"Of course not. You were a young man then—hot-headed and impetuous. It's a different thing now. No," the caller summed up, "we can't do anything until we see the summary of evidence against Bobby. By the way, did you reply to that letter from Marie Roget?"

"No."

"Did you keep it?"

"No."

"Wise man. Well, Alan, I must be off. Call on me at any time you like. I shan't let you down."

"I knew you wouldn't, old fellow." Once again the two friends shook hands.

Chapter XVIII

Sensation In Pall Mall

Never within the memory of the oldest members had such excitement been caused in the various Service clubs as on the day when the court-martial for trial of Lieutenant Robert Wingate, of the Tank Corps, began. It seemed impossible to credit such allegations as those made against this young officer. For an Englishman, holding the King's commission, to scheme deliberately to sell secrets of military importance to a foreign country—and a country, at that, with whom the nation might shortly find itself at war—why, it was utterly fantastic.

And yet, as the front pages of the evening newspapers showed, it was true.

There, printed in heavy type, were the stunning words of the barrister-soldier, Major Arthur Bingham, from the Military and Air Force Department of the Judge-Advocate General, who was acting as prosecutor:—

> I will be frank. It is the contention of the prosecution that Lieutenant Wingate betrayed his country for the sum of £100.

Long before the trial was due to start in the large library of the Chelbridge barracks, it had become known that the proceedings would be invested with much of the meretricious glamour peculiar to the cinema and popular fiction. For instance, evidence would be given by Secret Service agents whose names and methods could not be disclosed; the evidence of those who had brought the alleged traitor to justice would be given and special precautions taken to keep their identities secret. The chief actors on the enemy's side, it was known, were a reputedly beautiful woman agent and a man who had been prominently connected with the German Secret Service during the World War.

Altogether, a feast of unparalleled sensations was promised—and those who had waited sufficiently long to be fortunate enough to get seats among the "Public" were not disappointed.

There were two principal charges against the accused, stated the Judge-Advocate in opening the proceedings: the fact that the accused "did on or about the eighteenth of September, 1935, for a purpose prejudicial to the interests of the State, give to another person certain designs of a military importance which might be useful to an enemy," and the second, "that on September 22, 1935, he did collect at Woolvington certain information which might be useful to an enemy power, the said information dealing with the construction of a new type of tank."

In reply to both charges the prisoner replied in a firm, clear voice the plea of "Not Guilty."

The prosecutor, a short, thickly-built man in uniform, addressing the Court, which was presided over by Major-General Sir Somerset Faunthorpe, K.C.B., C.M.G., D.S.O., then proceeded to outline his case.

After using the words quoted above, he said:

"The accused is a Lieutenant in the Tank Corps and has been stationed with his unit at Woolvington. Up to the time that suspicion was first cast on his actions he had the reputation—it is only right that I should make this statement—of being a keen, efficient and zealous officer.

"Early in September he applied for leave and, as this was his due, permission was granted. I would point out that, in making his application, he stated that he intended to visit Paris; no mention was made of his proceeding to any other country. No doubt he was aware that if he had asked for permission to visit Ronstadt, leave of absence for that purpose would not have been granted; and yet, as the evidence of certain witnesses (witnesses whose statements are very necessary, but whose identities will not be made public) will go to show, the accused certainly *did* go to Ronstadt—in short, to Pé, the capital of that country.

"While in Paris, he applied at the British Embassy for a visa to visit Pé. He did not disclose the fact that he was a military officer; he posed, while making this application, as a civilian. It is an important point to be noted.

"Evidence will be brought before you to prove that, while on the Paris-Pé express, the accused got into conversation with a man named Ritter, a person employed by the Ronstadt Intelligence Service, and that the two of them spent considerable time talking together in a secluded part of the dining-saloon.

"Arrived at Pé, the accused did not sleep at the Hotel Poste, where he registered, but proceeded to a guest-house, run as a kind of annex to the hotel.

"Now it will be proved to the entire satisfaction of the Court, I believe, that this guest-house is a meeting-place for all branches of Ronstadt Secret Service operatives," proceeded the prosecutor, raising his voice from its previous monotone; "and it was during his first evening at this guest-house that the accused met, and became friendly with, a very attractive woman calling herself Minna Braun. She was a successful spy for the Germans during the last war, and is now known to be in the service of the Ronstadt Intelligence. That much will be proved to you on the evidence of reliable witnesses.

"The two of them—this professional seductress, for that is her mission in life, and the young British officer, who was in Pé ostensibly as a civilian—became very friendly. The accused does not deny that he spent the whole of the following day with her, visiting cafés and a cinema. Although he himself did not realise the fact, eyes were watching him, and there was no single moment of that day when he and his fascinating companion were not under the closest supervision. Even"—and here the speaker paused, weighing every word—"when she went to his room at something after one o'clock in the morning."

At this point it was noticed that the girl shorthand-writer, for whose presence Sir Brian Fordinghame had applied in order that a complete "note" of the evidence might be obtained, leaned her head on one hand, while her face became very pale.

A reporter, more omniscient than even the average of his kind, leaning towards his neighbour, whispered: "Her name's Rosemary Allister; daughter of the banker. Engaged or something to Wingate."

"And his old man is a Colonel in M.I.5—boy, *what* a story!" came the rejoinder. "Well, the kid's taking it on the chin all right. He doesn't *look* a swine."

"No." The journalist who had opened the conversation glanced at the notes he intended to incorporate into the descriptive sketch he was due to write of the proceedings for the *Morning Meteor*. *"Accused, handsome, soldierly bearing... looks anything but a traitor...serious but composed."*

The voice of the prosecutor continued:

"What happened at that meeting I cannot tell you. It may be that the woman offered the usual price in such transactions, but the contention of the prosecution is that it was at this moment that the accused handed over the designs of the new anti-tank weapon, the selling of which forms Charge No. 1 and the most important part of this prosecution.

"At any rate, there can be no possible doubt that either then or on the following day the accused was handed two fifty-pound notes, representing either the whole or part payment for the treachery of which the prosecution contends he was guilty. While a great deal of the evidence in this case is—and I admit it at this early stage—circumstantial, I shall hope to prove quite clearly that these two notes of fifty pounds each were paid to the accused while he was in Pé and by a certain agent of this foreign power. Later you will have his banking account placed in front of you, and you will be able to see that at no time during the material period were any other payments of similar sums made to him. I reiterate that the accused, for this sum, and possibly the promise of others, betrayed his country. It is a very grave accusation to make against any one, let alone a man wearing His Majesty's uniform, and it is one which should not be made unless there is evidence to support it. There is evidence to support it, as you will hear.

"After receiving the payment, the accused did not linger in Pé; possibly he had received definite instructions from those with whom he had done business; at any rate, we find him travelling back to Paris the following morning by air liner. He had not wasted much time in the Ronstadt capital.

"He was observed standing about in the rue Danou in Paris, looking for what may have been an address or a certain person. Perhaps realising that he had rendered himself liable to a certain amount of suspicion, he returned the next day to London, also by air. His leave was not yet up.

"Now comes a very significant fact: although, as I have said, he was not due to rejoin his unit for some days, he proceeded straight to Woolvington. Is it too much to presume that, acting on the instructions of his paymasters, he was anxious to obtain other information of a military nature which they in turn were eager to secure? The reason he gave his brother officers to explain why he returned to Woolvington was that he was to attend a dinner of the Old Boys' Society of his Public School, Repington. Although he took his mess uniform away with him the following day (he spent that night at Woolvington), he did not attend this dinner—he was otherwise engaged.

"Now, as it happened, on the morning following his unexpected arrival at his unit, a new type of tank was to be demonstrated at Woolvington. Evidence will be brought before you to show that he attended these trials and later went to the engineering shops and asked a good many questions from the sergeant-instructor in charge. That afternoon he returned to London. This was the twenty-second of September.

"Proceeding to his club, he was handed a telegram. The club porter will say in his evidence that he evinced considerable agitation after reading the telegram. Perhaps he did not expect to be summoned abroad again so quickly. That message summoned him to a meeting—an immediate meeting—at The Hague. Who but his paymasters could have required his presence in Holland? That night, the accused caught the eight o'clock train from Liverpool Street Station to Harwich, and took the night boat to the Hook of Holland. Before he went, being perhaps still in a state of agitation, he gave the case containing his mess uniform in charge of the club porter, explaining that he was obliged to 'cut' the Old Boys' dinner; he was going abroad.

"At shortly after ten o'clock on the morning that he arrived at The Hague, his destination, he was observed seated in the lounge of the Hotel Continental, which is situated just off Zeestraat, the main street. A page-boy handed him a note, and in obedience to this obvious summons he went to a room on the second floor of the hotel. In this room he handed to a man, who will be identified by reliable witnesses as another Ronstadt agent, a certain package. Immediately afterwards he returned to London. Directly he rejoined his unit he was placed under arrest, removed to the Tower, and there interrogated.

"He answered all the questions put to him, but the examining officer was not satisfied that he was telling the truth. For example, he found it difficult to believe that the two fifty-pound notes were paid him as the result of visiting a gambling club in Pé and being extremely fortunate in a game of poker—a game at which, he admitted, he was not proficient, having few opportunities to play it. As regards the woman calling herself Minna Braun, who will be identified, as I have said, as a well-known Secret Service agent now working for Ronstadt, he told an astonishing story. He claimed that this woman represented herself to be a French agent and that she came to his bedroom that night because she was anxious for the safety of a package containing certain documents which she had been able to obtain, documents the loss of which she was afraid had been discovered. Fearful of being arrested when these papers were in her possession, she handed them over to him 'because they are vitally necessary to the future of our joint countries.' That is his story. I will leave it to the Court to express an opinion on it. It is a fact that plans of a new military weapon to be used against tanks have recently been stolen from this country, and that they have been traced to a certain foreign power—namely, Ronstadt. It is also a fact that their loss coincided with the period during which the accused went to Pé. These facts, in conjunction with his subsequent visit to The Hague, the handing over by him of a certain package after he had witnessed the trials of a new type of Tank, cannot be regarded in any other than a very serious light.

"The accused contends that his visit to The Hague was solely for the purpose of handing over to the woman who called herself 'Minna Braun,' but who has many aliases, a certain package which he says she entrusted to his care on the occasion when she visited his bedroom in the early hours of the morning. The woman herself did not meet him—as he had expected from her wire—but sent an emissary, who was duly handed the package. He further contends that he is entirely innocent—on the two main and all the lesser charges."

◇◇◇

The officer from the Judge-Advocate's office who questioned the accused on the morning after his arrival at the Tower was an early important witness. After agreeing with the prosecutor's statement that he was not satisfied with the prisoner's replies ("although he spoke with great frankness"), he was cross-examined by the Accused's Friend.

Considerable surprise had been expressed that the prisoner's father had not engaged a well-known professional pleader like the famous Casson, until the President asked Mallory if he would care to be addressed by his military rank of Major, to which he was still entitled.

"He's an ex-Regular, then?" whispered one pressman to another.

"Yes—that's why Wingate's old man's given him the job; he'll know all the tricks."

"You have said that the prisoner answered all your questions with great frankness?" Mallory began.

"That is so."

"Then why were you not satisfied?"

"I felt he was keeping something back."

"The two facts are scarcely compatible, surely?"

The witness flushed.

"I have told the Court my impression."

"What gave you this impression?"

"I cannot say exactly. It may have been an occasional hesitancy on his part."

"He admitted having met the man who called himself Sandor on the train?"

"Yes."

"Can you give me any reason why the accused, who knew nothing of Intelligence methods, should be able to recognise on sight a Secret Service agent of another country?"

"No."

"Can you tell me why a young man, on holiday in a foreign country, should refuse the company of an attractive visitor at the same hotel?"

"No, providing—"

"I was coming to that," cut in the Accused's Friend; "providing, of course, that he is entirely ignorant of the fact that, to use the picturesque if somewhat lurid words of the prosecution, she is a 'professional seductress' and a character borrowed from the realm of fiction. Granted those premises—and the accused in his evidence will swear that he had no idea of the lady's real mission in life—can you advance any reason why Lieutenant Wingate should not have spent a day in her company—or have entertained her in his bedroom?"

The witness, conscious of a growing titter at the back of the Court, flushed a deeper red.

"The woman was a foreign spy," he said at length.

"Will you please answer my question and not make comments?"

"You must answer the question," prompted the Judge-Advocate.

"Since you put it that way—no," replied the witness, turning to his cross-examiner.

"Thank you. Now you realise, of course, the extreme importance of the interview you had with this young officer?"

"Yes—from his point of view."

"Did it occur to you at the time that you might be called as a witness?"

"No."

"You swear that?"

"Yes."

"Very well." The man acting in the capacity of defending counsel sat down, and shortly afterwards the Court adjourned.

◇◇◇

At the Senior Services—the club which had been the scene of so much animated discussion of the case during the previous three weeks—the talk was of nothing but the court-martial that evening. In one corner of the smoking-room, a particularly heated argument was proceeding between a young "ace" of the R.A.F. and an elderly major who had "Indian Retired List" written all over him.

The major was spluttering.

"Damnable.... I hope he gets five years... deserves it... ought to be publicly flogged as well...."

The younger man flicked the ash off his cigarette.

"Hold your horses, Major," he returned, a steely look in his grey eyes; "the fellow hasn't been found guilty yet."

"Guilty! Of course he's guilty! Do you think the authorities would have brought him to trial (and letting in the civilian public, too!) if they hadn't overwhelming evidence—if they weren't absolutely certain of a conviction?"

"Then it's something like shooting a sitting pheasant," was the irreverent reply. "Well, all the same, Major, I don't mind making a small bet with you that Wingate gets off."

"Do you want to lose your money, young man?"

"I don't mind giving a fiver a run."

"I'll take the bet; it will teach you a lesson. But I should like to know the reasons for your absurd confidence."

"I haven't any reasons; I'm just backing my fancy. It's ridiculous, in my opinion, to think that a fellow like Wingate (you should have seen him to-day) would be a traitor—especially for a paltry hundred quid. He isn't the type."

"Traitors have sold their country before this young man for less than a hundred pounds."

"Well, I maintain that the whole thing is just so much cock-eye. Any one would think the Army crush were staging one of old man Sardou's spy-dramas: why do they insist upon the foreign witnesses being cloaked?"

"You damned well don't know what you are talking about!" exploded his opponent, rising from his chair and stamping from the room.

"I'll make it a tenner if you like," was the flying officer's parting taunt.

◇◇◇

Down in Fleet Street, the editor of the *Evening Sun*, returning to the office after hours in order to plan the next day's campaign, was holding a secret conference with his star reporter and his most intrepid photographer.

"There's a story behind these hooded witnesses, and I want you to get it," he said.

The reporter, who combined the most extraordinary name in Fleet Street—Cuthbert Clergyman—with the keenest nose for news, shook his head.

"Very dangerous," he said.

Blackburn fumed.

"What's the matter with you?" he demanded.

"There's nothing the matter with me," he retorted, "but there will be with *you*, Blackie, if you start printing any of that stuff. It's dynamite—and it'll blow you to kingdom come and back. The Secret Service people *have* to keep these witnesses cloaked; I happen to know that they've taken extraordinary precautions to hide the identities of these people, some of whom are probably Ronstadt nationals, hidden.... Ever heard of the Official Secrets Act, Blackie?" he concluded with a sly chuckle.

"Go to the devil!" cried the baffled editor.

Chapter XIX

The Prisoner Gives Evidence

Bobby endeavoured to keep his voice firm as he took the oath. He realised that every eye in the crowded Court was fixed on him—at that moment, he was probably the most discussed person in the whole world: throughout every country where the printed word could be read, men and women were eagerly debating the subject of whether he was innocent or guilty.

He did not disguise the truth from himself: the evidence prepared against him by those British Secret Service witnesses, who had given their testimony while wearing those melodramatic costumes that covered both their faces and bodies, looked utterly damning. Even though he was entirely innocent, he knew that every one who had heard those stories of his conduct at Pé must believe him to be a traitor.

He had gone through hell during the last month. The strain had been terrific. Yet, when his father had come to see him he had always tried to give the Colonel the impression that he would emerge a free man. The woman he had always looked upon as his real mother had sent him many messages of love, sympathy and confidence.

"She is behaving marvellously," Colonel Clinton had said. "She tells me that you are not to worry on her account at all."

It had been this fact, perhaps more than any other circumstance, which had kept him going; otherwise, with what seemed hopeless odds against him, he must have weakened.

Rosemary, too, had been a brick. Although—ironically enough!—she was working for the enemy (wasn't she employed in the office of the very man who was endeavouring so strenuously to secure his conviction?), she had sent messages through his father to the effect that she believed in him absolutely. "Tell him also," she had said to Colonel Clinton, "that I should like to write to him, but that perhaps it would not be wise."

During the whole of that morning, he had been sitting directly opposite the President of the Court-Martial, listening to the evidence being piled up against him. Witnesses had testified that the man he had known as Sandor was actually a well-known Secret Service agent named Adolf Ritter, formerly employed by Germany, and now working for Crosber, the Ronstadt Chief of Secret Police; he had heard further that the woman who had called herself first "Minna Braun" and later "Adrienne Grandin," was also a Ronstadt agent, working in association with the man Ritter; he had heard how Fordinghame, the Chief of Y.1, had been able to trace the two fifty-pound notes he had received from "Sandor" to Adolf Ritter's account at the Norodny Bank in Pé, since their issue by the Bank of England.

He further had to listen to the full story of his movements from the moment he left Pé—there was a British agent on board that Paris air liner—until the moment when he handed over the "dummy" package to the supposed emissary of Adrienne Grandin in that second-floor bedroom at the Hotel Continental in The Hague.

Altogether, it had been a comprehensive and thoroughly exhaustive indictment, and one which bore ample testimony to the brilliant way in which the British Secret Service discharged its duties.

◇◇◇

And now he himself was in the box.

Peter Mallory, who had worked so hard on his defence, started to examine him.

"Your name is Robert Wingate and you are twenty-four years of age?"

"Yes."

"Have you ever attempted to obtain, have you ever obtained, or have you ever disclosed any information, appertaining to military matters or otherwise, which might be prejudicial to the State?"

"Never."

"Have you ever been hard-up for money?"

The witness was seen to smile.

"Like most fellows, I've known what it is to be a bit short; but I've never been really hard-up—nor in debt," he said.

"Has any previous complaint ever been made against you as a soldier and an officer?"

"Not to my knowledge."

"That is the young man who, you are asked to believe, has betrayed his country in such a despicable manner," continued the defendant's representative, in a scathing tone.

Mallory now asked the accused to tell the Court, in his own words, exactly what happened—from the moment he left London on his leave, until the time he arrived back in Harwich after handing over the dummy package at the Hotel Continental.

"Coming to this package," said Mallory, "why did you take it?"

During his imprisonment Bobby had given a great deal of thought to the answering of this question. He could not give the real reason why he had gone to The Hague—namely, to try to induce the woman Minna Braun to return to England so that the plot against his father might be cleared up; and so he had decided to tell a white lie. In the circumstances, he considered that he was justified.

He squared his shoulders and replied:—

"On the night before I left Pé, the woman calling herself first 'Minna Braun' and then 'Adrienne Grandin' came to my room. She was very badly frightened—or pretended to be. She explained that she was really a French Secret Service agent, that she had been sent to Pé on a dangerous mission, that she had succeeded in this mission, but that the Ronstadt Intelligence people had evidently become suspicious of her and that she was expecting to be arrested at any moment. She dared not run the risk of being searched, so would I take charge of the package containing the information she had collected?"

"Did she give any reason why you should run this grave risk?"

"Yes. She said that the information vitally concerned England (she knew I was an Englishman) as well as France."

"You believed her?"

"I believed her implicitly."

"And so you took the package? What did you do with it?"

"I put it inside a newspaper and posted it to England."

"Why did you do that?"

"Because I was afraid, after what the woman had told me, that it might be found in my luggage."

"Which, as a matter of fact, was actually searched?"

"Yes—by the Secret Police."

"And it was this same package which you took across to

The Hague and handed to the man who gave you a letter signed 'Adrienne Grandin'?"

"Yes." He had to go on with the lie now.

"Did this woman know you to be a British officer?"

"No—I never mentioned my military rank."

"Did the man who called himself 'Sandor'?"

"No. I pretended to be a civilian. He, on the other hand, claimed to be a foreign agent working for the British Secret Service."

"The prosecution has had a great deal to say about your going to Pé as a civilian. Tell the Court exactly why you went."

The witness was observed to smile. Bobby, as a matter of fact, was reflecting how cynically amusing the turn of events had proved to be.

"I went to Pé as a civilian because I realised that, with the present tension between the two countries, I might be suspected if I proclaimed myself to be a British officer."

"Exactly why did you go?"

"I was attracted by the information I had read about the new Ronstadt tractors for tanks."

"And you hoped that you would be able to gather a little further information at first hand?"

"I thought perhaps I might."

"But you didn't?"

"No."

"Why?"

"Because, directly I arrived at Pé, I realised I was probably being watched. I became sure of that when my baggage was searched."

"And you decided to get back to Paris?"

"Yes."

"So that what it amounts to is this: that, instead of intending to sell Ronstadt military information, as the prosecution contends, you went to Pé with the fixed idea of doing a little amateur spying yourself?"

"Since you put it that way—yes."

"And now with regard to the banknotes. You swear you received these from the man calling himself 'Sandor' as the result of an afternoon's poker-playing at his club?"

"I do."

The President at this point took up the questioning.

"That was rather a lot of money to have won, was it not?"

"I was very lucky, sir."

"Do you still believe the woman Minna Braun to be genuine?"

"No, of course not, sir, after the evidence I have heard."

"But you believed her story at the time?"

"Yes, certainly."

"Why did you go to that guest-house?"

"At the request of the manager of the hotel. He said that, owing to the Musical Festival, there was no available accommodation at the hotel."

Then followed a lengthy cross-examination by the prosecutor, Major Bingham.

This went on and on. The prisoner began to feel that he had ceased to be a human being and had become just an automaton—a mechanical figure that answered questions after being wound up and set going.

He could not decide whether his story—or, indeed, any part of it—was believed. To his right, taking a shorthand note of everything that was being said, was Rosemary—but she never looked his way. What were her private feelings? How could she sit there, hour after hour and day after day, having her feelings tortured by the foul and untrue suggestions against the honour of the man she had once said she loved? What was she thinking about that package? She knew he lied there. He could not understand it. Women seemed able to stand any amount of self-torment. And they even found consolation in it!

Now the voice which had grown so hateful boomed again.

"If," asked the prosecutor, "you were merely fulfilling a duty you had promised to perform, why were you so agitated at the Hotel Continental?"

"Was I agitated?"

"You have heard the evidence of witnesses Number Sixteen and Number Seventeen. They have told the Court you were very agitated, both while waiting in the lounge of the hotel and again when talking to the man in the bedroom."

"If I was agitated,—and I am not prepared to admit it in spite of the evidence of your witnesses—it was because I wanted to make certain that the man had really come from the woman who had given me the package."

He was allowed to step down from the witness box at last. His legs felt that they must give way. The only encouragement he received was a smile from his father. The governor—bless him!—must think he had come through the ordeal well.

Tea was taken shortly afterwards, and he was grateful for the chance to have a talk with his father. The three of them—Mallory, the governor, and himself—sat by themselves.

"You're doing splendidly—both of you!" declared Colonel Clinton.

Mallory shook his head gloomily.

"I shouldn't be too confident," he returned. "We know it's merely circumstantial evidence; we know, also, all the charges are absolutely groundless; but the stories these witnesses told will want a lot of disbelieving. Did you notice the Judge-Advocate's face? I was watching him all the time. I wish you had given me your confidence when I saw you in Pé, Bobby."

"I don't see how I could have."

"If you had, much of this present business would have been avoided."

"I don't follow that," commented Colonel Clinton sharply. "How could it have been avoided?"

Mallory, his mind evidently fully occupied with the many problems that thronged it, made an evasive reply.

"I didn't quite realise what I was saying," he murmured. "I shall have to see you after the Court adjourns," he added to the prisoner.

It was when he had reached the Tower that the man who was defending him said: "What I meant back at the Court was, why didn't you tell me about that package in Pé? By the way, what actually happened to it?"

"I told you in the Court this afternoon."

"But that wasn't the truth."

"Not the truth? Of course it was the truth."

What forced the lie from his lips he did not know; he only realised that something stronger than himself had prompted him.

But that Mallory still believed he had lied could be read in the man's face.

Chapter XX

Kuhnreich Decrees

Kuhnreich's scowl deepened. This was not a good morning with the Dictator of Ronstadt. What in the early days had seemed a mission from on high (not that Kuhnreich bothered much about religion) was now becoming a daily treadmill of vexation. Like others before him—and men gifted with much more brain power—Kuhnreich was beginning to realise that ruling over some sixty millions of people was not an enviable task.

When he took over power, Kuhnreich had stated that he was out to create a new nation—a nation infinitely stronger than the one from whose ashes it had sprung. All the demoralising forces which had caused so much misery, distress and national humiliation were to be rooted up; once he was in the saddle, with his loyal helpers around him, Ronstadt would be the strongest force in the world: the rest of Europe should act as its footstool.

The work was done—while the horror-stricken world shuddered as it read of the kind of methods used in the cleansing process. But the poison that, according to Kuhn reich and his counsellors, had lurked in the veins of the country for so long, devitalising the body politic, was eradicated.

All, then, should have been well. But it did not work out that way. With unemployment increasing and the nation generally having to tighten its belt, the promised millennium took on the aspect of a mirage—and the murmurings of those who had become disillusioned increased. These mutterings might be put down with a stern hand, but the economists whom Kuhnreich called in could not offer him much consolation.

"A population that is faced with starvation next winter cannot be expected to cry 'Hosanna!'" declared one bluntly.

The Iron Man, as the carefully censored Pé newspapers united in calling him, was torn; he became the prey of two conflicting schools of thought. Those who had marched to power with him—a curious collection—were all for putting down the discontented elements with the sword; on the other hand, the Dictator (who was said to be sleeping badly) knew that the shedding of blood, even on a big scale, never had been a cure for empty stomachs.

But, gradually, the fire-eaters ("The Murder Gang," as their enemies called them) gained the upper hand. Steiber, Minister for Propaganda, as the result of many private conversations with the Dictator, had planted a fertile seed in that megalomaniac's head.

"What we want, your Excellency," he had said in his shrill, disturbing voice, "is another war! For war will distract the mind of the masses. It will create a yet newer wave of nationalism. Once we are at war, they will forget their real or imaginary troubles—besides, we shall be victorious this time, and the indemnities we shall demand from France and England will make us the greatest Power in the history of the world."

Kuhnreich had wanted to believe it—how badly he had wanted to believe it! But it meant that in order to relieve one desperate situation he would have to plunge into another vortex. Yet out of this fresh maelstrom he might—yes, *might*—emerge a still stronger power. After all, he told himself, war was the natural destiny of the Ronstadt people. It had always believed in war, and would always believe in it. For, from time immemorial, its rulers had preached the gospel of the sword and fire.

"Yes—yes...." he had murmured.

Steiber's views had been supported by the Minister for Propaganda's deadliest enemy—Muntz, the Chancellor. Between these two had existed, from the moment Kuhnreich had elevated them to power, a gnawing rivalry. They had paraded side by side; they had stood on the same platform; they had issued proclamations signed jointly—but the man in the street was not deceived: he knew the truth; and the truth was that either would have sacrificed the other without the slightest scruple—given the right opportunity.

Carl Muntz had his own private and separate dreams. A soldier by profession, he naturally believed in war. Once hostilities broke out, he confidently assumed he would be made commander-in-chief of all the Ronstadt forces. What a position! And what a vision—to see himself riding through the Arc de Triomphe in Paris at the head of a triumphant army!

So, secretly, instructions had been given that preparations were to be made on a giant scale for the war which might break out at any moment. The information which the agents of France and England sent back to their respective countries proved that Ronstadt believed her only possible future lay in a victorious army.

◇◇◇

Once he had set his hand to the war plough, Kuhnreich concentrated all his energies in that one direction. The approaching war became his gospel and his creed. Fired by the intoxicating pictures which his brain provided, he thought of nothing else.

It was due to this that he gave the impression of being more than normally distraught on this particular morning. Sleep-starved nights had fretted his nerves and brought him to the pitch of hysteria.

Before him, undergoing a fierce cross-examination, was Crosber, the Chief of the Secret Police.

"Tell me the exact position," he cried. "Have I to do everything myself? Can I trust no one around me? Must you all be blunderers?"

The sallow-faced one tried to be conciliatory.

"It was most unfortunate, Excellency," he replied, softly. "Our most trusted agent in England certainly did secure designs of the new anti-tank gun of the British. He brought them himself to Pé and handed them to Aschelmann, the manager of the Hotel Poste, to be passed on to Ritter. At the same time, a package was prepared for the woman, Minna Braun, to hand to this young British officer, Wingate, on whom we had hoped to secure a hold. Unfortunately, the two packages became mixed, so that the one containing the plans for the anti-tank gun was handed to Wingate—"

"Why did you want to go to all that trouble?"

"Excellency, it was because we wished the young man to fall in love with Minna, and hoped by this means to arouse his chivalry. She pretended to be a French agent—"

"Enough! Get on with your story."

"Yes, Excellency. It seems that Wingate, according to the evidence at his trial, must have posted the package back to England enfolded in a copy of the *Tageblatt*."

Kuhnreich exploded.

"We must have those plans again—it is vitally important.

Tanks will play a very prominent part in the next war, and.... But enough: don't worry me any more."

"Yes, Excellency."

"Wait a minute! Aschelmann, for his blunder, must be punished. You will see that he is sent to prison for three months."

"Yes, Excellency."

"And instruct your agent in England—what is his name?"

Crosber whispered it.

"Well, if you are sure he can be thoroughly trusted, send him definite instructions that he must obtain that package—or duplicate plans—without delay. That is all."

Crosber withdrew.

This man, slinking down the East End street, would have been taken by any one for a derelict of the night—one of that myriad company who had better never have been born. Even the men and women who passed him on the wet pavement looked askance—they had no wish to rub shoulders with such as he.

Not that he minded. Pulling the collar of his shabby overcoat farther up round his neck—although the night was warm—he slipped down an alleyway, slithered up a court, and thus came to a paint-blistered door flush with the street. From fifty yards or so away there came the unceasing murmur of the great city; but here, as he put a hand into his pocket and withdrew a key, it was as quiet as a churchyard.

The door opened, showing a flight of uncarpeted stairs leading upwards. Closing the door behind him and fastening its patent lock, the man waited momentarily for any possible sound. None came. He was safe.

Then, picking up a letter which had fallen through a slit to the floor, he moved swiftly up those bare stairs, arriving, when he reached the top, at a door which opened into an unexpected room—unexpected in the sense that it afforded a striking contrast to the rest of that derelict slum dwelling. It was comfortably furnished: there was a turkey carpet on the floor; a good-sized gas fire was flanked by a couple of leather easy-chairs. Altogether, this room gave the impression of being lived in—which happened to be the case, although its occupant arrived only by night.

Closing this second door behind him, the man emitted his breath in a sigh of relief. This room might have been a sanctuary for either a hunted criminal or a fugitive from life itself. In any case, its owner now changed. Throwing off the shabby overcoat, he relaxed and, after mixing himself a drink and lighting a cigarette, lowered himself into a chair.

It was not until the cigarette was smoked to a mere stub that he opened the letter, which he had placed on the table behind him.

He read with a frown the few words on the single sheet of paper. The message was in code, of course—and the new one, which had only been in force for a few days, had been used. This would mean some digging out.

But there was no evading the task, so, rising, he went to the small bookcase to the right of the fireplace, picked out a volume of Masefield's poems, worked the combination of the small secret safe, hidden so unexpectedly behind the books, and, when the door swung open, took from this hiding-place a small, black-bound book.

Twenty minutes later he had deciphered the message:—

Imperative you obtain plans new anti-tank gun.

There was no need to decide the identity of the sender; he already knew that.

He knew also that the origin of this command was Pé, the capital of Ronstadt, the country for which he worked.

The man, who for years past had acted as the chief spy of Ronstadt in London, leaned back in his chair. This demand represented a problem and it required serious thought.

Like many other people in London intimately connected with espionage, he had been following the trial of that young officer, Lieutenant Robert Wingate of the Tank Corps, with very keen interest. As a matter of fact, he had been in the court throughout the proceedings.

And, as a result of much concentrated mental effort, he had come to one definite conclusion: that, through bad blundering on the part of his employers, he would have to do the same job all over again! It was he who had obtained the designs of the new British anti-tank gun in the first place, and he himself had taken them to Pé. What crass fools they had been to mix up the packages!

Where was the original package of plans now?

Lighting another cigarette, he went over the evidence he had heard in court that day. There was no possible doubt that Wingate had handed over a package to the man sent to meet him at the Hotel Continental in The Hague. But, if that had been the original package (the one Minna Braun had handed him at Pé) then the trouble would have been at an end and he would not have received this present imperative summons. Then, what was the conclusion? That the original package was still in England? Most probably.

That meant, then, that Wingate had lied. What had he done with the package? Had he really sent it to England enfolded in that copy of the *Tageblatt*? If so, to whom had he sent it? To himself? To his father? Or—to that girl with whom he was said to be in love?

There was another possibility. During the brief talk this Chief Spy had had with Minna Braun at Pé he had come to the conclusion that this still very beautiful woman had been dragooned against her will into working for the Ronstadt Intelligence. Was it possible that she had double-crossed them? Had she discovered beforehand that the supposed dummy package she had been ordered to give to the young British officer was extremely valuable, and had she found a purchaser for this information in another country? In any case, it was very obvious that the right package had not yet been received by Crosber in Pé.

Minna Braun? Was she a traitor? No; further thought persuaded him that the package with the duplicate plans had probably been received in England. With the original plans now so carefully guarded, it would be hopeless for him to endeavour to get another duplicate set. No, his job was to lay his hand on that package.

But where was he to find it?

For the next hour he scarcely moved in his chair; and when he left his hideaway in the East End he had to throw at least a dozen cigarette stubs out of the window before locking the door.

◇◇◇

At the Senior Services Club that night discussion raged concerning the verdict at the conclusion of the court-martial.

"I can't imagine what the boy's father was up to," blared one critic. "Why didn't he engage a pukka counsel instead of that fellow Mallory? His cross-examination of those witnesses from Pé was all wrong, in my opinion—certainly he had no right to ask whether the fellow who spoke about seeing the woman—what was her name—"

"Minna Braun," supplied a listener.

"Ah, yes, Minna Braun—Well, as an ex-officer, Mallory ought to have known better than to try to make that witness say in what capacity he was in the house—whether he was there as a guest, or as a servant."

"I quite agree, Colonel," supported one of the group gathered round the fire. "Damn it, if the identity of those witnesses leaked out, our Secret Service organisation in Ronstadt would be at an end. I can't imagine what Mallory was thinking about."

"Trying to get his pal's son off, of course—don't you know that he and Clinton have been friends ever since the war?"

"Well, any way, friendship is one thing, but behaving like an absolute ass another," came back the first speaker. "I was glad to see how the President jumped on him on that point. He pointed out that the witness had just stated on oath that he saw Minna Braun enter the room of young Wingate—"

"The prisoner never denied that she came to his room."

"It seems to me," drawled another voice, "that Mallory must have had some idea at the back of his head—of trying to discredit these witnesses altogether. Well, I think it's ten to one now on the young fool being convicted."

That, with many ornamentations, appeared to be the view of every one present.

Chapter XXI

The Intruder

Would the night never pass? She had heard the clock strike one...*two*...Switching on the bedside lamp, Rosemary saw that the time was now twenty-two minutes to three. Another four hours and a half, at least, before she could get up.

It was the incessant strain of the last month that had brought this insomnia. How could she possibly sleep when her mind was racked with so much anxiety? Sometime the next day, the decision would be given in the court-martial; she, with the rest of the world, would know whether Bobby Wingate was to go to prison or be allowed to walk the earth a free man.

She had done something that night which she had never done before—but the drug which was to induce sleep had not worked; she was as wide awake as though it were broad daylight.

In the endeavour to keep her mind occupied, her father had given a dinner-party that night. But the company had been dull—and, inventing some excuse on the spur of the moment, she had slipped away while the men were at their port, put on hat and coat, and driven in a taxi to the Rosy Dawn Night Club. (Anything to forget! Anything to force her brain to become sufficiently blurred so that this awful period of waiting might be bridged.)

But when she arrived at that fashionable Bond Street rendezvous, every eye had seemed to be fixed inquisitorially upon her; all the world must know by this time, she supposed, that she was in love with Bobby Wingate.

Several of the more irrepressible girls present came up and demanded to know the latest news. Did she really think Bobby was guilty?—and a dozen other hateful questions. Had these people no mercy?

But then, the consciousness had been forced home to her that she herself was to blame; she should not have come to this place, where scandalous tongues wagged and a devouring curiosity about other people's affairs existed. She should have realised that Bobby Wingate was the most discussed person, not only in London but throughout the country, at that very moment.

Ashamed, she had rushed away as quickly as she had come, feeling like a hunted creature.

Bobby continued to dominate her thoughts completely. Every phase of the trial returned in vivid and poignant detail. The woman, Minna Braun? Oh, she didn't mind her. This was 1935, and she prided herself on being broad-minded. Although it had hurt her at the time to hear Bobby declare that he was attracted by the woman, yet she would not have had him any different—the disclosure showed that he had courage and was not afraid to speak the truth. After they were married…Well, that would be different.

Married! That consummation seemed a long way off. It was only if the unexpected happened—and she had to admit that it would be the unexpected—that she could expect any sort of happiness herself. If he were declared innocent, then she would walk by his side and show the whole world how proud she was and how her courage had never faltered. But that would only be possible if the stigma was lifted—and what was that she had heard as she left the court that day? The crowd were betting ten to one against him? Oh, dear God!...

Why had Bobby lied to her? That was the wound that hurt and would not heal. He had lied in court, too. About the package. Why? She had had no opportunity to ask him, but he must have had some purpose. Although he had sworn that the package he had taken to The Hague and given to the man at the Hotel Continental was the original package, she knew differently. For was not the original package locked away in that bureau drawer on the opposite side of her bedroom? Why she had kept it, she did not know, since, on tearing aside the oilskin covering and opening the envelope, she had found it contained nothing but two perfectly blank sheets of paper. Yet, because of those words which Bobby had scribbled on the outside, "*Keep this safe for me*," she had refused to throw those sheets of paper away. After the trial there would be some explanation, no doubt—meanwhile she was safeguarding them. Yet she wished—oh, how she wished!—that he had not lied to her.

Her thoughts switched to the man who was defending Bobby. Peter Mallory, for some reason which she could not understand, had been pressing his attentions on her during the last few days—ever since, in fact, the trial had started. There had been nothing objectionable in his behaviour, and, considering the circumstances, perhaps it was only natural that he should go out of his way to try to keep her spirits bright; but, no doubt because she still could not overcome her original antipathy to this man, his frequent talks with her had been difficult to tolerate.

How sick she was of everything! How she longed to get away from the staring crowds, the whispering tongues, the gossiping scandalmongers—with Bobby.

Gradually her further thoughts became confused; there followed a blur and a wiping-out of the chaos that was in her mind.

◇◇◇

She must have slept, for she could remember nothing more until a noise near at hand made her spring up.

She saw—dear God, what was it? Glaring into her eyes, making them blink, was a fixed, relentless light. It was fixed to something which a dark shape—was it that of a man?—held at the end of what looked like an arm.

"Who are you? What do you want?" In the short interval which had elapsed between her awakening and now she had been able to get a grip on her senses.

There came a swift outrush of something from the object the burglar carried in his hand, and the next instant she was fighting vainly against a fast-failing consciousness. The gas pistol had done its work.

Waiting only long enough to ascertain that the girl was unconscious, the intruder resumed his task. He had come to search for a certain package, and he could not go until it had been found. The chances of its being in that bedroom were problematical; but, if the scanty information he had been able to collect on the subject was reliable, Rosemary Allister had kept the thing under her own eye instead of handing it over to her father to put in his library safe.

Those papers on the table by the side of the bed?...No, the two sheets he wanted weren't there. Then, where? That bureau? Possibly. But when he tried the top drawer, he found it locked. Curse it!

What was that? Had some one heard him moving about? He strained his ears to catch the significance of the faint sound that was drifting up from below. Every now and then he looked at the open window leading out to the balcony where he had crouched for so long before making an entry.

His desperate need drove out every other sense after a couple of minutes. He must open that top drawer; already in fancy he could see the two sheets of pale blue paper, perfectly blank to the ordinary person, on which so much depended.

His right hand went out again. He seized the handle of the drawer furiously, dropping his gas pistol, on the upper barrel of which still gleamed the small electric light by which he worked.

Still the thing was immovable. He would have to use a jemmy.

But before he could pull this from his pocket the unmistakable sound of stealthy but heavy footsteps climbing the stairs came to him.

Picking up his pistol and switching off the electric light on the upper barrel, he stepped out through the window and on to the balcony.

It would be useless to stay; he would be able to knock out the fool of a butler, no doubt, but Matthew Allister kept a couple of stalwart footmen as well.

No, he would have to get away while there was still time.

◇◇◇

Rosemary stared at the familiar face of McColl, the family doctor. That worthy Scotsman was looking very perturbed, she noticed.

"Why, what the—?" And then she remembered. "Where is he?" she gasped, and, as no one answered: "The burglar, I mean! The man who squirted something at me out of what looked like a pistol. He was here a moment ago...."

"Young lady," she heard the unmistakable Edinburgh tones of Anthony McColl explain, "please try to calm yourself. The man has been gone these four hours, according to what Thomas, your butler, tells me—and it's taken the better part of that time to bring you back to consciousness. If I had the power I'd put that dirty scoundrel away for a term of years, whoever he might be."

"Can you remember anything about him, pet?" It was her father speaking now. "Do you think you could give any sort of description to the police?"

"No, father—he was just a dark shape. Besides, he had a mask on his face."

"A burglar, of course. But what could he be wanting in your bedroom?"

Rosemary laughed.

"Is that a very tactful thing to say?" she asked. "He must have heard of my devastating beauty—the shape that set a thousand ships a-sailing—"

"Be sensible, pet," gently chided the banker. "This is a very serious business. I rang up the police directly I was told what had happened, and there is an officer downstairs now waiting to take a statement from you."

"I have no statement to give him. All I can say is that I woke up suddenly, saw a dark shape by the side of the bed—and then got snuffed out by—"

"Some form of gas, I should say," supplied McColl. "The police-sergeant downstairs says it is the latest device used by the up-to-date burglar."

"Burglar." The repetition of the word rang in her ears. Of course! Then....

"Excuse me!" she cried, and, to the gaping astonishment of her father, if not of McColl, whose practice lay largely among girls of Rosemary's age, station, and outlook, she jumped out of bed and rushed across the room.

"My keys!" they heard her shout. "Where are my keys?"

It was not until she had gone helter-skelter to a wardrobe, rummaged there, and come away with a bunch of keys jingling in her hand, that she would vouchsafe any explanation.

"Wait!" she cried to her father. "I'm worried."

They watched her insert one of the keys into the lock of the top drawer of the bureau standing to the right of the fireplace and then pull the drawer out vigorously.

Rosemary thrust a hand inside.

"Ah!" she said after a pause, and there was a deep note of thankfulness in the exclamation.

Chapter XXII

The Summing-Up

The Court was crowded when the Judge-Advocate began his summing-up.

Addressing the members of the court-martial in a voice that was serious to the point of actual gloom, he said:

"We have now approached the end of a case the gravity of which was, of course, apparent to you from the moment of the start of the trial.

"I need not point out to you that the future of a brother officer lies in your hands, and that both you and he know how much depends on your verdict.

"You have all sworn you will well and truly try the accused according to the evidence given before you, and that you will duly administer justice without partiality, favour, or affection. It is a very responsible task which has been committed to you, and I know you will not shirk it.

"Now, it would be useless for me to deny that the allegations made against the prisoner are most grave. For, in the words of counsel for the defence, they charge this young man of standing, who holds a commission in the military forces of his Majesty and has the honour to serve in a famous corps, with acts of downright treachery to his country."

After a brief pause, while he consulted some papers before him, the Judge-Advocate proceeded.

"Now, the whole case for the prosecution is that the accused received money, and it does not require much intelligence to suppose that he would not have received a *quid pro quo* for those services which the prosecution alleges unless he had collected, obtained, and communicated something to those persons who paid him the two notes of fifty pounds each.

"There was no doubt that the accused did receive these two notes, that they were paid him by a certain person in Pé, and that they were afterwards passed through his banking account. That is the first important fact to be considered.

"The second is that, a short time after he returned from Pé, he travelled to Holland and there, in a hotel at The Hague, handed over to a certain person, who has been identified as an enemy agent, a certain package. Neither of these facts is denied by the prisoner, although he puts a very different complexion on the circumstances attached to them.

"I would remind the Court that it must not act on surmise or suspicion alone: the duty of the prosecution is that the charges preferred against the accused must be brought home with such a measure of certainty as to exclude all reasonable doubt about his innocence or guilt. Unless the prosecution, in your opinion, has fulfilled that duty, then the accused must go from the Court a free man."

Referring to the prisoner's visit to Ronstadt, the speaker reminded the Court that the prosecution did not say that he went to Pé with any traitorous purpose, or with an idea of doing anything deleterious to the interests of his country. Indeed, on the other hand, he, with the purpose he said he had in mind, ran a certain risk of encountering danger in an entirely different direction.

"He has told you what seems to be a very straightforward story about the man who called himself 'Sandor' but who has been identified by reliable witnesses of the prosecution as a person who has been connected with international espionage since the last years of the late War. It is possible that the prisoner's story concerning how these two met is correct; it is also possible that the submission of the defence, that this young officer was beguiled by Ronstadt agents into a position where they could have some kind of future hold over him, is correct. You must remember that, even at the present time, twenty-four years is not an age of great sophistication. I mention this particularly when we come to consider the evidence given concerning the prisoner's association with the woman who called herself 'Minna Braun.' The prosecution has told you that the record of the woman shows that during the last year of the War, namely 1918, she was acting as an agent for Germany and performed the usual *rôle* of such women in this connection—namely, that of a seductress.

"The defence—which, if I may be allowed to say so, has been conducted with marked ability by Mr. Peter Mallory—contends that the very fact that this woman became so friendly with the accused is supporting evidence of the plot against him hatched by Ronstadt agents. There is certainly much in that submission. The prisoner, on oath, has stated quite frankly that he was considerably attracted to this woman, although he would never have considered the possibility of marrying her. You, as men of the world, will recognise the nice distinction.

"How much hold did this woman gain over the accused? That, it seems to me, is a very important factor to be considered—I will even go so far as to characterise it as the crux of the whole case. Was it because she had promised him her future favours that he returned to England—before his leave was up and when it might have been thought that he would have been very content to remain in Paris, if only on the off-chance of meeting this woman again?

"Now, why actually did he return to England? The prosecution alleges that it was because, having already received a hundred pounds, he had been given orders to obtain further information. You know that the prisoner actually returned to his unit at Woolvington, that he explained his unexpected appearance by stating that he was going to attend an Old Boys' Dinner, that he remained the night at Woolvington and the next day witnessed the trials of a new type of tank. Straight upon that, he returned to London, and that same night crossed to Holland.

"He has a very plausible reason for making that journey. He has told you that, believing 'Minna Braun' was what she pretended to be—namely, a French secret agent—he considered himself bound to return to her the property which she had entrusted to him. That is the reply of the ordinary man of honour. It is for you to decide whether his explanation can overrule in your minds the allegation of the prosecution—namely, that, instead of returning 'Minna Braun' the package which she had handed to him in his hotel room at Pé, he supplied the Ronstadt Intelligence with further information, namely, details of the new amphibious tank, the trials of which he had witnessed the day before at Woolvington. We have here two conflicting stories, each of which might be correct.

"The prosecution has told you that the evidence in this case is mainly circumstantial, and certainly there is no direct evidence that the accused ever took to Ronstadt or Holland any books or documents containing references to military matters.

"You have observed the accused during the days of the court-martial. You have had ample opportunity to form your own opinions about him. Now the time has come when you must decide if he is, in your opinion, an honourable man, with a keen sense of duty (as the defence has put forward) or whether he is that contemptible creature, very low in humanity's scale, who, for the sake of money, would betray his country. That is the issue you must decide.

"The accused has told you that his journey to The Hague was entirely unpremeditated; that, if he had not received the wire signed 'Adrienne,' he would not have returned to the Continent. The prosecution, on the other hand, claims that his paymasters had sent him home post-haste and that he took advantage of meeting an old school friend on the Croydon air liner to provide him with a sufficient excuse, when he got back to his unit, of explaining his unexpected return. Whether he ever intended to go to the Old Repingtonians' dinner or not, the fact remains that he cancelled the appointment.

"You all, as military officers, are acutely aware of the state of tension existing between the different European countries at the present time. You all possess sufficient military knowledge to realise that each nation is eager to obtain the military secrets of its neighbours—whether it is living on friendly terms at the present time with that particular neighbour, or whether it anticipates being engaged in warfare with the same country at an early date. Consequently, I cannot stress with too much emphasis the fact that, if the accused *did* give information concerning military weapons, as set out in the two main charges against him, he was guilty of a most heinous crime.

"With regard to the new type of tank—the subject of the second main charge: this appears to have been officially secret, although it had been exposed to view in manœuvres. It is natural to assume that this young officer, who, I would remind you, has always borne the reputation of being a very keen soldier, would take the greatest possible interest in this new type of tank. There is as much to be said in support of the defence as there is in support of the claim of the prosecution.

"Stress has been laid on the fact that, although, according to his own statement, the prisoner went to The Hague for the express purpose of handing over to 'Minna Braun' the package which she had entrusted to him at Pé, he, in point of strict fact, did not do so. The package was handed to a third person. In reply to this, the accused has told you that the messenger brought with him a letter which he was able to identify as being in the writing of 'Minna Braun,' and consequently he considered that this emissary would do just as well as the woman herself. It is for you to say whether you believe that statement or not.

"To conclude, my last words to you are these:

"Has the case for the prosecution produced in your mind such a measure of certainty as to exclude such reasonable doubt as would cause you to hesitate to take an ineradicable step in some event of great importance in your own lives?

"Mr. Mallory, in his final speech for the defence, warned you of the terrible responsibility resting on your shoulders. The entire future of this young officer is in your hands. Declare him guilty, and he will be banished into that outer darkness from which there can be no possible recall; acquit him of these grave charges, and there is no reason to suspect that he will not be taken back into the confidence and friendship of his brother officers. No reason whatever. His fate rests with you.

"On the other hand, it is my duty to tell you that no personal consideration should deflect you from the path of your duty—in other words, if the evidence you have heard leads, in your own minds, to an inevitable conclusion of guilt, then the decision you are bound to face, however distasteful, is to pronounce sentence strictly according to the oath you have taken.

"If you cannot bring yourselves to such a conclusion, a conclusion which the prosecution must bring home definitely to your minds, then the accused officer will leave this court free of the dreadful imputations which these charges involve, and it will be borne to the world outside that he has not been proved by a court of his fellow officers to be guilty of any act of treachery."

There was a deep silence as the Judge-Advocate sat down.

The Court then adjourned.

Chapter XXIII

The Secret Writing

As the different members of the court-martial rose and went out by the door behind the President, Rosemary felt her temples throbbing. She realised she would have to abandon hope. There could be only one result of the trial, and that would be a verdict of "Guilty."

She had been sustained until now, but the whispered words of her Chief, Sir Brian Fordinghame, as he sat down by her side, brought both fear and desolation.

"The experts say there is nothing on either," Fordinghame stated, passing over the two sheets of lightish blue paper over which she had expended so much hope.

This was the end, then. Her intuition—that same intuition on which she had so prided herself—had been proved wrong; it had let her down badly.

The night before, disregarding the protests of both Dr. McColl and her father, she had got up from bed as soon as she was able and, dressing, had gone down to the library. There was a book there which she wanted to consult. During the few hours that remained before the court-martial proceedings restarted she would read up everything possible on the subject of spies and secret writing.

It was that night's intruder who had given her the idea. The man must have been after the package. There was nothing else in her room of any value, apart from a few jewels, and he had ignored those. No, he must have come for the package.

Why?

Because—the answer, to her mind, was obvious—it was of vital importance to some person or group of persons—to a foreign country. Then, if it had this importance, it must also be of paramount value to the court-martial.

She had imagined she could see more or less clearly now what before had been so dark: Bobby must have been given this package *by mistake*. How this blunder had been committed she could not tell, of course, but, as she continued to throw on a few clothes, her heart seemed to stop beating when she realised how narrowly the papers had escaped total destruction.

On the night that Bobby had refused to give her his complete confidence—when, for some unaccountable reason, he had lied to her—she had been strongly tempted to throw the wretched package into the fire. Why not? The whole thing was a bluff. What possible value could there be in two perfectly blank sheets of paper?

Sir Brian Fordinghame would be able to decide, of course; but, before meeting her Chief at the office, she herself had wanted to master, as far as was possible, the fascinating subject of Secret Writing. For that was what these sheets contained, she had felt certain—*secret writing*. That seemed the answer to the puzzle.

Locking herself in the library (she had still felt groggy, but had fought hard against the sense of nausea), she had gone to the shelf on which she remembered having seen the book, and had taken down a heavy volume, on the back of which was printed *The Arts and Crafts of Modern Espionage*. How Fordinghame would have smiled if he could have seen her! Everything between these two covers was known to him, she supposed.

Still, she hadn't minded about that; she had wanted to discover the possible secret for herself. The thumping of her father's hand on the door had been disregarded.

"Look here, Rosemary, Dr. McColl isn't at all pleased with you—neither am I," she had heard her bewildered parent wail.

This was intolerable.

"Oh, do go away, father, and leave me alone!" she had cried. "Haven't I told you I have some important work to do?"

"What—at this time in the morning?" Matthew Allister's business hours were ten to five and he rarely exceeded them. On the few occasions that he broke this rule he protested that the end of the world must be coming.

"Yes; it's to do with the court-martial and its secret."

Outside the door, the banker turned to look at Dr. McColl and shook his head.

"She always did do what she wanted to do—I wish her mother hadn't died."

With her eyes fixed on the print, and her fingers swiftly turning the pages, Rosemary had become absorbed in the chapter devoted to this special branch of modern espionage. With morbid fascination she had read of the tremendous use to which various kinds of secret inks had been put by spies in the Great War. While the many forms of sympathetic or "invisible" inks had been known for centuries, she discovered, their development for Secret Service purposes had not been generally utilised until after 1914. Even the Germans, who were supposed to be past masters at every branch of espionage, had not developed this particular kind of spy communication to any great extent. There was one case of a German agent, she read, whose life—and, what was of more concern to his employers than his life, the vitally important information he had secured—might have been saved if his instructors had given him, in the early days of the War, even an elementary insight into the uses of secret ink.

Rosemary, feeling more certain every moment that her intuition was correct concerning the two sheets of paper resting by her left hand, had then become informed through the medium of the authority she was reading that the German Secret Service, once they realised the importance of invisible inks, used at first very informally onion, lemon-juice, and even saliva. These liquids, whose properties were physical rather than chemical (the writer continued) could readily be made visible to the counter-spy either by treatment with iodine vapour or by colouring baths.

She had stopped to look at the two sheets of apparently blank paper which, before many hours were past, she was determined should be placed before experts. Did the honour and freedom of the boy she loved depend on whether her surmise was correct? She believed so.

Turning back to the book, she had read:

> It was early in 1915 that the first of the truly invisible inks began to appear. For it was not until then that the Germans discovered how easily their secret correspondence was being read by the Allies. Once this discovery was made, they called in many expert chemists—but there were equally clever brains on the other side, and as quickly as a new ink was invented the secret was solved by French and British chemists.
>
> It naturally followed that the inks with which German spies were provided became more and more scientific....

She had stopped reading again. Her brain was becoming bewildered; the references to preliminary baths in solutions of hyposulphite and ammonia, solutions of metallic or organic salts, organic silver compounds, and proteinates confused her. Ronstadt had taken over many of Germany's former secrets and, no doubt, had raised them to a much higher degree of proficiency. Would the British chemists, to whom those two sheets of paper would be submitted, be able to find out their secret? The possibility of their failing almost prostrated her.

It was only when the print had begun to swim before her eyes and her head ached intolerably that she had risen from the chair. She had realised then, that it would be impossible for her to do anything by herself. She must wait until she saw Sir Brian Fordinghame....

The Chief of Y.1 had listened to her intently.

"It's a very remarkable story," he had commented, "and I should not be the least bit surprised if you were right, Rosemary." (He had dropped into the habit recently of addressing her by her Christian name.)

"Then you will get the papers tested for any secret writing, Sir Brian?"

"Immediately."

"Oh, thank you."

Fordinghame had given her one of his honest-to-God stares.

"You still believe Wingate innocent?"

"Of course—I've never allowed myself to think anything else."

The Chief of Y.1 then had picked up the two sheets of lightish blue paper and risen from his chair.

"It may sound a strange thing to you, Rosemary—but so do I," he had remarked....

Ten minutes later, the time had arrived for them both to go to the Court. Fordinghame had assured her that, while they were at the court-martial, every known test would be applied to the papers and that, if they did contain invisible writing, it would certainly be exposed.

With what hope she had waited!

And now all that hope had been dashed to the ground. According to what the Chief of Y.1 had just told her, every re-agent known to modern science had been tried out on both the sheets of paper and no result whatever had been obtained.

The whole scheme was a complete washout.

And she had been so confident of success! She was not going to allow Bobby to sacrifice himself through his loyalty to a woman whom he had known for only a couple of days and who had made no effort at all to come forward and testify on his behalf at the court-martial. Neither had Minna Braun, or Adrienne Grandin, or whatever her name was supposed to be, sent a single word, so far as she knew, of regret at having ruined a promising boy's career before it could really be said to have started. As for what Bobby might say afterwards about her action, she completely disregarded this factor; there was only one thing to be considered and that was how to clear him of the odious charge of which, unless a miracle happened, it seemed certain, after the Judge-Advocate's summing-up speech, he would be declared guilty.

She lowered her face, unable to meet Bobby's eyes. What torture was reflected in his face! What he must have suffered! And now she could do nothing to help him. If only these sheets had revealed their secret, she would have insisted on giving evidence—Sir Brian Fordinghame had promised to give his support in this—and then she would have told the whole story of the package so far as she was concerned. Fordinghame had told her that the President would allow her to be sworn: any evidence for the defence would be taken right up to the finding of the Court being announced. The accused was always given the utmost latitude in this respect: that was the invariable law at all General Courts-Martial.

It had been merely a mirage…a vain hope…a mocking illusion….

◇◇◇

The members of the Court were filing back. The verdict that they had decided to bring in could be seen written on all their faces. Rosemary had no need to take a second look: Bobby, she knew, would be declared guilty!

In her distress she swung an arm out convulsively. A touch on the shoulder by Sir Brian Fordinghame made her realise what she had done: a small bottle of fountain-pen ink, from which she had been accustomed to fill her Waterman, had tipped over, and the contents were flowing all over the desk.

"Your sleeve, my dear!" said the Chief of Y.1 commiseratingly.

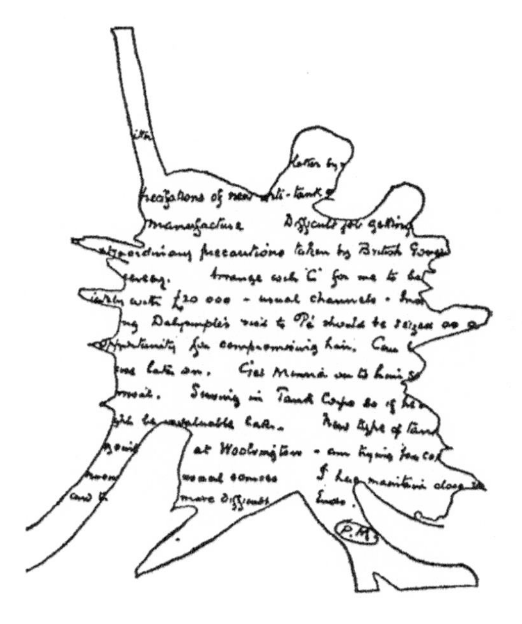

Rosemary paid him no heed: her attention was fully occupied. She continued to stare at the ink-stained sheet of paper—one of the two contained in the package.

A miracle was happening—the miracle of which she had dreamed, but of whose fulfilment she had utterly despaired: through the deep ink-stain which had formed, *writing was coming.*

Chapter XXIV

The Traitor

Rosemary sprang up.

"Sir Brian! Look!" she cried—and caught hold of his arm as though she had suddenly been driven mad.

Fordinghame was quick to act. He took one look at the sheet which the girl extended to him so excitedly and then his voice rose high above the excited buzzing in the Court.

"I wish to apologise to you, sir, as President of the Court," he said to the frowning chief official, "for this interruption, but something entirely unexpected has occurred."

"May I inquire what it is?" The Accused's Friend, Peter Mallory, had crossed to the speaker's side. "What is that paper?" he asked.

Those sitting or standing near wondered why Sir Brian Fordinghame's voice had grown so stern.

"It is a very important document which has just come to light," he said.

"Has it anything to do with the defence?" inquired Mallory, his face white.

"Yes."

"Then I demand to see it."

The answer was so strange that it infuriated the listener.

"I must refuse to allow it out of my hand, Mr. Mallory."

Pandemonium suddenly broke out. If some one had not seized him from behind, Mallory would have struck the speaker. As it was, struggling in the grip of two court officials, he glared at Fordinghame as though the latter had turned from a friend into an enemy.

"I demand the fullest explanation of this extraordinary scene!" called the President. He was forced to shout to make his voice heard above the hubbub.

"I will make myself responsible for supplying it, sir."

"You, Sir Brian?"

"Yes, General."

While every one stared, the speaker proceeded:

"A piece of evidence, bearing strongly on this case, has suddenly turned up. May I have your permission, sir, to call a new witness?"

"Certainly—but I don't understand. Have you undertaken the defence of the prisoner, Sir Brian?"

"So far as the furnishing of this new evidence is concerned—yes, sir."

Sensation.

"Call your witness."

Fordinghame touched Rosemary Allister on the arm, and the girl walked towards the witness-box. In doing so she was forced to pass the prisoner. Everyone in the Court noticed that she gave Wingate an encouraging smile.

The Chief of Y.1 addressed the President again.

"Before I put any questions to this witness, sir, may I ask that the doors of the Court be closely guarded?"

"Are you afraid of some one trying to escape, Sir Brian?"

"Yes."

After a nod from the President, Major Bingham, the prosecuting counsel, himself gave the necessary order. He looked completely bewildered as he returned to his seat.

"Now, Sir Brian," said the President.

Fordinghame faced the witness.

"Your name is Rosemary Allister?"

"Yes."

"You are the daughter of Mr. Matthew Allister, the well-known banker?"

"Yes."

"For the past month you have been employed as assistant personal secretary to myself as Chief of the Y.1 branch of British Intelligence?"

"Yes."

"Am I correct in saying that you have been for some time a close personal friend of the prisoner?"

"Yes."

"Did you receive on the twentieth of September a package addressed in Lieutenant Wingate's handwriting?"

"I did."

"Of what did that package consist?"

"It consisted of two sheets of paper enclosed in an oiled-silk covering and placed inside a copy of the Ronstadt newspaper, *Tageblatt*."

"From where did Lieutenant Wingate send you that package?"

"From Pé."

"Do you know for what purpose?"

"He wrote on the outside—that is, on the outside page of the newspaper—'*Keep this safe for me.*'"

Waiting for the Court to digest this piece of information, the man who had so unexpectedly superseded the Accused's Friend in conducting the defence (thereby transferring himself from a powerful member of the prosecution into an ally) proceeded.

"Now I want you, Miss Allister, to tell the Court in your own words exactly what followed your receiving this package."

The witness looked straight at the prosecuting counsel as she replied.

"I realised that Lieutenant Wingate must have had a very good reason for sending it to me, and when he came back to London I questioned him about it. He told me that the package had been given him for safe-keeping by a woman in Pé who had said that it was vitally important to both their countries—that was, England and France—that it should be kept safe. Mr. Wingate went on to tell me that this woman had said she was a French Secret Service agent, and that he believed her."

The President interposed a question.

"You have been in Court throughout this court-martial?"

"Yes."

"You have therefore heard all the evidence?"

"Yes."

"Then why have you not brought the contents of this package to the notice of the Court before?"

"I will explain," promptly replied the witness. "Curious to know what was inside the package, I took the liberty of opening it, but was disappointed to find that all it contained were two perfectly blank sheets of paper. This made me come to the conclusion—later, of course, when I heard the full circumstances—that Lieutenant Wingate had been fooled by this woman."

"But you still kept the sheets of paper?"

"Yes."

"Why?"

"Because, in the first place, the prisoner"—she hesitated a little over the word—"had entrusted the package to me, and then, secondly, because I had a vague feeling always that I ought not to throw them away. I cannot give a better explanation than that. That was why I kept them locked in a bureau drawer in my bedroom. Last night"—she spoke more slowly now—"I had my intuition confirmed."

"Please tell the Court what happened last night, Miss Allister," said Sir Brian Fordinghame.

"A man broke into the house and entered my bedroom. He was masked, so that I could not see his face, but I knew why he had come: his purpose was to secure the two sheets of paper which had been in the package. It made me realise that there must be some secret attached to them—and now we know what it is."

"They contained secret writing?" interjected the prosecuting counsel.

"Yes. Sir Brian Fordinghame will show you."

It did not seem in any way unusual that this remarkably attractive girl of twenty-two should have become the strongest character in the Court and that she should be dominating the proceedings. Even Sir Brian Fordinghame seemed to recognise that their previous relations had been changed; in any case, he obeyed the request of the girl and walked towards the seats occupied by the President and the Judge-Advocate, placing before them the piece of paper on which the ink had formed such a large blob.

Both officials were seen to lean forward to study the document intently.

Then they looked at each other, amazed. The President beckoned Major Bingham; and the prosecuting counsel, who had been frowning during the short time that it had taken Rosemary to give her evidence, walked quickly forward.

The paper was passed to him; he read it and whispered something in the ear of the President. The latter, after conferring briefly with the Judge-Advocate, nodded.

"Gentlemen," he said, addressing the other members of the court-martial, "it is my duty to inform you that very important evidence—evidence which you must hear before I ask you for your findings in this case—has just come to light. I call upon Sir Brian Fordinghame."

The Chief of Y.1 went to the witness stand and took the oath. Meanwhile, the reporters turned curiously to each other; this case, which had already been crammed with drama, looked as if it would provide an extraordinary dénouement.

Strangely enough, it was the prosecuting counsel who started to question this new witness. Standing at some distance away from every one else, the man who should have undertaken the task—Peter Mallory—surveyed the proceedings with what looked like a sardonic smile on his gaunt face. He had one hand in his coat pocket.

"You are the Chief of the Y.1 branch of British Intelligence?" Major Bingham asked the new witness.

"Yes."

"In that capacity it has been your duty to prepare the facts for the present charge against the prisoner?"

"Yes."

"You corroborate all that Miss Rosemary Allister has already told the Court?"

"I do. May I go on?"

"Yes, please, Sir Brian."

"Directly I arrived at the office this morning I found Miss Allister in a great state of excitement. She told me of the attempted burglary the night before, and said that she had spent several hours reading up all the available facts about secret inks. She implored me to put the two sheets of paper in question to every possible test—which I did."

"With any result?"

"None. All the usual re-agents failed."

"And yet ordinary fountain-pen ink brought out the writing?"

"That is so."

Major Bingham took some time before asking the next question. When he did so his voice sounded like the voice of doom.

"Sir Brian Fordinghame, I have now to put to you a very important question: do you recognise the handwriting on this paper?" holding it up.

"I do."

"You must tell the Court what person, in your opinion, supplied this secret information—namely, the very facts on which the first charge in this prosecution against Lieutenant Robert Wingate has been based—to the Ronstadt agents."

The answer seemed dragged from the witness. He evidently spoke with the utmost reluctance.

"I am sorry to say," he returned slowly, "that these details concerning the new anti-tank shoulder weapon, which Lieutenant Robert Wingate was supposed to have supplied to Ronstadt, are in the handwriting of—"

He was obliged to stop. A heavy crash—like that which might have been made by the sound of a body falling—had diverted not only his attention but the attention of every one in the crowded court.

A man was seen twitching in agony on the floor.

"My God!" shrieked a reporter, forgetting all professional decorum in the excitement of the moment. "*Mallory was the traitor!*"

Chapter XXV

Press Club Gossip

It was Cuthbert Clergyman who made that dramatic announcement. For a reporter with his experience to commit such an offence against newspaper etiquette and elementary good manners was unpardonable, of course, but this was the story of the century, and he was half-way across the room (*en route* to the nearest telephone) before the President could voice his displeasure.

"Stop that man!" he called.

"But I'm a reporter!" protested the indignant pressman. Then, as he watched Sir Brian Fordinghame, who had rushed to Mallory's side, straighten himself and announce, "He is dead!" he calmed himself. He might not have had all his facts—the most heinous crime a reporter can commit—if he had been able to get away before.

Now it was the Judge-Advocate speaking.

"He poisoned himself?"

"Yes."

"This is his writing, you say?" inquired the President, tapping the sheet of paper he held.

"Yes—that was why he wanted to get possession of it."

"But it's incredible—simply unbelievable!"

"There is the proof, sir," returned the realist, pointing to the corpse.

Major Bingham spoke his last words for the prosecution.

"I ask the Court to declare the prisoner Not Guilty," he said.

The President tried vainly to stop the storm of applause. He was forced to wait until this had subsided before making his announcement.

"Lieutenant Robert Wingate, it is the verdict of this Court that you be discharged."

◇◇◇

Cuthbert Clergyman was a man of deeds rather than words (unless seated at his typewriter, punching out a good news story), but to-night, as he sat in his favourite corner of the Press Club, a pint pot of beer by his elbow, he allowed himself to expand.

"Yes," he said; "it was a whale of a good story. Somehow, I'd suspected that fellow Mallory from the beginning."

"Liar!" chorused his listeners.

"All right; have it your own way."

"What about the hooded witnesses?" asked a man sitting on the fringe of the crowd.

Clergyman smiled.

"As I told Blackie," he returned, "we couldn't possibly use the stuff because of the Official Secrets Act, but now that it's all over I can pass the story on to one of the American papers and get a good fat cheque for it. Of course, what troubled Fordinghame, of the Y.1 Department, was that he would be required to produce the actual agents who had furnished him with the reports on young Wingate's activities in Pé. That must have made him do some pretty serious thinking, for of course he realised that unless great care was taken he stood a good chance of losing some of his best men—the Pé undertakers would be called in. The absence of the Ronstadt nationals from Pé would render them liable to be suspected by the Ronstadt Secret Police, and if this did not definitely put them on any kind of death list, it still would mean that (as Bingham said at the court-martial) they would not be able to render any further service to the British Government. In short, they would be scuppered.

"However, the presence of these witnesses was absolutely necessary; so there was no way out. The charge against Wingate was so serious that a conviction was absolutely necessary.

"I knew very well," Clergyman went on to declare, "that Fordinghame would be nervous about the Press—and so it turned out. He decided, after a good deal of thought, that the five agents whose presence was wanted in London must, prior to their leaving Pé, each provide a good alibi and then get out of the country by separate and devious routes, reaching London alone."

"How did you know that?"

The reporter withered his interrogator with a look.

"Fordinghame himself told me so," he replied, amidst a gale of laughter. "Once they were here, he had them accommodated in separate hang-outs. I don't know whether you fellows," getting well into his stride now after another hearty pull at the pint pot, "are aware that Secret Service agents are never allowed to know each other, even although they are from the same town or district.

"All right. I got as far as telling you that the five agents had reached London separately. Now, although the evidence of these witnesses was given *in camera* and every possible precaution taken against their being identified, Fordinghame must have realised that every newspaper in the country would risk a good deal if it could get a story about these witnesses. For instance, look at the fit Blackie threw when I told him that such stuff was dynamite. And in order to prevent any clue concerning any of these agents from leaking out, Fordinghame resorted to pure melodrama. He hit upon the idea of putting them all in robes that the Ku Klux Klan boys of a few years back would have been proud to own. That was all right so long as they were in the court—but how were they to get there without being seen? The sight of a bloke going round dressed as a K.K.K. chieftain, even in a taxicab, was likely to cause something of a riot. Righto! The only thing for it, then, was to exercise a little more strategy. Fordinghame is a wily old bird (he ought to be, after his experience) and he bethought him of an old Sinn Fein trick back in the days of the 'Trouble' in Ireland. He arranged for a laundry van, with a large-sized skip, to be waiting outside the back entrance to each house in which one of the witnesses was staying. Getting into the skip, the witness was duly collected, and deposited at the rear door of the library at the Chelbridge Headquarters."

The reporter broke off to chuckle.

"I got on the trail of one of those damned vans on the second day," he said, "but just as it was entering the barrack gates, out from a side street came a fellow pushing a little hand-truck on which rested the longest ladder—it looked the longest—in the world. My taxi was held up for a couple of minutes—and by that time, naturally enough, the witness had been smuggled in."

One of the listeners interjected a question.

"Did the Sinn Feiners, you say, use that ladder trick?"

"They did, my boy, whenever they were out to ambush a car in the streets of Dublin. I was there and I know.... Well, it's me for bed—and I think I've earned it."

"It's your turn for the next round," said a complaining voice.

"That's why I'm going."

Chapter XXVI

In Which a Good Deal Is Explained

Sir Brian Fordinghame looked round the room, crowded with high Government officials—the Prime Minister himself had slipped away from Downing Street for a few minutes—and made a weary gesture.

"I want you all to realise," he said, "that what I am going to tell you is not an agreeable task. I had known Peter Mallory for over twenty years. He had been not only my personal friend but also one of my chief operatives for at least half of that time. Even now that the evidence of his guilt as a traitor is so conclusive as to leave no doubt, I find it difficult to credit the truth.

"The double-spy is not unknown in espionage, of course; but rarely does one encounter one in such a social position as Mallory's. There was a famous instance, of course—that of Colonel Redl, Chief of the Austrian Intelligence, who was bought by the Russians, and who shot himself with a revolver left by his brother officers so that he might be saved from a firing squad. He met a better end than Peter Mallory.

"It was Rosemary Allister who started my suspicions of Mallory. Poor child, I shall never forget the indignant way I answered her on the day that she first brought up the subject. It wanted courage, that action of hers."

Colonel Clinton was heard suppressing an exclamation.

"Mallory was a queer man. His diary reveals that his mentality was quite abnormal, bordering even on madness," went on Fordinghame. "It was not until his effects were searched and the strongbox he kept at a safe deposit opened that this came to light. I confess the knowledge was a terrible surprise to me. And yet, looking back, Mallory from time to time had given, unconsciously perhaps, hints of insanity in his conversation that ought to have set me thinking.... But the man was such a friend that the thought of his being abnormal in any way never once occurred to me."

Bobby Wingate groaned.

"And you say it was Rosemary who first told you?"

"Yes. Miss Allister, who was acting, as you know, as my secretary, told me that Peter Mallory had taken her to the Savoy Grill for supper and she...well, noticed certain things. She was suspicious of him, not quite sure that he was 'straight.' And told me so. 'I'm going to keep my eye on him for I'm certain he's a darned sight more guilty than Bobby Wingate.' Those were her exact words.

"After that she apologised for 'wasting the office time,' as she put it, and went into her own room to work. I suppose I should have dismissed the whole occurrence as being preposterous—Mallory, a man I had known and trusted, a man, moreover, who had brought off several very valuable coups; why, it was fantastic. And yet—well, Clinton," looking at the M.I.5 Colonel, "you know how it is, in our job: we have only to hear a word and—didn't I move heaven and earth to get this boy"—walking across to Bobby and placing a hand on his shoulder—"who might have been my own son, convicted? I tell you, this is a hellish trade we're in," frowning heavily.

"I began to ponder, to look into things. I had a talk with a Harley Street surgeon—McAllister; you probably know him, most of you—and he gave me positive proof that if Mallory *did* belong to the abnormal type he might be suffering from a psychological kink. I had my duty to do: if Rosemary Allister's amazing suggestion (based partly, I agree, on feminine intuition) were true, then one had the utterly astounding situation of the man who was defending an alleged traitor being himself guilty.

"I felt I couldn't take any chances, and I had Mallory watched. I realised I had to go very carefully. Moreover, he was acting as young Wingate's defending counsel—and appeared to be doing his job very well."

"He was—I will say that for him," put in Bobby; "even when he persisted in asking me about the package I sent Rosemary from Pé, I only thought he was anxious to get me off."

"Whereas we know now," said the Chief of Y.1 grimly, "that all he was thinking of was how he could get hold of it and return it to his paymasters in Ronstadt. Incidentally, of course, he was afraid of being discovered.

"It was a clever idea to make ordinary fountain-pen ink a re-agent," the speaker went on musingly; "no one would be likely to try ink, of course, for fear of spoiling the paper altogether, and as regards the second sheet in the package—the one showing the actual specifications of the anti-tank gun—once the ink was used it became a perfectly good blueprint."

"Very ingenious; but where I am beaten," confessed Colonel Clinton, "is why a man like Mallory should turn traitor. What was the inducement? It couldn't have been money; he was successful at his business; he was a bachelor, with comparatively inexpensive tastes; and even if, as you have said, he was abnormal, that, surely, in spite of whatever McAllister may have told you, was not instrumental in turning him into a traitor. Why, if that rule held good, hundreds of supposedly patriotic men in London alone would be rushing over to Ronstadt, offering to act as spies!"

"Quite so," agreed Fordinghame, "but there were helping factors in Mallory's case. To begin with, he was wounded in the head during the last war (you will remember he frequently made a joke about 'that bit of shrapnel wandering about in his brain'), and then—and this will surprise you, Clinton—he had a step-brother shot during the Irish trouble in 1916. Oh, I admit he kept it a dead secret—I didn't know it myself until I began to make every possible kind of inquiry about him—but the fact is on record, nevertheless. My own belief is that his wound completely changed his character. McAllister told me of an ex-officer who, through a similar disability, murdered the wife he adored."

"Mallory went to Pé frequently, didn't he?" asked Major Bingham.

"Yes, I used him as my 'post-office,' or connecting link with the resident agents of Y.1. That gave him a unique opportunity to pass on information, although exactly by what means he obtained possession of the design for the new anti-tank shoulder-weapon we haven't yet been able to discover."

"But we will," said Colonel Clinton grimly.

"Yes; between us we undoubtedly will, and then it will be rather bad luck for another traitor.

"Whether this kink in his moral character was the determining factor in making Peter Mallory, who used to be one of the best fellows alive, turn traitor, we shall now never know; but my own belief is that it played a big part. However," touching a bell, "it is time we stopped talking and did something more practical. Bring some whisky and a siphon, Brooks," Fordinghame added to the servant who now entered the room.

When the various glasses were charged, the host—this talk had taken place in Sir Brian Fordinghame's office—gave a toast.

"To your future happiness, Wingate!"

"It's very good of you, sir." Bobby's hand trembled slightly as he watched the others drink.

The two men faced each other.

"Now for the truth, Bobby," said Colonel Clinton. "I've waited a long time.... Just a minute," he broke off, as the boy seemed about to reply: "I've a confession to make to you. Seventeen years ago—"

"Please, governor!" came the interruption. "I know all about it."

Clinton stared at him.

"And was it because of that—"

Again he was interrupted.

"When I was in that guest-house at Pé, I heard some one talking in the next room one night. Of course, it was part of a plot to get hold of me, but I didn't realise it at the time. I thought you were going to be blackmailed."

"That was the original intention, no doubt—the woman you knew as 'Minna Braun' sent me a letter."

"They must have got the wind up once I was arrested. Well, governor, I don't blame you; she's attractive enough now; I bet she was a stunner seventeen years ago."

Colonel Clinton fidgeted with his cigarette.

"I've never stopped feeling the worst kind of cad—I should like you to know that."

"As if I didn't know.... But it's time to forget it now."

Clinton had his arm round the boy's shoulder when Hannah entered.

"Miss Allister is on the telephone, Master Bobby—and she seems terribly impatient."

It was only then that the haggard expression on the Colonel's face changed into a smile.

◇◇◇

Rosemary stopped the two-seater by—of all places in the world—the side of the Serpentine. The October night was gracious.

"We can talk here, Bobby," she said; "we might be millions of miles away from London. If any one sees us (not that I should mind that!) they'll think we're just a shopgirl and her boy. . . . Well?" for the young man at her side was silent.

"Really, we should have been at the Berkeley—with the whole world looking on," she continued.

"I couldn't have let you face it."

"What fools men are!" she told him. "They don't realise that when a girl is proud of any one she wants to show him off. And I'm damned proud of you, Bobby, let me tell you! *Well?*"

He slipped an arm round her.

"I can't talk," he said.

"No—it would be a waste of time," she agreed, offering her lips with a frank, glad surrender.

To receive a free catalog of Poisoned Pen Press titles, please provide your name and address in one of the following ways:

Phone: 1-800-421-3976
Facsimile: 1-480-949-1707
Email: info@poisonedpenpress.com
Website: www.poisonedpenpress.com

Poisoned Pen Press
6962 E. First Ave. Ste 103
Scottsdale, AZ 85251